AMADEA
One Spring in France

Michelle Granas

*

All the characters, all the events, and many of the places in this story are fictional.

*

I am grateful to Araminta Whitley of the London literary agency Lucas Alexander Whitley, whose enthusiastic reception and representation of this work in 2002 encouraged me to keep writing. It was, she said, the only manuscript to reach her during a postal strike. Thank you, postal workers of Great Britain.

*

The passages from Jean Froissart's *Chroniques* are from the 1806 translation by Thomas Johnes, *Chronicles of England, France, Spain*; the passage from Chateaubriand—volume 1 of *Mémoires d'outre-tombe*; on black dogs and treasure—Éloïse Mozzani, *Le Livre des Superstitions*, Editions Robert Laffont, Paris, 1995.

LCCN: 2015903595
Copyright © 2015 Michelle Granas
ISBN: 9780988859210

1

Madame la marquise was leaving Paris. There was a bustle in the hallway of the d'Alembert mansion in the Rue Monsieur. Joseph, the marquise's eighty-year-old chauffeur, had not yet finished taking out the luggage. Madame's son-in-law came down the stairs, brisk and upright in spite of a certain elderly portliness. He was wearing a city suit and carrying a briefcase. He kissed his mother-in-law on the cheek and suppressed an urge to help Joseph with the bags. He held the door as the man struggled out with the last of them.

"*Madame ma mère*, you must get younger servants or lighter luggage."

He had always gently kidded her and Lucien did too. She liked it. She shook her head slightly and smiled. "Never—but you must be off; do not wait for me; your taxi has been honking there these ten minutes."

"Yes, yes, I have a board meeting. It started five minutes ago. But I'm worried about you. It will be some time perhaps before a new companion can be found ...Well, we've been over that. I must run. Lucien will be waiting for you." And he trotted to his taxi.

Madame was helped into the car by Joseph and the housekeeper. She smoothed the cashmere shawl over her knees, and raised a fragile hand in greeting to young Loïc, the housekeeper's son, who had just come from school. Then she folded her hands over her silver-handled cane and nodded to Joseph. "We can go." He started the engine and pulled slowly out into the street.

Loïc followed his mother back into the house.

"What's for lunch?"

But his mother gave a shriek. "Heavens! She's left her medicine case behind. Quick! Loïc!"—She thrust the case at him—"Run! Maybe you can catch up with them."

Loïc stood gaping at his mother for a second, but she opened the door and pushed him out. He dropped his youthful torpor then and clasping the case to his chest entered into the spirit of the chase. The big gray car was just ahead of him. He tore along the sidewalk, his mother's cries behind him, lending him wings. The car stopped at an intersection. He was almost up to it. No, it was pulling away. His legs were pumping faster and faster—no, he'd never catch it. He dodged a passerby to the left, this one to the right. The car was getting away. No, it was stopped in a line of traffic again. He leapt into the street and banged on the car's window. The marquise's startled face swiveled round and Joseph was also turning in his seat. Loïc was already red from running, but now he blushed too. Maybe one didn't bang on a marquise's window. He pulled open the door, thrust in the medicine case, and was about to beat a hasty retreat, but—

"Wait!" cried the marquise, eyeing the box with amusement. "So very kind, my dear young man." She lifted her purse slowly, and slowly delved in it. The car behind honked its horn. Several cars honked their horns. Loïc squirmed.

"No, no, they can wait," said the marquise, in her slow, incisive voice. "Virtue must be rewarded."

She selected a twenty-euro note and held it out to him; then she waved a deliberate hand in apology to the racing engines behind. Loïc stammered a thank you, closed the door, and felt himself making a curious bowing gesture towards her. She had that effect on him. The car moved off and he skipped back to the pavement.

It was unfortunately not the sort of thing one could brag about to one's friends, but the little adventure had improved his day. He felt gallant. He didn't mind the money either, of course. Whistling, he sprang up the steps of the d'Alembert house.

"All the same," he said to his mother, as she dished up lunch for him in the kitchen. "If she'd had a cell phone there wouldn't have been all that brouhaha."

"Mmf," said his mother.

"All the same," said Joseph severely over his shoulder, "if you'd had a maid, madame, it wouldn't have happened. You should have got a replacement when Madame Giroud retired. I've always said so. And I don't hold with these companion girls, either. Six months and off they go, all of them."

"True, true," said the marquise soothingly. Joseph had come into her employ sixty years ago. He only came out of retirement these days when she was in Paris. She was well aware that she was the central figure in his life, eclipsing even his own wife. She was his property, in a sense, and as such she knew she had to be tolerant. And then, yes, when one was ninety, one had to be tolerant. Everyone else was so much younger than one. She smiled slightly to herself, but Joseph was still grumbling.

"And what are you going to do alone there at the *manoir*, madame? Me, I tell you frankly, I don't like it."

"Madame Sabadie will be there, and Monsieur Sabadie. I shall not be alone."

"Madame Sabadie. *Bon*. But that Yves. I don't know that I'd trust that Yves."

"Indeed," said Madame pacifically, ignoring the insult to the eminently respectable Yves, "he has only been at the *manoir* for twenty years, but he has never given cause for complaint."

Joseph said something that sounded like "Mmf, madame."

"And Lucien will be there."

"Ah, *oui*, Monsieur Lucien." The gray head nodded in a way that meant Lucien would pass.

*

Amadea Heyward, newest and youngest teacher at the E.N.P.C. Private Institute of English, was about to become unemployed. She did not know that, however, and so she stood hesitatingly and unsuspectingly on the edge of a group of teachers who were gathered in the hall between classes. She was always on the edge. Having been born Franco-American and shy, the edge was her birthright.

Students milled passed, laughing, carrying notebooks. The Institute was run on a short course system, and it was late February. There was a general end-of-the-term, exams-are-over feeling of relaxation in the atmosphere. Everyone was joking. One of the teachers was asking another, "So does anyone know what E.N.P.C. *stands* for? I've been here for two years and I still can't find out."

Someone answered, "I asked Duquesne once and he just shrugged and said, 'What does it matter? We French like initials'—and he's the director."

"Yeah, well," drawled Charles of England, tossing his forelock out of his eyes, "I think it means 'Entirely Nugatory Progress Cited.'"

"Mademoiselle Aiourd?" said Monsieur Duquesne from ten feet away. Everyone jumped a little and with rather guilty smiles at one another hastily departed in separate directions.

"Mademoiselle Aiourd? A word wiz you, pleaze."

Somewhat startled, Amadea followed M. Duquesne down the corridor to his office. He closed the door and waved her to a seat. Then he sat down behind his desk. He was a small, round-headed man in a dark suit and a dark moustache. He picked up a packet of cigarettes and played with it, then a pen. He shuffled some papers.

Amadea waited a trifle nervously. What could he want? Something to do with the exams, she supposed, although he seemed to be having some difficulty in saying whatever it was. He cleared his throat, then bending over his desk, dropped his chin in his hand, and fidgeted still with one thing or another. Amadea studied the top of his rather balding head. She had had little contact with him, but her private opinion—which she would never have expressed to anyone, being infallibly kind—was that he was a rather dry, unimaginative man. Now he was talking though.

"Mademoiselle, *je regrette*—he spoke French away from the students—I'm sorry, but, when we hired you, we thought you would be like the other Americans we have here—like Liz, or Jennifer—so full of—how shall I say it?—so full of '*bounciness*.' Yes, that is it. Mademoiselle, you have no *bounciness*. In your lectures, your drills, in your lessons in general, there is no *bounciness* at all. Not a speck." He looked embarrassed. Amadea saw that she had wronged him and that he had enough imagination to feel sorry for her. Being French, he thought an analysis of the situation would help. He went on, his fingertips pressed together, "And this lack of bounciness is composed of a certain indefinable dryness, a failure of imaginativeness perhaps, shall we say, an unceasing propensity to be—bah, mademoiselle, you know—to be boring..."

Amadea put her hands behind her back and felt for the support of the chair. She leaned back against her hands and stared out the long window behind M. Duquesne's head, into the light well, and barely listened to the long explanations that followed about unemployment, and hard times, and diminishing enrolment, and the temporary nature of her contract, etc...And, oh, he'd forgotten. He'd been told that Mademoiselle Aiouard had given her students poetry to learn? But this was an English institute, in the twenty-first century! No one wanted to learn poetry; they wanted to have fun and learn how to write business letters.

"But..." said Amadea, but he was continuing: It was just an example of how ill-suited she was to the work of the Institute.

It was over at last. She rose, said a few civil words of regret and farewell, walked out into a mercifully empty corridor, collected her belongings, and left the E.N.C.P.

*

Hugo Trencavel, sitting at a rickety table in a small house to the west of the lower Pyrenean village of

Maugrebis, eyed his father with distaste. His glance swept over the shoddy little interior of his father's dwelling with its molding and molting plaster, its heaps of farm tools and masonry tools tossed helter-skelter into corners, the stained work clothes hanging on pegs. Even the books—and there were many books—lying among the bric-a-brac with torn covers and dirty, thumbed pages, lost here their quality of intellectual status symbols and became just so much more clutter. His father—he watched the older man take a blackened pan off the burner and pour water into two enamel cups, watched him bring the coffee to the table and set it down with slightly trembling hands.

"Not your usual drink, is it?" Hugo said, and then felt dissatisfied with himself. He had to keep the sneer out of his voice, however he felt.

Raymond sat down and stared at his two hands lying on the table. Why had his son come? he wondered. He hadn't seen him for—five or six years, was it? He eyed his son: the expensive casual clothing, the expertly cut hair, the arrogant expression.

"Why did you come, I wonder?" he said aloud, but as if to himself.

Hugo looked at his father in pretended surprise. "To see you, of course."

Hypocrite, thought Raymond, but he said nothing and concentrated on stilling the shake in his hands. And yet, he thought, my son. This handsome man with the unpleasant curl to his lip is my son, and it can't stop mattering to me, even though I wish it would. He felt a dull ache, as always when he thought of his son. The shaking would not be stilled. He shrugged his shoulders and raised his cup.

"You'll burn yourself," said Hugo.

Raymond took a sip of the boiling liquid. It did burn him, but Hugo was watching, so he drank again, without flinching.

Hugo shrugged in his turn, and drummed his fingers on the table. Fathers and sons talked to each other, didn't they? He had come all the way from Bordeaux to this ramshackle hut in this godforsaken corner of the Pyrenees because, in fact, he had something to say. He had plans for this godforsaken corner, etc. There were people who would pay good money for godforsaken corners for their secondary homes, and he was a real estate developer. And the ramshackle hut— that would go, of course. But he couldn't get right at these plans because, however brilliant, obvious, and sensible they might be, his father was incalculable and his acquiescence necessary. The land had been left to the two of them, but his father had the right to it during his lifetime.

A little cozy chat would be the best way to lead up to it. He cast about in his mind for something to say. His eye fell on his father's enormous black mongrel, which had just jumped off his father's bed with a thud and padded into the kitchen in hopes of a hand-out.

"Where'd you get that beast? I've never seen such an ugly dog in my life."

"He's a good dog," said Raymond, patting his companion's broad head. "A good watchdog." He played with the dog's collar, scratching letters in the leather with a fingernail, so as not to have to look at his son.

"Good dog, good dog, maybe," said Hugo, "but why do you let him sleep on your bed? You'll get fleas."

"I already have fleas," said Raymond, smiling inwardly as Hugo, with a look of disgust, drew in his well-shod feet and squirmed a little in his chair.

By evening matters had progressed little. Asked about his farming—if one could call it farming, thought Hugo to himself, subsistence gardening rather—Raymond answered merely, "I'm surviving." Asked about the books that lay about, Raymond just grunted. Hugo picked one up. He had bought books too, when he was in his early twenties: the latest Goncourt prize, whatever was being talked about at the moment, whatever would impress young women. Then he had made money. He had this big utility vehicle. He didn't need to read. The book in his hands was a history of the Albigensians in Languedoc. He could play the Cathar card in his promotion of his father's hillside; he hadn't thought of that.

"I suppose you're reading this because the Cathars lived in poverty too, didn't they?" He tried to keep his lip from curling, but it would of its own accord.

"No, only the Perfect ones among them renounced the material world," Raymond answered quietly.

Hugo was never taken aback for long. "That's so ridiculous. Perfection and poverty have nothing in common. One could even say they are mutually exclusive."

Raymond considered, with pain, that his son could serve as a perfect illustration for the Cathar belief that materialism was the root of all evil. He also had a fleeting thought for the bigotry and cruelty that, so many centuries ago, had put an end to the belief system of most of Languedoc. But his son wasn't interested in either religion or history, and so he merely nodded his head as if he were agreeing.

Encouraged, Hugo went on rapidly: "Listen—
Papa. (He never called his father 'Papa' to himself, but
always 'Raymond.' However, there were times when
one had to put aside one's feelings.) Listen, Papa, I've
thought of a way to get you out of poverty." Rapidly, he
outlined his plan for the subdivision of Raymond's
acres into vacation homes. He had a partner who took
care of the construction. He could sell this property like
hotcakes, like *des petits pains chauds*. The fresh air, charming medieval village—

"It isn't," said Raymond.

"Isn't what?"

"Isn't medieval—not most of it, anyway."

"Okay. *Bon.* Period. And there was that *manoir*
just down the road, okay, *bon,* a few kilometers down
the road; okay, okay, quite a few kilometers down the
road. It belonged to a marquise or something, didn't it?
That would be a selling point. Renaissance, wasn't it?
Or something like that?"

Raymond nodded.

"Renaissance! Excellent! And the castle in Foix,
and Montségur not so very far away, and the fortress of
Carmonjaloux—perhaps if the trees were cut down one
could see it? No? There was a mountain in the way?
Well, *tant pis*, it was close. Land prices around castles
always skyrocketed, sooner or later. He could get a
good price here, too, he knew. Did Raymond know that
10% of French families had vacation homes? That
meant that 90% were still in need. Then there were the
English, the Irish. And besides, it didn't really matter
what the virtues of a location were, his hard-sell tactics
were guaranteed to get the job done. He was *un vrai pro*.
He knew how to get around sticky land-use commis-
sions, too. In fact, no one said no to Hugo Trencavel...

"So what do you say, Papa?"

"No."

There was a silence. Raymond had listened in silence, he was still silent. He wished he had a drink.

"*No?* Just *no?*

"Just no."

No, by evening things had not improved. Hugo was to stay the night. He really, really, didn't want to: a twenty-minute drive would take him to a decent hotel, and his father's bed, with its sagging springs, ragged blankets, and no doubt, fleas, filled him with repugnance. But he knew the importance, in this type of negotiations, of not letting up the pressure. He had come to carry a point and he was determined not to leave until he had succeeded. He would—he could—keep talking till his father gave in. Weaker parties always gave in to superior forces. And Hugo had no least doubt that the superiority was all on his side.

So he prepared for bed with only that degree of bad grace that he felt suited someone of his caliber who is asked to lie down in dog hair and dirt. Of the comfort of his father, who took two blankets and went off to sleep in the woodshed, he never thought.

It was sometime after midnight when the peace of the Pyrenees foothills was split by a roar of indignation: "Get off, *enfant de chienne!*"

Raymond, in the woodshed, smiled to himself a little as he rolled over. Was it his fault that the window was open, or that Guilhabert, the dog, was used to come in and out the window, or that Guilhabert liked to sleep in a bed?

The dog slunk into the shed with an injured air and lay down with a sigh by his master. "Should have bit him," Raymond muttered, and pulling the blankets around himself, went back to sleep.

2

Amadea had been looking for work for weeks. There had been interviews that came to nothing, applications that were never answered. What does one do if one has a degree, even two degrees, in literature and one doesn't want, or isn't able (and Amadea was wincingly aware that this was the case) to teach? The overworked owner of a café in a peripheral quarter agreed to give her a try as a waitress.

Amadea, poised in front of a group of clients among the crowded tables of the Bistro Au Goinfre Ailé, considered that looking for a job was hard, but perhaps having a job was worse.

"So that'll be two *cafés filtre*, two *mousses au chocolat*, an *absinthe*, a *café au lait*, a *baba au rhum…*"

"No, mademoiselle, I changed my mind, I wanted a *café serré*, not a *café filtre.*"

"So one *serré*, one *café crème*, one…"

"No, that was two…"

"Mademoiselle, mademoiselle," another customer was calling. "How long do I have to wait?"

"Little faster, mademoiselle," said the proprietor between gritted teeth as he passed with an order. Amadea nodded. She was trying hard, but she was painfully aware that she was all thumbs where trays and glasses were concerned, and too easily flustered to be able to remember orders. It was not to last long. Hurrying with the *café filtre*, *café crème*, *absinthe*, *mousse au chocolat*, etc., she collided with the proprietor carrying an equal load. A man, coming through the door, had his trousers liberally splashed. He was annoyed and said so. The owner, bending to fish glass out of the sticky pond, was also annoyed. He said: *"Eh bé*, mademoiselle, you're fired."

"I'll help to clean it up before I go," she quavered.

"No, no, no. Just go away. Go." He waved impatient hands at her. She collected her coat and left the Bistro Au Goinfre Ailé.

So there she was, alone in the world and jobless. She was of mixed parentage. Her mother was French, and part of her childhood had been spent in France. Her father had been an American businessman, and after her mother had steamed off, under full feminist flag, to pursue her own career and affairs, they had lived in America. Or Amadea had, at least: first in one boarding school or another, then at Swarthmore. Her father's bankruptcy and suicide a year previous had left her at a loose end.

She had come back to France partly because she missed the French language: the intrinsic sensual pleasure of a language where, if one only asks for the lavatory—*"excusez-moi madame, y a-t-il des toilettes ici?"*—it sounds like a phrase one might have proffered to Madame de Maintenon at the court of the Sun King.

And partly she had come in the hopes of re-finding a homeland, of finding a place for herself in the world. She had found neither a homeland, nor friends, but in that, she told herself, she was no worse off than before, and maybe she was better situated. Paris is the best place in the world to be lonely. So many million other people are feeling the same all around one.

But, however congenial for melancholy singleness Paris may be, it is also very expensive. Pay at the E.N.C.P. had scarcely done more than cover the bare necessities of life; when her work as a waitress reached its crashing finale, she had only a few weeks' savings left between herself and destitution.

So there were more rounds of applications—applications submitted with the apologetic feeling that in accepting a job she would be doing her employer a disservice—and days of wandering lonely as a cloud, and of palely loitering, and of all the unrewarding activities with which the jobless fill their days. Amadea knew that although the French have a very nice word—*flâner*—for this kind of aimless strolling, in her case it was the restlessness of anxiety. She worried along the congested streets, and up and down in the Parc Monceau, and along the paths of the Jardin du Luxembourg, where exhaust-blackened moisture dripped off the city's trees, and Polyphemus in the Medici fountain tensed his muscles against the cold, while Acis and Galatea shivered below him.

Somewhere it was spring, but Paris hadn't heard about it yet. The wind bit as it whistled, and Amadea turned up her collar and huddled together in her thin coat as she stood on the *quai* and watched the sluggish brown waters of the Seine roll past.

Who was it? Yes, Mirah in *Daniel Deronda*, who, alone and penniless in England, goes down to the Thames and wets her coat in the water. But if I tried to drown myself, thought Amadea, no fine young man would come along to save me singing '*Nessun Maggior*

Dolore'—nor even 'I Wanna Hold Your Hand'—I'd just make a botch of it and end up in a psychiatric ward. Her father now—*No*. She wouldn't think of that. Hastily she made an effort to turn her thoughts elsewhere. She faced away from the river and watched the traffic for a while. In any case, if she was not so optimistic as to think the future might be happy, perhaps at least it would be interesting? Surely it was an interesting fate to starve to death in Paris in the 21st century? Did people? Or was there an association like the Humane Society that would come around some day and scoop her up off the sidewalk and take her to a soup kitchen?

She became aware that someone was hailing her, was, in fact, crossing the street to speak to her...Monsieur? Monsieur? Monsieur Somebody. He was a frowsy-looking man of forty who had been in one of her (apparently unappreciated) classes at the E.N.C.P. He was standing in front of her now, stammering slightly, inviting her for a cup of coffee. He wanted to practice his English, he was shy—both were factors that made Amadea put aside her own shyness to be kind. She hazarded a busy intersection at his side and soon found herself ensconced in an empty café. The coffee, the first she'd had for some time, steamed up warmly between her hands. M. Somebody beamed at her. She wondered what to say that he would understand.

"It is very windy today."
"*Oui, oui.* Vairry vindy."
"Winter has lasted very long."
"Er?"
"I wish spring would come."
"Ah, *oui*, spring."

Conversation rather stuck, so to help it along she began to tell him about her job-hunting. Yes, he had heard that she was no longer at the English Institute. He politely supposed that they'd had to—how to say it in English?—make people leave because of the bad economy?

She didn't refute it, but sat pondering the word 'boring,' which had sprung up to darken her day. She wasn't listening though. She forced her attention back to her acquaintance, who, all goodwill and desire to help, was telling her that the thing to do was to leave. She regarded him with mild surprise. He hadn't seemed like a France-for-the-French type. But no, no, he didn't mean leave France—no one in his right mind would want to do that—he meant leave *Paris*. Life in the provinces now—so much healthier, so much greener, so much slower. Sometimes it was easier to find a job there these days, as so many people had left for the cities over the past decades. In fact, he was from the south—ah, *oui,* you might not think it—but he was from a little village to the west of Foix, Maugrebis, in the highlands, a beautiful place. He had been there just last week, in fact—and do you know?—there had been a help-wanted sign in the bakery that had been there since his last visit—oh, months ago. So it just went to show—not that she would want to work in a bakery, of course—he didn't mean that, of course, only that it proved there was work in the provinces.

The subject dropped, they talked of other things, but Amadea, in the uninspiring days that followed, thought more and more frequently about the bakery in the beautiful Pyrenean village, with the help-wanted sign.

*

At Raymond's house, near the beautiful Pyrenean village, the father-and-son reunion was not about to receive the *Légion d'honneur* for progress. By noon of the second day, harmony had not been achieved, nor had Hugo carried his point.

Hugo, resigning himself to a long siege, gave up any hope of a dialogue, and set himself to talk. He could talk endlessly—it was a sales tactic—and he did. He carried on a monologue covering the weather, the region, politics both foreign and domestic, his work, other people's work, his vacations, other people's vacations, the need for vacation homes: anything, so long as there was noise and his father was held captive, listening. Because every so often the noise would veer away from the weather, the region, the politics, etc., and glide into the wonders and wealth awaiting them if only...

"No!" said Raymond for the eighth time. And the talk would slip back into the weather, last year's weather, the mountains, vacations in the mountains, the need for vacation homes...

In the evening, after his eleventh refusal, Raymond rose and left the house. He did not slam the door, although he wanted to, he just got up quietly and left, as if he were going out to feed the chickens.

Hugo remained sitting. His father had gone out to feed the chickens or something of that nature, he supposed. He waited more or less patiently, drumming his fingers on the table. Half an hour later he was feeling much less patient. He rose and went to the door. The dog was chained to his house, but his father was nowhere in sight. He stepped gingerly around the yard, not wanting to soil his shoes on the raw earth and grass. There were spotted chickens pecking about in a pen, but his father was nowhere to be seen. Hugo cursed, and went back into the house, slamming the door.

A brisk walk, hurried perhaps by a slightly euphoric feeling of escape and a stronger feeling of need, brought Raymond to the farm of his acquaintance, Pascal.

Pascal appeared at the gate, but looking back toward the house, he shook his head; he didn't dare to today, and his wife had the stuff under lock and key.

Nodding, Raymond turned away. He would have to go all the way to the village then. He set off, glancing occasionally over his shoulder when he had to follow the road, in case Hugo should come after him in that big truck thing of his. Why couldn't he just tell the boy to go away? Because Hugo was his son, and because, because—Raymond admitted it to himself—he wouldn't go anyway. How the boy—boy?—how the man—he was thirty-five, wasn't he?—how he loved money. How could he have had a son like that? But no, better not to think about such things. The memories were too painful, too full of bitterness and regret. After all, he hadn't had much to do with Hugo's upbringing. But wasn't that his fault, too? When he had inherited the land, Odile had not wanted to move here from Bordeaux, but he had insisted. He had had a good position as a history teacher in a prestigious school, but he had imagined a happier life for them here in the wilds, à la Jean de Florette (only, of course, he wouldn't get hit on the head like poor, dumb Jean, or anything like that). Odile had had other ideas of happiness. He had been hurt by her attitude. "A godforsaken hole," she had called it. "It isn't a hole, it's a mountainside," he had answered. She had screamed in irritation, "A hole, a hillside, a horrible hovel—it was still in the middle of godforsaken nowhere!" How could anyone prefer a dusty, crowded city to this wooded Arcadia, with the wild delphiniums and the nesting birds and the mountains all about? Godforsaken? No, he was sure God inhabited the hills more than the plains. "I shall lift up mine eyes unto the hills, from whence cometh my help," said the psalm.

But in the end, Odile had taken Hugo and left. And he had suffered because he had loved her and he had loved Hugo, who was only five and didn't understand. Then, when he had given in and followed, it was too late, and she had sent him packing back. He too, had thought something more important than a human being. *Dieu*, how he needed that drink. He had seen little of Hugo since then. He supposed it was poetic justice: he had destroyed his family for the sake of the land, and now Hugo wanted it back from him. He stopped in the road, weighing this thought, because he was a man with a fine sense of justice, and a Mediterranean feel for the dramatic gesture:

"Here, son of my loins, take the land and let it be quits between us!"

He stood still, savoring the idea. But no, no. He would give up the land, and then? Hugo's planned housing development would go slicing across his cherished woods, toppling the trees and churning under the poppies and the gentians and the lilies of the meadows. Then there would be all those mock Provençal *mas* with shiny cars in front of them, and smug city-dwellers carting in expensive groceries—all that olive oil!—at the weekends and eyeing him askance, and whispering that it really was a scandal—that old drunkard in the decaying house, with the rusty tractor, and the unkempt yard: wasn't there a zoning law against, against—well, they wouldn't say against *him*, but that's what they would mean. Never! It was the land of his forebears, and there had been a manor house too, once, there on the hill behind. Let it all go? Never!

He hurried into town by a roundabout route in case Hugo was looking for him. The bistro was open and he nodded to the few patrons. They were not his friends. With the exception of Pascal, his sometime drinking companion, he had no friends here. He had come to Maugrebis as a stranger, thirty or more years ago, and somehow he had always remained one in the eyes of the villagers. And although he frequently did odd jobs of work for some of them, a little carpentry or masonry, he had never joined the community. He was nearly a recluse.

He rarely came to the bistro, preferring, on the times, once every ten days or a fortnight, that he needed to get drunk, to buy the requisite bottle and take it home. He had his dignity. He might have been seen stumbling along the road from Pascal's house, but he had never yet been found drunk in the village street. He sat down at a table with a glass and a bottle of cheap wine in front of him. What would Hugo do if he were to find his father lying in the gutter? Drive off and pretend he didn't know him, that's what. Raymond smiled wryly to himself. He thought awhile, then he lifted his glass and toasted himself. There was a time for everything: a time to reap and a time to sow; a time to lie sozzled in the street.

When he stumbled home the next afternoon, cold, filthy, and feeling sicker than he could remember feeling for a long time, he was somewhat comforted by the absence of Hugo's vehicle in front of his house. It had not been for nothing then, his heroic flouting of his own dignity. He imagined Hugo driving through the town searching for him, seeing a body lying crumpled against a wall, slowing, looking again, thrice, recognizing his father, then his foot going down hard on the accelerator as he sped out of town. Yes, that was how it must have been, though, truth to tell, he couldn't remember how or where he'd spent the night. He fed his hungry animals with the last of his strength and will power, then went into the house and fell down upon his bed. When he would wake everything would be back to normal, and now, oblivion was bliss. He slept.

And yet, when he opened his eyes sometime later, Hugo was there, sitting on a chair and watching him. Raymond closed his eyes again and was about to groan but the thought of Hugo stopped him. Then he thought that groaning would annoy Hugo so he groaned, and then again, loudly.

"Stop that!" Hugo controlled his irritation with difficulty.

Raymond groaned again, to show that he was his own man, then, feeling rather ashamed of himself, he rolled over and pretended to sleep again.

Hugo rose from his chair, banged it against the floor and left the house. A moment later the car started and rolled away. But in the evening, when Raymond had risen and was running cold water over his head, the car was back. And Raymond knew that Hugo was not going to give up. And this was the evening of the third day already.

On the fourth day, the talk recommenced, and Hugo dogged Raymond's footsteps. On the fifth day, Hugo had to leave for Bordeaux to get back to his real estate business: he had matters that needed his personal attention. Bruno, his partner, was good at the construction end, but Bruno was a bit heavy, a bit...well, Bruno frightened people a little. There were matters that it was better he took care of himself.

But before many days had passed he was back, and the pressure was on again. Raymond became rude: he told Hugo to go away. Hugo ignored him, except that he dropped all pretence of politeness. Raymond considered asking the authorities for help. But this was his son and he didn't like the authorities anyway. They'd think him an old drunkard; he knew it showed on him. What luck would he have explaining the situation to anyone? He got a bottle from Pascal, brought it back, and drank a good part of it in the woodshed. Hugo found him there.

"Wake up! *Ohé!* Wake up!" No response. Hugo gave his father a nudge with the toe of his shoe. "Wake up! We have things to talk about!" No response. Hugo left the woodshed. Guilhabert was standing at the end of his chain, straining at it slightly, ears pricked in the direction of the woodshed. He growled faintly at the sight of Hugo. He didn't like Hugo. The feeling was mutual. Hugo would have liked to kick the dog as he passed him, but he didn't quite dare.

There was a tray of water in the chicken pen. He lifted it out, returned to the woodshed, and dumped it over his father. He'd been patient long enough. Raymond awoke sputtering and spitting. He sat up and lifted dazed hands to his face: they came away wet. His son stood in front of him, dangling the chicken pan.

Hugo spoke icily. "Get up. We have to talk, and I'm getting tired of all this. You're going to do as I say."

But for Raymond too, the time for patience had come and gone. He staggered to his feet, and supporting himself with one hand on the wall, shouted: "Get out! Get out of my house!"

Hugo looked at his father disdainfully. "'Housh,' 'housh.' Get out of your shed, you mean. You don't even know where you are, you old wino."

"Get out of my housh; get out of my sh-shed; get off my land; get out of my life!" Raymond was trembling with rage. Outside, Guilhabert, hearing his master's shouts, was barking and lunging at his chain.

"I don't have to listen to you! *You* have to listen to *me!*" shouted Hugo. He put his hands on his father's chest and pushed. Raymond, unbalanced by the alcohol, fell backwards, slipped on kindling wood and tools, and tumbled with a crash into the woodpile. Guilhabert broke his chain with a mighty lunge, came rushing to the rescue, and arrived to see his master fall. He jumped at Hugo, but Hugo had time to snatch up an axe and he swung it at the dog. Guilhabert dodged and circled, snarling furiously. Hugo swung the axe again, and missed. But now Raymond, seriously frightened for the dog, was urgently shouting "No! No! Down!" at him. Bewildered, the dog backed out of the shed, barking thunderously. Hugo came after him purposefully. To drive the dog out of his son's reach, Raymond took up a piece of wood and threw it at the dog. "Go away! Go away!" It hit the dog on the side, and he yelped and ran off a short distance. Raymond stumbled forward out of the shed, found a rock, and threw that too. "Go away!" Hugo strode across the yard with the axe raised. Raymond threw another stone. It connected, and another. The dog, with a last shocked look at his master, turned and disappeared into the bushes.

Raymond squatted on his heels and leaned against the chopping block outside the shed. He wept.

He was weeping not for his dog, but for his son, and the tears were very bitter. His last hope that his son was not as awful as he suspected had just evaporated. He had no son and he had very little wish to live.

So when Hugo came striding toward him with the axe he felt no particular fear of his impending murder, only a deep sadness. Hugo, his face hard, swung the axe up over his head. This was it, the end. Raymond closed his eyes. The axe came whistling down and smacked into the chopping block.

Raymond opened his eyes and began to laugh a weeping and hysterical laugh. Hugo, realizing in a flash of intuition what his father had imagined, felt a cold rage take hold of himself. Anger was a very good remedy for shame.

"*Voilà.* I've got rid of your dog, and I can get rid of you, too."

Raymond said nothing, but continued to chuckle and hiccup.

"All old people should be euthanized."

Raymond said nothing.

"Tomorrow, you will come to the notary's office with me." |

Raymond said no.

Who could have believed the old man could be so stubborn? Hugo couldn't stay here forever. He had business to attend to. He took out his cell phone and called Bruno. Bruno frequently had good ideas. They might need a little polishing to bring them into line with the law, but they were good ideas. Bruno's idea this time was that he should send over one or two of the security guards who watched over his construction equipment at night. They were burly fellows. He used them sometimes for collecting money owed. The sight of them should be enough. Hugo hesitated and said that threatening people was a criminal offence, and besides, he added with a touch of unwilling admiration, he didn't think it would work with his father.

"*Bof.* Have it your way," said Bruno.

Hugo thought for a while. His father was an alcoholic and needed tending. Someone really should be around to look after him, and incidentally make sure he didn't talk to people, and, by the way, remind him there was no escape: sooner or later, he'd have to give in. If his father managed to talk to the police, it would just look as if he, Hugo, were a concerned son trying to take care of a difficult parent.

*

Guilhabert, when driven out of his home, had fled only a small way, then come back. He stayed out of sight until in the evening he saw Raymond outside again. Then he emerged, crestfallen, from the bushes, and with drooping tail and apologetic grin, tried to approach his master. But his master bent, took up a rock again, and made as if to throw it. Hugo was not to be trusted. Perhaps the dog would find a home at one of the farms down the hill. He would ask Pascal to look out for him—if he ever got a chance. Guilhabert took the hint and turning, trotted away down the drive. He kept trotting for a long time, looking neither to the right nor to the left and having no idea where he was going. He passed various houses: dogs barked at him and he went on, until at last, sore in foot and mind, he lay down under a tree and slept until dawn. He spent the day wandering, hungry and tired. Once he managed to slip into a yard and eat some food put out for cats, but he was soon chased away. People, when they noticed him, gave him a wide berth. He was not an appealing character. In the evening it began to rain, and this displeased him. He came to a house and circled it: no one was there. The door was shut, but one of the windows was unlatched and a bit ajar. Guilhabert knew from experience how to insert his toenails into the cracks of unlatched doors or windows. He scratched and pulled. The window resisted, then swung open. He heaved his considerable bulk through. Here it was dry and safe. It was a house and he was used to sleeping in a house. He flopped down upon the floor and slept the sleep of nervous exhaustion.

*

Some hours after Hugo had made a second phone call to Bruno there was a dreadful mechanical growling outside Raymond's house, and a motorcycle gnashed its way up the bumpy drive. Bruno's thug had arrived. He was a large and beefy man of indeterminate but probably youngish age, wearing a black leather jacket and very little hair. He had a scar on one cheek and a tattoo on one wrist. He grunted in greeting to Hugo, pushed his bike into the woodshed, came into the house, surveyed Raymond without a word, and grunted again in response to Hugo's directions that he was to keep watch over Raymond—not to let him near other people, and particularly not to let him go to a notary's office or the police. Hugo left.

The thug sat down and stared at Raymond. They were alone in the house; outside there was silence except for the soughing of the tree branches in the breeze, or the occasional clucking or crowing of the chickens.

"Some job, eh?" said Raymond to the thug.

The man shrugged his shoulders and shifted his dead-alive gaze to the floor. Raymond sighed and picked up a book.

3

Amadea, tramping along a gritty gray pavement on foot to save the metro fare, was thinking hard about her immediate future. The faces of the passersby looked stressed and hurried. So, no doubt, did hers, she reflected. She could leave the city and go to the country. Spring would come there, with all its hope and flowers. It began to seem like a good idea. Provided, of course, that she could find work. By the time she had climbed the four flights of rickety stairs to the miniscule and shabby cubbyhole she was renting at an enormous price, it seemed like a better idea yet. She could not afford another month's rent. She pulled the door shut again without entering and went back down the steps and out to the nearest post office. She went into a phone booth there and asked for the operator. "The bakery in Maugrebis, please," she asked, hoping there was only one. It seemed there was: La Boulangerie Nareix.

She took a deep breath and dialed again. The voice that answered assured her that yes, he, Benoit Nareix, was the owner of the bakery—and what might madame be wanting? She explained that she had heard he was looking for an employee; an acquaintance from the village—it was unfortunate she couldn't remember his name—but he had told her that the bakery was hiring. Was it still?

"Well, yes, but..."

No, she had never worked in a bakery, but he would find her very eager to learn and hardworking. (It was easier to be brave over the phone than in person, she found.) M. Duquesne of the E.N.C.P. English Institute in Paris would give her a reference for reliability, she felt tolerably sure. Oh, she was a teacher then? She had a degree?

"Yes." (True, it was not a degree in bread-making, but still, the French are impressed by diplomas.)

Only if madame had a diploma, then why did she want to work in a bakery?

She was tired of teaching and tired of the city. She had heard so much about the beauty of Maugrebis, and the cordiality and hospitality of its citizens. (This was an uncharacteristic bit of deviousness on her part, but it answered.) From an attitude of suspicion, the bakery owner relaxed gradually into friendliness. Why not? He had, indeed, never hired anyone over the telephone, but, after all, why not? He wasn't having much luck by the usual methods: three months now he had been looking for someone to help out in the shop. There had been two applicants. Neither had stayed for more than a week. Having decided to take a chance on his caller, he put himself out to be helpful. She would need a place to live if she was coming from Paris, and now—wasn't it lucky?—he had heard that old Vaturin's place near the *manoir* was to let again. The last tenants had just left. He didn't think the rent would be much. It was a converted barn, a ways outside the village, but the walk wasn't far. Or maybe she had a car. No? Well, just a moment while he searched for the number. He knew

Vaturin's sons. They all lived in Paris now, so she could talk to them there. Here it was. He gave her the number. He would expect her then within the week.

As easy as that. Amadea hung up the phone and immediately, before the impetus flagged and failed, dialed again. M. Vaturin sounded elderly and a little confused, but he was quite willing to let his barn; she could come anytime to collect the key.

*

It was morning in Maugrebis. The sun came into the kitchen over La Boulangerie Nareix. Madame Nareix snapped off the gas, lifted the pan off the burner, mixed the milk and coffee with a dexterous hand and pursed lips, and banged the bowl of *café au lait* down in front of her husband.

Monsieur Nareix sighed. He rubbed the spilled coffee off the table with the palm of his hand and wiped it on his pants. He had been up since four baking and he would have preferred a meal now, but his wife insisted that mealtime was midday and that to eat anything but coffee and bread before that was an inadmissible break with tradition. So for nine hours he ate croissants and *chocolatines* off his own racks to stave off hunger and he had been getting heavier and heavier since his marriage two years ago, but his wife was inflexible. He had found her through an advertisement in a Toulouse paper. A baker didn't have time to go looking for a wife, and he wasn't young anymore. At first he had been quite pleased, because she was tolerable-looking and could be charming when she chose. Unfortunately, since their marriage she had seldom felt like being charming, or even very pleasant. In short, she ruled him. He knew it, and it bothered him a little, but he couldn't seem to do anything about it. Anyhow, it was better than being alone, and maybe it was easier if she made all the decisions for him. He sighed again, and reached for another roll, but his wife snatched them out of the way.

"You're supposed to be watching your weight."

"*Oui, chérie,*" he said meekly.

And then there was the problem of the bakery. None of the villagers would work there with his wife. That was why, when the woman had called from Paris, he had thought, after the initial hesitation, that she might be a godsend. One person was not enough to mind the shop, his wife was always telling him, and he was busy with the baking, and now, too, he was starting to deliver to neighboring villages as well. Yes, they needed a third worker, perhaps even a fourth. But his wife had objected to his having acted on his own, he supposed. Indeed, that had been wrong. He should have let her handle everything; life went more smoothly that way; because no sooner had he told her about the woman with the strange name from Paris then she had flown into a temper and said she had already invited her niece to come from Toulouse to work for them (and, in fact, later he had heard her dialing her sister, and there had been a long—several long—telephone conversations.) Sylvie, the niece, had dropped out of school, was out of work, and one had to help one's own flesh and blood, didn't one? said his wife. Of course, of course, he had agreed, although he could never remember her speaking with charity of this niece before. However. The worst of it was that he had no way to call back the Paris girl and tell her not to come. It was very embarrassing. And his niece, who had come down to breakfast late after spending three-quarters of an hour in the bathroom, and was now sitting opposite him with a sulky pout on her brown-lipsticked mouth, did not look to him exactly like an eager beaver of a worker. However. He would let his wife handle her. He ducked his head into his cup, drained it, and went back to work.

*

Amadea's first thought, when she opened her eyes a few days later, was that this was her last day in Paris, and perhaps the first day of a new life. If it was not better, it would at least be different. She smiled to herself as she thought of the duc de Lévis' maxim: "Man tires of the good, seeks the better, finds the bad, and submits thereto, for fear of worse."

But hopefully that would not be her case, she told herself firmly as she made a hasty breakfast. Outside, a gray drizzle filtered down between beige buildings. In Maugrebis the sun would be shining. Her bag, bulging with books and a few clothes, stood ready by the door. She took a last glimpse around the room and caught sight of herself in the mirror. Thin hair that was almost, but not quite, blonde, a thin figure of no particular defect or attraction, a face that was nearly beautiful—but only if one liked that kind of a face. It was a dispiriting glimpse. I look like an Edwardian governess, she thought, peering at herself with a slight frown; and that's not a very good thing to look like at the beginning of the 21st century. She was a century out of date in looks, thought, and manners. And it was only in novels that the lives of governesses were anything but wearisome. She gave herself a mental shake. Enough self-pity! Onward! The bakery shop awaits! She picked up her bag, locked the door, and went down the stairs.

The bus from Toulouse chugged gradually upwards until it ran in among a close-packed settlement of brick and stone houses, a high bell tower, and a street of shops. It lurched into its stop just long enough for Amadea to descend. A hint of rain was being blown by a light breeze that brought the scent of snow down off the mountains. Even through the station odors of petrol, rubber, and people, there was a smell of wet earth and plants. Amadea swung the strap of her bag over her shoulder, stretched legs that were stiff from long sitting, and began to walk along the main street, where shop-owners were locking up and the pavement glistened wetly. So here she was. She felt both excited and wary; she rather wished someone would smile at her, or speak; but when she tried to catch, half-unconsciously, the eyes of the few passers-by, they merely gave her a cursory glance and hurried on their way. She knew she had no right to expect otherwise, and yet her arrival in this new place seemed so momentous to her, such a departure from the past, that she would have liked it to be marked by some human contact. She walked on. The traverse of the village took longer than she expected. She was beginning to grow quite hungry, and the bag was heavy. In fact, it banged against her legs at every step. She began to feel discouraged. The bakery was in this street. She would just see if it was still open. It should be around here someplace. Yes, there it was, but the shutters were already across and no one answered her tentative knock on the green-painted door. A sign in the window listed its hours: it must have just closed. Well, she would be back in the morning, early. In the meantime, she had the key to her new quarters in her pocket, and a map, drawn on a scrap of paper, showing her how to get there. She fingered the key to make sure it was still there. She had met the owner in Paris and made a down payment. It was just on the edge of the village, he had said. Quite near. She would get some groceries and go there—go home, was it? A combined grocery and *charcuterie* was still open. She turned into the welcome light and bought eggs. She had half a leftover loaf of bread with her yet—that would be enough for dinner. After an internal struggle she decided to forego a packet of coffee and a carton of milk.

The proprietor, a rubicund little man with a strong Midi accent, observed her with some curiosity. "Mademoiselle is new in town?"

"Yes." She hesitated, but after all, why be so reserved always? Here was the human contact she had desired. "I've come to work in the bakery."

The proprietor's eyebrows lifted. "*Ça, par exemple!*" was his odd comment; and then, "Where are you staying? There's no hotel in our village."

"At M. Vaturin's." She guessed that in such a small place he would know where she meant.

"*Ah, oui?*" Voices could be heard at the back of the shop and he suddenly lost interest in his new customer, only saying, as she considered the cheeses, that she should try his sausage or his very good cold cuts. Amadea shook her head. "Thank you."

The proprietor had one ear cocked to the voices. "Really, take the cold cuts."

"Thank you. I'm a vegetarian."

"*Ça, par exemple!*"

The bells on the door tinkled behind Amadea as she stepped back into the street. She heard the key turn in the lock while she stood studying her map. The town was almost entirely closed for the evening now, and it was quite dark. However, she had only to turn left at the next street, follow it to the end of the cobbles and then take a dirt road leading from the highway up the hill a short way. The owner in Paris had made it sound quite close to the town.

By the time, however, that she had stumbled and slipped to the end of the long cobbled street, she felt she had been walking for quite a while. The little glow left by the slight exchange with the grocer had long since disappeared, to be replaced by a growing emptiness. The houses, right on the street or tucked away behind small gardens, had petered out, and with them, the light. Amadea did not like the dark; she could hardly see the path that led from the end of the street to a paved road curving away in both directions. She followed the verge. The strap of the bag was cutting into her fingers now, and although the rain had stopped, it had already soaked her shoes and the bottom of her skirt. A car came quickly round the bend, its lights blinding her for a moment before it sped on. She suddenly felt rather like crying. Long habit had made her used to being alone, but only, so to speak, in a crowd. She had never taken a lone country walk before, in the night, in the rain, to nowhere, it seemed, in particular. And she had never, she felt, been good at coping with the unexpected.

She came to what she supposed was the "track up the hill" that led to the converted barn. It looked very dark and led between fields into a stand of trees. She stopped and stared at the hillside. Imagination began to suggest strange ideas. Suppose it was all just a plot to get her to this out-of-the-way place to murder her? She shuddered, and then reason reasserted itself: Nonsense, don't be silly. No one tried to get you here, you decided to come. And poor M. Vaturin, her landlord—he had seemed very elderly and slow-moving and not very clear-thinking when she had travelled out to the proletarian suburb of Vitry to meet him in his tiny house. He had had difficulty in remembering why she'd come, and had seemed to think it had all been arranged a week previously, although their telephone conversation had been only the evening before. They had gotten it straightened out, however, and he had given her the key, and assurances that the barn was furnished—oh, yes, mademoiselle, all the pots and pans and bed linen. And so near the *manoir*. There was a path through the woods. They would show it to her, no doubt. It was very convenient. It was the marquis who had converted the barn and given it to him. He was a very good man, the marquis, and his grandson, now, he was a very good man too, a real gentleman, very attentive to his grandmother, too, not like most young people these days, never thinking of anything but themselves...She had smiled and nodded and paid little attention to his talk about the honorable grandson or his grandmother or paths that didn't concern her, and eventually she had managed to steer him back to the barn. Yes, the last tenants left it in good order, he'd been told. Not like the ones before that. "Then there was a mess, I tell you...But you will not leave a mess, mademoiselle?" She had assured him she would not, and he had given her the key and various instructions—several times over— about the water and electricity, and this map. No, M. Vaturin could not have meant her any harm.

She shifted the bag and stepped resolutely off the pavement. The clouds had shifted, and there was a moon out, nearly full. Her eyes had adjusted to the dark enough to be able to follow the track easily and to tell that her shoes would be permanently the worse for the mud. The way led uphill, and, slipping occasionally, she walked on, resolutely still until the shadow of the trees reached out to greet her. She stopped. No matter how hard she stared into the greater blackness ahead of her, she couldn't make it diminish. Perhaps she could go around the woods? But if she lost the track she might never reach her destination. She took a faltering step forward, and then another. Werewolves came out in the full moon, didn't they? And what was that creature she had been reading about recently? The Bête de Gevaudan, that ate over 100 people in the middle of the 18th century. No, that was in the Massif Central, and this was in the Pyrenees, but still—still, strange things could happen in French woods. Stop it, she told herself, as her heartbeat increased and gooseflesh rose. Stop it! If she let herself think things like that she would shortly turn and flee in mad headlong flight down the track. Fortunately, a truck rumbled by below her. This was the age of trucks. Of course, there weren't wild beasts in the woods, or murderers, either. She took a good hold of herself, began to recite 'Invictus,' very fast, and marched briskly on.

> *"Out of the night that covers me,*
> *Black as the Pit from pole to pole,*
> *I thank whatever gods may be*
> *For my unconquerable soul..."*

Yes, well, don't try to see behind the trees, don't glance behind... "Out of the night that covers me"...It was dark, so dark she could only feel the ground beneath her feet, not see it. And here it was actually lightening a little, but surely there was something coming up behind her? Something reaching for her? "Out-of-the-night-that-covers-me-black-as-the-pit-frompoletopole ..." She was practically running; she *was* running, with the bag slamming against her legs and panic in her heart; but here the trees were ending. She was beyond them, uneaten, un-murdered, and she could see her way again. She slowed to a walk. Above her to the right, standing among fields, was a roofed structure. Hurrah. That would be the barn, right where it was supposed to be.

The converted barn, Amadea thought, as she followed a gravel path from the track to the door, was really more of a cow shed, but she was too glad to have reached it to be in a mood to complain. It appeared to be a mixture of stone and brick, with a wide, over-hanging roof of slate. The door was painted brown; the narrow windows were shuttered and expressionless. She put down her bag and fumbled for the key with hands that shook a little. Rather to her surprise the latches clicked back easily at the second turn and she pushed the door open. It was darker inside than under the trees even and the interior exuded a smell of damp and cold. It struck her that she had never asked any questions about the heating at all. She fumbled for a light switch; surely there would be one here beside the door? Her hand ran over the wall and encountered nothing, nothing. Ah, there it was. She flicked it—nothing happened. Perhaps the bulb was out. With a sinking feeling she stepped into what she took to be the entry. In the next room, surely, there would be light? A few steps took her into the house. The door swung shut behind her and left the darkness almost complete. Here was another doorway. Her hand fumbled against the wall. No switch. She stood still, feeling the pulsating silence of the house as her eyes struggled to adjust to the darkness. She could just see that in the center of what must be the living room a white pull cord hung from a ceiling lamp. She felt loathe to leave the wall to reach it. It seemed to her that she could hear something breathing in the room. She stood frozen, trying to hear, as the hackles rose on the back of her neck. She took a deep breath. The sooner she reached the cord, the sooner she could put her overworked imagination to bed. She took two firm steps forward, put her foot down on something that—horribly—moved beneath her foot, and the room exploded in noise.

Something rose from the floor with the sound of a chainsaw starting up. Amadea shrieked and something heavy floundered against her, while something that brought to mind a flashing image of a wolf trap closed around her arm and then released it. The arm felt wet. Blood! She staggered backwards. A few seconds of total confusion, and she became aware that the noise filling the room was a deafening barking, drowning out even the sound of her own sobbing breaths. She clamped her teeth together to stop the sobs, and stood very still, stifling the urge to call for help. There was no one to hear her. She was alone with the creature. That it was a dog of enormous proportions and vicious propensities was obvious even in the dark. A werewolf would have been preferable.

She stood still and tried not to shake. Any moment the dog would spring. It would rend her legs, her arms, she would fall, and its teeth would close on her throat...The barking had switched to a low angry growl that was somehow even more menacing. She could see its eyes glistening as it stared at her from across the room. If she turned and ran she would never reach the door before it caught her. She closed her eyes and stood still, very still, concentrating on steadying her breathing. It seemed to work. After a long period of utmost tension, the dog appeared to get bored. It stopped growling. It sat down, and then it yawned noisily. Amadea opened her eyes. The dog stood up and came slowly towards her. She closed her eyes and listened to its footfalls padding closer, closer. She opened her eyes. Its enormous broad head was six inches away. She could feel its breath. It made a low rumbling sound in its throat. She closed her eyes again. The dog considered her for a moment, appeared to give her up for a loss, turned away, lifted a leg, and peed on her shoe.

An outraged "Hey!" broke from Amadea before she could stop it. The dog gave her a startled look, woofed over his shoulder, and retreated to the other side of the room. Amadea began to back away, slowly, slowly, the dog watching all the while. When she had reached the first doorway he burst into barking again, but she turned and sprang for the outer door: a moment's scrabbling for the doorknob, and she was through and slamming the door on the noise behind it. Then she fell over her bag.

She got up and stood panting in the misty moonlight. What to do now? Where to go? Whose dog was it? And why was he in her—supposedly—house? Perhaps she had the wrong house? But no, this had to be the right one: the keys had turned in the lock. What she needed was to call old M. Vaturin and ask him what it was all about: if it was his dog and if he'd just forgotten it? But no, it had been over a month since M. Vaturin left Maugrebis for Paris. The dog wouldn't have survived that long, surely? This one didn't give the impression of being on its last legs from hunger. Anyway, the only thing to do was to call M. Vaturin. Where could she make a phone call? She looked around her through the night. Near, there were only fields and the darker bulk of trees; away to the left were the occasional lights of the village, partially obscured by the woods and a little rise in the ground; across in the other direction, fairly close, were the lights of another house: the *manoir*, she supposed. But she couldn't go there; and if she walked to the village, would she find a phone? And where would she get a phone card? Surely it must be possible to call from somewhere? And then what? Out of all the possible answers M. Vaturin might make her, was there any that would lead to her being able to sleep in this house, this night? "There's no hotel in the village," the grocer had said. She shivered, then picked up her bag and stood hesitating. Then, oh joy, here were the headlights of a car coming slowly along the road from above. She rushed to the end of the path. Perhaps she could ask for a ride to the village? The dangers of hitchhiking faded entirely from her mind amongst her other worries. But she did not need even to hold up a hand or stick out a thumb. The car, a battered-looking jeep, was pulling over and parking beside the low stone wall that separated M. Vaturin's yard from the road. A man slid out of the driver's seat and stepped towards her.

"*Bonsoir*, mademoiselle—Lucien d'Alembert," he introduced himself. Stunned, Amadea held out her hand automatically and he bowed slightly over it. "We weren't expecting you until tomorrow, but M. Vaturin telephoned and said you had the address and were coming today. So I came over to see if everything was all right."

So this was the baker? He was unlike anything Amadea had imagined. She had expected the baker to be middle-aged and rather bulging, to have large burly forearms and to carry with him the aura of baguette. This man was in his mid-thirties, and though he may have been muscular, he did not bulge obviously in any direction. He was wearing a suit and polished shoes and he gave an impression of grace and cleanliness. The aura was of a top hat and white tie. Amadea gaped at him.

He, however, was looking down at the hold-all bag at her feet, taking in the small shopping bag clutched in her fingers.

"So you've just arrived, then? Shall I open the door for you?" He reached politely for the bag.

"No!" She found her voice then. "No. You can't go in. There's a dog in there."

"You brought a dog, mademoiselle? Does it bite?"

"Yes. No. I mean," Amadea stammered, "I don't know whose it is. I went in and I couldn't turn on the light and then I stepped on something and it rose up and bit me—but not very hard—and then it barked and snarled and I thought it was going to kill me, and then it—it, er—then I ran away and shut the door on it, and now I can't go back in and I don't know what to do, because there's no telephone and no telephone card, and what could M. Vaturin do anyway, and is it his dog, do you know?"

The man's eyebrows had raised slightly as she poured out this hopeless mish-mash, but he waited patiently for her to finish. Then he said kindly, "I don't think M. Vaturin has a dog. Perhaps you'd like to sit in the car while I check things out?" He moved over and opened the off-side door for her. Amadea slid in, feeling stupid but grateful. He picked up her bag and carried it back to the house, pushed open the door, and went in. Amadea slid out of her seat again. He didn't realize what kind of a dog it was. She couldn't just let him go in and perhaps get mauled. But the house was quiet. A light sprang on.

Amadea got back in the car and sat quietly. The dog couldn't have just disappeared, could it?

M. d'Alembert reappeared and came around to Amadea's side.

"Mademoiselle, there's no dog in the house."

"There was one. Really there was. He was huge. And black—black like 'the Great Gorgon, prince of darkness.'"

"*Ah? C'est interessant, ça.*" The black eyes regarded her with amusement.

She pushed her sleeve up (it was wet with saliva) and looked at her arm. Unfortunately there didn't seem to be any bite marks there. M. d'Alembert paused a moment and then walked back to the house. She could hear him calling:

"Here Fido, here Fido, here Fido," and there was laughter in his voice. How embarrassing. She wished the dog would appear from nowhere and, well, not bite him, of course, but chase him to the door, perhaps. He was back beside the car.

"Not even a poodle, mademoiselle." The tone was still neutral, but the laughter note was definitely there. "Everything seems to be in order. I've switched on the heater for you." He paused, then conceded: "A window was open, and a dog could have got in, I suppose. I've closed everything up."

Amadea swallowed. "Thank you. It's very kind of you to have bothered." She opened the car door and got out, turning to look for her shopping bag. Something flat and viscous lay on the seat. She had sat on the eggs.

She lifted the dripping parcel out. It left a stain across the seat. Wishing she were dead, she turned to M. d'Alembert, and said, miserably but quite calmly now, "I'm terribly sorry. I've sat on my eggs and it's left a stain on your seat."

His eyebrows shot up and she could see he was struggling not to laugh. She said, "I'll go in the house and try to find something to clean it with." She stumbled past him, but he stopped her.

"Mademoiselle, I assure you, it is no matter at all. One stain amongst many. It is not worth bothering about."

She stood dangling her squashed groceries in her hand. She said, looking at the ground, "I stopped by the bakery when I arrived this evening, but it was already closed. What time do you want me to come to work?"

She looked up at him. The amusement had died out of his eyes and he was regarding her seriously. It came to her that he was suddenly wondering if she were in her right mind.

"I'm not crazy, you know. There really was a dog."

"Of course."

He didn't believe her, she thought.

"Well, my grandmother doesn't get up very early. Perhaps you could come around nine? You can find your way by the road? It's not far. Tomorrow in the daylight we can show you a shortcut."

"All right," she said, rather mystified. What did his grandmother's rising have to do with her work? "Thank you again for coming. It was very kind. Goodnight."

"Goodnight, mademoiselle." He nodded and withdrew gracefully. The jeep started up, the headlights swept an arc that lit up tall dead grass in the field opposite, and then the taillights bounced slowly away.

Amadea turned and went back into the house. She felt too ridiculous to be afraid any longer. The dog seemed, indeed, like a figment of her imagination. The little house was still cold, but in the light it was almost cozy. After the small entryway, there was one rather large room, which was the living space. It held a sofa and a small wooden table and chairs. There was a fireplace: that would have been an addition to the cowshed, she supposed. It was empty, but on the hearth a large space heater had been plugged in. To one side of the room was a kitchen area. She opened a cupboard. There were a couple of plates and a few pots and pans. She turned back to face the room. The dog had been right there, beyond the table. Maybe it was a ghost dog and would silently appear when her back was turned. Stop it, she told herself sharply, you don't believe in ghosts. And besides, there was a small puddle on the floor—a ghost surely wouldn't have done that.

She dropped her spoiled groceries on the counter. Tomorrow she would have to see about a garbage container. Tonight there would be no dinner. She was tired, hungry, and cold. Something from the Bible came to mind: "in the morning thou shalt say, Would God it were even! and at even thou shalt say, Would God it were morning!"

She went over and crouched in front of the heater. M. Dalembaire—or was it d'Alembaire?—was like a character in a romantic novel, she thought. And then it struck her: the baker's name wasn't Dalembaire at all. The man with whom she had spoken on the telephone was called Nareix. Nareix of La Boulangerie Nareix. So who was this M. d'Alembaire? Or d'Alembert? And then the voice of her landlord came back to her.

"M. d'Alembert, the grandson of *madame la marquise*, comes often to the *manoir*....*oui*, mademoiselle, I worked for thirty years for the marquis." He had been the caretaker, but now he preferred to live in Paris, close to his sons. "Yves Sabadie is the caretaker now, and his wife does the housekeeping; they have their own rooms there, in the *manoir*...You will like the marquise," he had said, forgetting that she was unlikely to have any contact with her. "She is old, though, older than I am, and I am 85, ah, *oui*, mademoiselle, older than I and I am 85...and M. d'Alembert comes frequently to be with her. No, no, I am wrong; it is young Lucien who comes. A very fine young man. He married a very beautiful woman. *Ah, oui,* beautiful. But they have no children. You can see the *manoir* from the barn when there isn't any mist..."

So why, she wondered, had M. d'Alembert come here and said they were expecting her? Perhaps M. Vaturin asked him to? That seemed the likeliest idea. And he was married—so much for the romantic novel. Not, she thought, that he would ever have been interested in someone like herself anyway. And what a fool she had made of herself, with her nonexistent dog and "I stopped at the bakery before I came here." What must he have thought? But he was married. That was fortunate, because it was surely less painful to be thought muddleheaded by a married man than by a single one? And hopefully she'd never meet him again. No, she really never wanted to see him again.

Her mood was not improved by not having eaten for what seemed an eternity. Goodness, she was hungry. If she picked the eggshells out of the mashed eggs, perhaps she could still make a—rather crunchy—omelet?

There was the sound of a motor outside. It stopped in front of the house. Footsteps sounded along the path and someone rapped briskly on the door. Who could this be? Amadea rose numbly and went to the door. An unknown man, smallish and nondescript, was standing there. He held out a small basket, which she took automatically.

"M. d'Alembert thought you might be in need of these," he said, and then he was retreating up the walk.

Amadea closed the door and looked in the basket. It contained eggs, a loaf of bread, croissants, a piece of cheese, butter, and coffee and sugar in screws of paper. "I would not spend another such night"—didn't it say that in Shakespeare somewhere?—but things were looking up.

4

In the morning, so long as she didn't think about the previous night's meeting with M. d'Alembert, things were looking up even further. She woke early, under the rafters of the barn's loft, in a narrow bed covered with a six-inch-thick eiderdown. She lay breathing in the scent of old pine boards and listening to the urgent squabbling of some kind of birds outside, under the eaves perhaps. Through a slit of window on the far side of the loft she could see that the day was going to be clear. Today was the start of a new and better life. She sprang out of bed, dressed quickly in the center of the loft, where there was just headroom, and clambered cheerfully down the rickety ladder.

She opened the windows and pushed back the shutters. There on the ground below her were paw prints. And there, somewhat lower across a highland plateau, and just visible beyond the trees, was a small and graceful manor-house. It rose golden out of the low-lying mist. Amadea gazed at it as she breakfasted on the remains of M. d'Alembert's hospitality. Never, she thought with a smile to herself, had she seen a building that could more appropriately be described as existing *entre rêve et réalité*—between the dream and reality—that phrase beloved by French critics and journalists. She finished her meal. Well, her own *réalité* was awaiting her at the bakery. She locked up the Cow Shed and set out for the village.

Amazing how quickly she tripped down the hill in the daylight. As she turned the corner of the cobbled side street she could see the last shutter of the bakery being flung back, and by the time she reached it, it was full of people.

The bakery had a very contemporary gilt-and-chrome counter, an old tiled floor, and blue-checked curtains in the window. A delicious scent of bread and sugar met one even before one stepped in the door. A half-dozen people were standing in line to buy their morning baguette or brioches. A girl in her late teens perhaps, with dyed-blonde hair over one eye, a very tight sweater, and a very bored manner, was handing the bakery goods down from the racks. Amadea waited a little nervously at the back of the shop, not liking to push forward through the line, but when the rush showed no signs of diminishing she stepped forward and said, "Excuse me, mademoiselle..."

Mademoiselle resolutely ignored her, while the customers tossed her indignant or curious glances, and pressed closer to the counter.

"Mademoiselle, excuse me..."

Mademoiselle did not turn her head.

Amadea tried again: "I wish to speak to M. Nareix, if you could just tell me whether he's here or not?"

The customer at the counter took pity on her. "She wants to talk to your uncle," he declared to the girl.

The girl rang up the change, then called over her shoulder, into the back regions of the bakery, "*Ohé*, *l'oncle!"* and to Amadea, without really looking at her, she said, "You can go on back."

Amadea, not precisely encouraged by this rudeness, walked around the counter into the bakery proper. Here there were ovens rising to overhead and heat and racks of long dough. A red-faced man in an apron came towards her, rubbing his hands on a cloth: M. Benoit Nareix. He was middle-aged and rather round, with large muscular arms. The aura of baguette was all around him. He was also flustered-looking. Amadea introduced herself. Benoit shifted from foot to foot and sighed and rubbed the back of his neck.

"Ah, yes, well. About the job. I'm afraid...You see...The fact is..."

A woman appeared from the back of the bakery. She was red-haired and shrewish-looking and she began in a shrill and truculent voice, "Well? Have you told her?"

She turned to Amadea. "Madame, you can't work here. Who ever heard of just calling someone you don't know from Paris and being given a job? How do we know who you are? My husband is crazy, I tell you. But fortunately one of us has his head screwed on properly. We don't know anything about you; we've never even set eyes on you before, and you think you can just walk in here and go to work? Thank you very much. We've already given the job to my niece. We can't just have strangers coming in here like this. And those references you gave—do you think we can spend money on long-distance phone calls? What this good-for-nothing" (gesturing to her husband) "was thinking of I'll never know, but I can tell you one thing..."

Amadea and Benoit, during this tirade, had been retreating silently backwards and in opposite directions, away from the storm center. Behind his wife's back, Benoit shrugged his shoulders, gestured to his wife, raised his hands in a repeated gesture of helplessness. He rolled his eyes at his wife and ran an expressive finger across his throat. His eyes begged Amadea mutely for forgiveness.

She forgave him, but, oh, what was she going to do now? Within minutes she was back in the street; the green-painted door closed behind her. She took a deep breath. The beauty had gone out of the day. What on earth was she going to do now?

Mechanically, she stopped at the grocer's to pick up the day's food, limiting herself to the cheapest items. Did the grocer know of any work? He shook his head. Regretfully, there was very little to do in Maugrebis; the young people left or commuted. And was she not going to work at the bakery?

"No, Madame Nareix appears not to want a stranger."

"Ah...try my cold cuts." He was sympathetic but he had other customers. Amadea trudged away from the village.

Back in the Cow Shed she sat still for a long time, not even taking off her coat, trying to decide on the best course of action. She had the price of two weeks' groceries left if she stayed here, but here there was no work. She would go—she would have to hitch-hike—to Toulouse: it was not as far as Paris, and hopefully prices would be lower. She would look for work while staying in a youth hostel. She would lose the month's rent on this little house, but that couldn't be helped.

Well, she needed to take the basket back to M. d'Alembert, then she would leave. It was after nine. His "grandmother would be up by then." It occurred to her that she had been so caught up in her own mistakes that the oddity of his answer had escaped her. He had said, "Come around nine." What had he meant? Really, Maugrebis was a disturbingly odd place, and the sooner she left the better. She picked up the basket, and without even brushing her hair or straightening her clothing, trudged slowly around to the *manoir*.

*

"Madame, madame," said Céleste Sabadie, coming into the marquise's dressing room with a rather flurried look on her face. "The new companion has come already. Shall I help you to dress?"

"No, thank you, Céleste, I've just finished. If you would hand me my cane, I'm ready to go down. But do you not think she will wait for me, if I am slow? You seem worried."

"No, no, madame, of course not." Céleste's private opinion was that the new companion looked like a tartar (and she had experience of tartars, being married to one), but, no doubt, she reflected, Madame would be able to handle the woman. And if not, there was M. Lucien.

"Tell Lucien that we're here, please," said the marquise, as Céleste opened the drawing-room door for her and she went in to meet the arrival.

By the time Lucien reached the drawing-room it was obvious that the interview was not going well. He had only a moment in which to be surprised that the new companion was a dark-haired, strong-jawed woman with an aggressive manner and not at all a thin, blondish, gentle one, only a moment in which to take in the look on his grandmother's face, and they had barely sat down after the handshakes, when the woman continued with a complaint she had obviously already been voicing.

"It's very smoky in here. We'll have to do something about that. She shouldn't be breathing it. It's very bad for elderly people." The woman looked accusingly at the fireplace, where there was a roaring fire, and then at Lucien.

If Lucien was surprised to hear his grandmother referred to as 'she' before her face, he did not show it, but sat quietly contemplating the newcomer. A close observer might have noticed that he and his grandmother were quickly assuming the looks of twin and dyspeptic hawks whose morning meal has not come up to expectation, but the newcomer was not observant.

Madame said, "We are both old, the fireplace and I—we suit."

The newcomer paid no attention. Indeed she had no interest at all in Madame's opinions; she saw in her only a very old and decrepit woman who needed someone to look after her while she waited for the grave. She noticed neither the intelligence, nor the humor, nor the long-practiced civility. She was resolutely unimpressed by her surroundings as well. She was an independent woman with opinions of her own; she aired them with great decision. Then, not getting much response, she reverted to the fire.

"I'm really going to have to ask that the fire be put out," said the woman, speaking to Lucien and ignoring the marquise.

"Ah, *oui,* madame," said Lucien, "but do you not think it will be rather cold here, without the fire?"

"You don't have central heating?" asked the woman, regarding him with incredulity.

"Ah well," said Lucien apologetically and untruthfully, avoiding his grandmother's eye, "these old houses, you know...We were thinking it would be part of your duty to rush around with the wood and keep the fires well fed. But anyway, it will shortly be spring, I hope, so it would only be a matter of say, five or six fireplaces to keep stoked—oh, say, not more than an armload a piece, every other hour."

"Ye-es. What?" The companion gaped at him. He couldn't be serious, and she didn't like to be trifled with. She shifted her ground.

"She"—jerking her chin at the marquise— "should have a walker, not that flimsy cane. She would feel much more secure, and I can't risk having her fall. There are other improvements that will have to made as well."

"Grand-mère," said Lucien, "we are about to be improved. How does the prospect strike you?"

"I am overcome," said his grandmother. "Lucien, a word with you, if I may."

Lucien sprang to his feet and helped her up.

"Then if you could tell me how to reach my accommodations?" said the woman. "I'd like to get settled in right away."

"Ah," said Lucien, "now that might prove a problem. If you would be so good as to wait here a moment." The tone was very pleasant, but so self-assured that the companion found herself, rather against her will, agreeing to wait.

*

Guilhabert, creeping disconsolately about in the woods, was suddenly attracted by strange cries. He turned in their direction with a lean and hungry look,

and found, as he came to the edge of the woods, that
there was a flock of birds, quite large birds, birds of a
shape he'd never seen before, moving about on a
meadow in front of him. Now Guilhabert knew very
well that he was not allowed to chase birds. He knew
they were protected by man, taboo to him. But Guilhabert had had nothing to eat for a long time, and a
hungry dog is an angry dog. The laws of man fell by the
wayside; Guilhabert the Hunter stalked his prey.

*

It was a beautiful building, thought Amadea,
coming up the drive, and had she been in a mood to be
charmed she would have been charmed. One passed by
a gravel road through tall entrance gates that stood
among trees and opened onto a long field. A peacock
with attendant hens strutted slowly about on grass that
was slightly too long to be a lawn. There was a terrace,
and beyond that, tall windows. It was not a large structure and looked perfectly in harmony with its surroundings. It was neither garishly modernized, nor
showing dilapidations: timeless and peaceful. A thing of
beauty is a joy forever. Particularly if it's one's own
property, thought Amadea, and then quickly stifled the
thought as being unworthy. Beautiful things should belong to good people. She was glad the *manoir* belonged
to someone kind. She kept this idea firmly in mind as
she strode resolutely toward the door.

But before she reached it she heard voices coming through a window. Amadea's code did not en-
compass eavesdropping. She looked back toward the
gate: should she retreat? It seemed ridiculous. Go forward? She wavered indecisively, moved toward the
door, and the voices went on. A man—it must have

been M. d'Alembert—was saying, "I've called the Agency
to find out who the other one is, though I think it must
just be a mistake and they've sent two. They should call
back any minute." The other voice was a woman's—
elderly, Amadea judged, by its graveliness, but concise
and decisive. "Well, this one won't do. She's much too
persnickety—she will try to patronize me, I won't be
patronized, and we will live in a state of permanent warfare." A little laugh. "She's too dull to make it entertaining. I will put her down with great politeness and
she'll never catch on. Oh, I suppose I should feel sorry
for her, because it's probably all the result of an inferi-
ority complex, or something. Let's try the other one.
She of the imaginary dog."

The man's voice said, "Yes, I rather took to that
one, but I'm not absolutely sure she's in her right mind.
The Agency has really let us down this time. I agree
with you about..."

The voices suddenly died away, as if the speak-
ers had moved away from the window. Amadea had
reached the door. What could they mean? "Try the
other one." The "she of the imaginary dog" was herself.
With burning cheeks she pulled on the ancient bell-pull
and it clanged somewhere within. She would just hand
over the basket, and then, the sooner she left Maugrebis, the better.

A few moments and the door was opened by
the smallish man who had brought the eggs the night
before. Was it only last night? He gave her a frigid
good-day and stood immovably in the door frame. He
looked so forbidding that Amadea gave up her idea of
asking for M. d'Alembert. She had wanted to ask if she
could leave the keys to the Cow Shed with him, but she
supposed she could mail them anyway. She handed

over the basket with some incoherent thanks to be conveyed and was turning away when the guardian of the port stepped aside to look over his shoulder. M. d'Alembert appeared in a doorway. Amadea had a glimpse of an interior composed of an unpolished marble floor with broad white stone steps rising gradually beyond. The man half closed the door and Amadea turned and walked away.

In a moment, however, someone was calling her.

"Mademoiselle?" M. d'Alembert was standing in the doorway. Amadea came back a few steps and thanked him shyly for the food. He listened patiently.

"You were unbeset by any further beasts in the night?"

"Quite unbeset, thank you."

He smiled, "Good, but I'm afraid we've got a little problem this morning. Come in, come in. You've arrived quite opportunely; I don't know why Yves was turning you away—but that's just the way he is."

Why did I ever leave Paris? thought Amadea, and must have given M. d'Alembert a wide-eyed look, because he smiled reassuringly and murmured something about having it soon straightened out. He ushered her through the entrance hall and held open one side of a tall double door that gave onto a lovely salon. Its full-length windows faced the terrace and the lawn beyond. It was ivory-paneled, sparsely furnished, and swam in light. There was a Savonnerie carpet and a small group of fawn *Régence* armchairs. In one of these, a very elderly lady was sitting. She was dressed in a pale blue-gray suit and her white hair was curled—or perhaps curled naturally—off her face. She was fine-boned and must once have been strikingly beautiful. The room's other occupant was a youngish woman wearing slacks, a sweater, and new boots. She looked decidedly irritated.

M. d'Alembert introduced Amadea to his grandmother, and next to the younger woman, whose irritation, Amadea noted, then encompassed her as well.

"Well," she was saying, "I'd really like to know what this is all about. I was expressly led to believe that an independent dwelling would be made available for me. I'd really like someone to explain the problem to me."

M. d'Alembert began calmly, "The Agency..."

"Wait please, Lucien," his grandmother stopped him. "The important things first. Mademoiselle Heyward, what do you think of my fireplace?"

Amadea stared wildly at the fireplace. The chimneypiece was of carved stone, two-tiered, with caryatids, pilasters, and scrollwork. "Er, um...it's very beautiful. Is it 16th century?"

"Not bad," said M. d'Alembert approvingly.

Madame raised a quelling hand. "Do you not see a problem with it?" she addressed Amadea.

"Um," said Amadea, starting to bite her fingernails and then stopping. What was this, an exam? "Um, I'm not sure. It's a different period than the paneling?"

"Not bad at all," said M. d'Alembert.

"It smokes," said Madame severely.

"I'm sorry to hear it," said Amadea faintly, dropping her eyes. Truly these people were all mad.

The smallish man appeared. There was a telephone call for Monsieur. M. d'Alembert disappeared and Amadea rose also. "You'll have to excuse me," she said to the marquise, "I really have to be going. I'm sorry there's a problem with your chimney, but I very much doubt that I could be of any assistance."

"Well," said the marquise, laughing, and rising with the aid of her cane, "if you are leaving you must let me show you my daffodils. They're just beyond the terrace. You will excuse us, Madame Lacroix?"

Madame Lacroix made a sound of impatience, but the older woman was already moving slowly away. Amadea followed her through a window. They walked slowly along the terrace until they were out of earshot of the drawing-room. Then the marquise looked up at Amadea with an impish grin. "My dear, there are no daffodils. I wanted to speak to you alone. I suppose there was some mistake at the Agency: they've sent both you and Mme Lacroix. But I much prefer you, so we will send her away and you can stay."

"But," Amadea was starting to say, "but..."

And then there was a terrible shrieking and barking behind them. Amadea whipped round and there was the beast of last evening in hot pursuit of a peacock. The peahens had risen, flapping heavily and screeching, into the air, but the peacock, hampered by his tail and startled, was leaping up and fluttering down again just in front of the dog, who, somewhat confused with the multiplicity of quarry and all the flapping, was yet bounding determinedly about with the obvious intention of catching something.

"My peacock!" shrieked the marquise, and Amadea bolted along the terrace and down the steps and caught the dog by the tail just as he sank his teeth in the long tail feathers of the peacock. The bird struggled mightily, the dog struggled mightily, the tail feathers came loose, and Amadea lost her grip. The dog doubled around her, spitting feathers, and was leaping for the bird again when he was met by Madame, who had hobbled up at top speed and managed to give him a whack with her cane.

The bird took refuge behind his mistress, and Amadea, afraid the dog would knock the marquise flat, made a flying tackle but missed and fell on her hands and knees in the wet grass. As she scrambled to her feet she realized that the commotion had reduced itself to one spot. M. d'Alembert had appeared from nowhere and was holding the dog with a firm grip on the scruff of its neck, while the dog had his teeth locked once more on the bird's tail. M. d'Alembert was risking the fingers of his free hand on the dog's muzzle, trying to pry the jaws away, while the dog squirmed and growled and the bird screamed bloody murder. The animals' combined capacity for noise was extraordinary, but the man remained calm in the midst of the fray.

"If I lose a finger, mademoiselle, you are to give it a hero's funeral," he gritted out and then laughed. "Lost in the cause of a peacock, several extraordinarily useful digits."

"Oh, don't!" cried Amadea, "Let me try." And she flung herself at the group, but fortunately at this point the dog yielded to strength and released the bird, which fell on its beak and then departed shrieking across the grass.

The dog's collar had broken and was lying on the ground. M. d'Alembert shifted his grip to the left hand and pinned the dog between his legs while with his right he tugged off his belt and held it out to Amadea:

"Mademoiselle, if I could trouble you to make a noose in that, I'll hang the creature."

Amadea did as she was asked with trembling fingers: "You won't really?" she said, before putting it into his outstretched hand.

"No, no," he said, his eyes smiling. "Nor shoot him, either," he said to Yves, who had appeared with a rifle. "You can put that away. Then come back with a rope or a chain for this beast."

Amadea had turned away to help Madame, who was bending precariously for her cane in the grass.

"Is this your creature of last night?" M. d'Alembert asked Amadea. She nodded.

"He looks like one of the mastiffs in Gaston Fébus' *Livre de la chasse*, but I think he's part *dogue*," he said, patting the animal, which, recognizing defeat, had ceased struggling and was wagging its tail.

Part dog? "I know it's a dog," Amadea answered, rather startled. She would not have suspected the man of such fatuousness. Then she blushed, "Oh, of course, in French." She had forgotten that a *dogue* was a bull-dog.

Lucien glanced at her for moment. "You are not French then, mademoiselle?"

"No, only demi-French."

"Hmm. How fatuous you must have thought me."

He could read her mind, thought Amadea, and answered, "Yes—No, I mean, no."

He gave her a glance and a grin.

Sometime later Amadea found herself waiting— she didn't know why, but she had been asked to wait— in a smaller sitting room on the other side of the entrance hall. It was from here that she had heard M. d'Alembert talking with his grandmother, she supposed. This room was on a more intimate scale than the long drawing-room and more cluttered with personal items. There were silver-framed photographs dating onwards from the turn of the century—that one must have been the marquis, she supposed—and, incongruously, a laptop holding down a stack of papers on a Louis XV desk with bronze *doré* fittings. Books rose in shelves almost to the ceiling along three sides. The chairs were deep and comfortable. The tall windows with their crisscrossing mullions and transoms looked out onto the meadow, where the peacock, obviously suffering a little in his nerves, was jerkily trailing his mangled tail back and forth, back and forth, followed by the hens. Yves appeared and threw food to them. The hills rose blue and deep blue in the distance. It must be wonderful to live here. But she had to get going; she had so much to do yet: pack her bag, straighten the house, walk to the highway, hitchhike to Toulouse, find lodgings, look for work. Nervously she raised her fingers to her mouth and then stopped herself again from biting her nails.

Here was the doorknob turning and M. d'Alembert was entering the room. He looked clean and unruffled. Amadea remembered that she would have to change her clothes now, too.

She rose. She didn't know why she'd waited, only that, like other people, she found herself compelled by his air of confidence.

"Please sit down," he said.

Amadea perched on the edge of a chair and he dropped into an armchair opposite.

"I won't take up too much more of your time," he said, "and I have an apology and an explanation to make—in my own name and in my grandmother's. You see, my grandmother arranged for a companion through the Domestiques de Rêve Agency. I arranged with M.

Vaturin to lease his house for this new companion. Last night, when I went to check on the house, I did not know the new companion's name, only that she was coming. I assumed you were she. This morning when Madame Lacroix appeared, I assumed the Agency had made a mistake and sent you both. However, I've just spoken with the Agency and they've never heard of you, and I've spoken with M. Vaturin, and he also thinks you're the new companion. You are not she—so I'm very sorry to have troubled you with my family affairs, but, if you'll allow me to ask, who are you?"

"And I thought you were the baker," said Amadea irrelevantly.

M. d'Alembert averred gravely that as he had thought *she* was Madame Lacroix, they would have to consider their mutual injuries avenged. This stopped Amadea for a moment, but then she went on to explain about coming to work in the bakery—"The bakery!" interjected M. d'Alembert, "*ça, par exemple.*"—and about M. Vaturin's house, and how M. Vaturin had seemed to confuse her with someone else. "I suppose, my call coinciding with your arrangements, he assumed, like you, that I was your grandmother's new companion."

M. d'Alembert was listening attentively. She went on, "I'm sorry if I've interfered with your plans in any way, but the job at the bakery has fallen through, so I'll be leaving—I should be off now, in fact." She rose. "So the house will be free. Perhaps I can leave the keys with you, once I've locked up?" (It would mean another trip back and forth, but as it was manifestly her destiny "to scorn delights and live laborious days," as Milton put it, then the sooner she got at it, the better.) She pulled her jacket around herself and stepped toward the door. He rose politely also.

"Where will you go?"

"To Toulouse, I think, to look for work."

"Hm. Could we sit down again?"

She sat. He sat.

"When we thought you were from the Agency, my grandmother wished to retain *you* in place of Madame Lacroix. Now we've sent Madame Lacroix away—"

"Oh. Poor thing," murmured Amadea.

"She will be paid for her time," M. d'Alembert shrugged, "and the position is still open. Are you at all interested?"

Amadea looked interested, so he explained that the position was half way between that of a lady's maid and a companion. Amadea would have nothing to do with Madame's clothes—the housekeeper, Yves' wife, did that—but she would help her dress when she was feeling less well, and read to her occasionally when her eyes were bad, and be around to fetch and carry. His grandmother had had a trusted attendant for decades, but when the woman had retired, it had been difficult to find a suitable replacement. And then, as his grandmother had been so much alone here, she had thought it would be entertaining to have someone young and educated with her. Only it was hard to get young women to stay. It was too lonely here and too confined. Not many women wanted to give up their independence and live in, which is why he had thought of renting Vaturin's house. He himself was often at the *manoir*, but then again, his work took him often away, and at such times it was good for his grandmother to have someone lively and entertaining about.

As he spoke, a hope had been growing in Amadea. Here was an end to her problems: a job, and in this beautiful place. But now she rose and did up her jacket. M. d'Alembert rose too.

"I'd love to stay, but if it's lively and entertaining you want then I feel compelled to tell you that I lost my last job, well, next to last job—I was teaching English—because I was thought to be boring. So I'll just be going. Thank you anyway for the offer."

"Please sit down."

She sat. He sat. He continued, "The liveliness is a bonus, but if you don't feel like being lively, well, too bad. Maybe my grandmother will have a good influence on you. The main thing is that someone should be around to deal with emergencies."

"I'm particularly bad at dealing with emergencies."

"You managed with the dog just now."

Amadea looked down at the mud caking her skirt.

"It seems to me that it was you who dealt with the dog." She sighed. "I'd love to stay, really I would, but I truly don't think I'm the person you want."

She stood up. M. d'Alembert stood too.

"You can't, at least, deny that you're well educated," he said.

"Yes, but I'm dull."

M. d'Alembert laughed. "I'm not bored. I haven't felt so much like a yo-yo in years."

Amadea gave him half a rueful smile.

"Mademoiselle," he said, "I'm glad that if you can't laugh you can at least smile."

So they settled it.

It was decided that she would begin work the next day, as M. d'Alembert thought it likely his grandmother would spend the rest of the day in bed after the morning's excitement. He escorted Amadea out of the house to show her the shortcut through the woods. Amadea's heart was high and a smile played about her lips; there was a slight spring in her step again. M. d'Alembert noticed the change and felt oddly gladdened as well.

They descended the terrace steps, skirted the building, and beyond a barn or garage, headed towards a stand of tall cedars to one side of the manor. The dog was tied there to one of the massive trunks. He stood watching them uncertainly.

"What will you do with him?" asked Amadea suddenly.

"Well, we'll ask about the neighborhood if anyone has lost a dog, but I doubt he's from around here. He'll have to go to an animal shelter, I'm afraid. If he's going to want to eat peacock, he can't stay here."

"Poor thing," said Amadea.

Yves came out of the building and approached them. He was holding a strap of leather. "Dogs that run animals in the Pyrenees have to be put down," he said sourly. "There's some writing on this collar. I don't know what it means, but maybe it'll help you find the owner. Then *he* can get rid of him."

Lucien took the collar and turned it over in his hands. "Curious," he said, "there's the name 'Guilhabert' and then '*digna canis pabulo*.' Do you know Latin?" he asked Amadea.

Amadea shook her head regretfully. "Only a little. Does it mean something like 'the dog is worthy of his food?'"

"Yes. Now why does it suddenly seem so much worse to send to the pound a dog that has a Latin inscription round his neck? It seems almost like an amulet to protect him."

"Does 'Guilhabert' mean anything?" asked Amadea.

"The only 'Guilhabert' I can think of at the moment is Guilhabert de Castres. In the days when the pope and the king of France declared a crusade against the Cathars of Languedoc—that is, against the population, as the majority were sympathizers—he was one of the Cathar 'Perfects.' He was a daring character who descended sheer cliffs by rope and stole through enemy lines at night in order to bring comfort to the believers. It's a fine name."

They surveyed the dog as he stood slowly wagging his tail. At the sound of his name he lowered his head and grinned apologetically at them from a wide and toothy mouth.

Lucien glanced at Yves. Yves stiffened. "I'm not taking him," he said instantly and belligerently. And yet Lucien knew and Yves knew that if Lucien asked him to keep an elephant he would no doubt—complaining bitterly—build it a cage and tear up grass for it. Yves was a simple character. He loved his country, his church, and the *manoir*; and his favorite pastimes were hunting, gardening, and grumbling. He was tyrannous with those who allowed it, but devoted to his family and friends.

"You could take him hunting," said Lucien. "He likes birds."

Yves muttered something dark-sounding under his breath.

"No? *Bon.* Thank you, Yves," said Lucien, and Yves took himself off, his shoulders indicating relief.

Amadea put a tentative hand out to the dog. He gave it a lick, squirming and squinting up his eyes. Her hand came away trailing long strings of saliva, which was rather disgusting, but it was obvious even to Amadea, who knew nothing about dogs, that the gesture was kindly meant.

"Well," said Lucien, "he doesn't bite."

"No," said Amadea, "perhaps he was only startled last night. Actually, until I stepped on him he hadn't even barked or risen." Perhaps the danger had been all in her imagination.

As if reading her mind, Lucien said, "Until he showed up today, I suspected you might be like that pathetic governess in *The Turn of the Screw.*"

"I'm afraid that's too close to the truth. He doesn't seem to be vicious at all." She hesitated then said, "Perhaps I could keep him for a while." She had accused him unjustly and must make amends. Besides, his mere presence should keep away werewolves and other figments of her fantasy.

Lucien regarded her with surprise and some approval.

"Mademoiselle, it would seem you have a tender heart."

Soon she was on her way back to the little house, with the dog Guilhabert, an omen of things to come, trotting confidingly by her side.

Lucien watched her depart, then turned back to the house. Well, he thought, he wouldn't hire her for a secretary certainly, but he believed she and his grandmother would do very well together. He had work to do, but instead of returning to his computer, he found himself heading for the Beckstein in the drawing-room.

He sat down at the piano and for fifteen minutes
played—for reasons unknown to himself—Mendels-
sohn's *Spring Song.*

*

Amadea tripped down to the village again and
entered the *Charcuterie.* She gave the grocer a big smile.
"I'm going to need..." What did dogs eat? Her
eye ranged over the sausages, the cold cuts...
"Ah, mademoiselle, I knew you'd come round."

5

Amadea's first day of work had passed with only a single fleeting moment of discomfort. It was Céleste who opened the door for her, and she had been very pleasant and encouraging. Following her directions, Amadea had climbed the stairs to the second floor and Madame's bedroom. Madame, lying in white lace under a canopy, was finishing her coffee. She greeted her new companion warmly. Amadea had helped her on successively with various garments; she had helped her downstairs; they had gone for a walk which consisted of sauntering at snail's pace up and down the terrace a few times; then they had retired to the drawing-room. So far Amadea felt she was performing her duties adequately enough, if clumsily.

"Now, if you would read to me," said Madame, lying back in her armchair. "That's right, place the blanket over my knees, thank you...Yes, go to the bookshelves in the small sitting room; you will find a copy of Barthes' *Mythologies*. Read the chapter on Dominici, and make me an *analyse de texte*. I am interested to hear the American approach."

Amadea stood as if riveted, staring at her. The marquise laughed. "My dear, you look terrified and I am only joking. Go and bring back something light."

In the days that came Amadea grew accustomed to the marquise's ways, to her humor and her wit, which was frequently astringent but never ill-natured. She did not know that she herself had excited a keen curiosity in the older woman, but she found that she looked forward to each day, to her employer's company, and to the family history which was revealed to her day by day: the marquise's childhood in a distant chateau, an early life composed of ponies and governesses and visits to the convent—and to the village, which had just lost most of its young men. (Ah yes, Amadea had seen them, the poignant memorials in nearly every village square, "*Aux enfants du village*," and the names of all those Camilles, and Marcels, and Henris, followed by dates—1914, 1915, etc.). Then there had been a gay youth in Paris, and marriage, and children. The war again—her brothers had been killed, her husband imprisoned. Later there had been the death of her daughter, Lucien's mother; her interest in her grandchildren, and her charitable activities, taken over now by Lucien's father. People that Amadea had never met before took on personalities for her; periods of French history that had previously lain dormant for her in dull tomes became suddenly a backdrop to one woman's private life. But she revealed little about her own self, and the marquise, as she told her grandson, had to piece together occasional bits of information.

For instance, observing once that her companion kept looking at an intricately worked silver object on a small table, the marquise asked her if she knew what it was. Amadea had a memory: she was a child trailing after her mother and attendants in an antique salesroom—was it Paris, or New York?—she didn't remember. There were paintings in gilt frames and porcelain on a table, and other items. Her mother had picked up an object: "Do you remember?" she had said to her small daughter. "We saw one last week. I told you what it was. Well?" The child that was Amadea had shaken her head sadly; she never remembered. Her mother had hissed, "It's a *pokal,* of German origin." Amadea said to Madame, "It's a *pokal,* of German origin."

"Ah, so you are knowledgeable about such things?"

"No, not really...it was my mother who knew."

"Was? She is dead?"

"No. Just departed."

The marquise gave Amadea a look over her glasses and a slight snort of amusement. "Mademoiselle, you are droll."

No one, thought Amadea, had ever considered her amusing before.

Of M. d'Alembert she saw little during the first days. From the marquise she learned that he was an expert on international law and served as a judge on international arbitration tribunals.

They passed each other in the entry or the driveway once or twice as she was leaving and he was entering. Once he informed her that his efforts to find the dog's owner had been in vain and did she want Yves to take it to the pound? This worried Amadea, for although she and Guilhabert had become fast friends, she was aware that with her own future so insecure it was unwise to take on a dog, and particularly a dog that ate like a horse, broke chains like a tractor, and bayed like the Baskervilles' hound. She bit her lip.

"No, poor thing. I couldn't do that to him. He's really very sweet. I'll keep him a while longer and try to find someone to adopt him."

"I hope he's proving useful at least?"

Amadea didn't pretend to misunderstand him. "Yes, very." Indeed, with Guilhie there she was not at all frightened to be alone in the house. Lucien passed on.

The next afternoon he came in while Madame slept in a chair and Amadea was bent over a book. She glanced up a little cross-eyed at his entry, so intently had she been studying, and he said quietly, so as not to wake his grandmother:

"What are you reading? It seems absorbing. Black magic, I suppose."

"No," said Amadea with a faint smile, "I'm not a witch at all."

He leaned over and glanced at the book. "Ah, *voilà*, you see, Latin. It's the last bit of evidence I need. Incantations in a dead language. You arrived mysteriously from nowhere on a dark and stormy night, you produced a black dog, you have put a spell on my grandmother, and I shall no doubt wake up one day and find I'm a frog."

"I arrived on the bus from Toulouse," said Amadea primly, "and…" She stopped suddenly—no, he might not think that was funny.

"And I'm already a frog?"

"Yes," said Amadea, confused and embarrassed, because it was what she had thought. "No—I mean, no."

Lucien laughed and left the room.

But his grandmother's companion was becoming a matter of some curiosity to him as well. It surprised both him and his grandmother that she had not asked for a television to wile away the long stretches of inactivity. She read Montaigne, and Malraux, and Emmanuel Todd, but did not appear to find Simenon beneath her. Celeste liked her, and even—the acid test—Yves had no fault to find. More, he seemed actually to approve of her.

Lucien had found Amadea and the marquise seated outside one sunny day. The marquise was dozing again, Amadea reading, Yves working in the shrubs nearby.

"Latin still, mademoiselle?" Lucien had bent toward Amadea's book.

"It was the dog's collar that reminded me I'd always wanted to learn," Amadea had confided shyly, "and then I found this grammar on the shelves and it seemed like a good opportunity."

Yves had suddenly lifted his head from the bush he was clipping and entered the conversation.

"I know Latin," he said, "I could teach you: *Viburnum opulum rosea.*" He went on expansively: "*Cornus alba. Berberis julianae.*"

Amadea laughed. "*Salvia, et,* um, *rosa.*"

"Ah, *oui,*" said Lucien, "*nasturtium,* absolutely.")

She was also, Lucien admitted to himself, not bad looking, if too somber. She was quite unlike the career women—sharp, defensive, and self-possessed—who made up most of his acquaintance. If she had not been his grandmother's companion, he would have asked her out—just from curiosity, of course. But he had no wish for domestic complications. Showing an interest in his grandmother's companion was too much like pursuing maids. So he observed her through his grandmother and rarely spoke to her. A visit from one of his grandmother's friends rather changed matters.

"Lucien," cried the marquise one evening, "a terrible thing—my friend Madeleine de Boissy is coming to lunch tomorrow."

"My sympathies," answered Lucien. "Must you see her?"

"Oh yes," the marquise replied dolefully, "I put her off with invented infirmities all last autumn. If I don't let her come now she'll be expecting to read my obituary notice."

"The comtesse de Boissy," Lucien explained to Amadea, "is a deplorable woman whom my grandmother has had the misfortune of knowing all her life."

"Well," said the marquise, striving for tolerance, "but she is eighty-two."

"Then she has been deplorable for eighty-two years," said Lucien. He considered Amadea with some misgivings. His eyes asked his grandmother: "And mademoiselle? Will she be there?"

"Yes," his grandmother answered aloud, "Mademoiselle will join us. I cannot face the woman alone." Besides, she added to herself, I do so want to know how she will manage...

Celeste appeared and soon she and Madame were deep in a passionate discussion over the various advantages of steak *au chocolat* or *poularde à la Néva*.

Lucien said to Amadea, "She won't like it that you don't eat meat." (Or anything else about you, he added to himself.) "If she tells you that Robespierre was a vegetarian too, you must tell her firmly that most of the Jacobins were *not*."

"I wouldn't dare," said Amadea, and faced lunch the next day with considerable trepidation.

Her jacket, and the purse that had been one of her father's last gifts, had been hanging in the hallway for some hours when the comtesse de Boissy, driven by her daughter, Madame Rolle, arrived. They came into the hall and Céleste helped them off with their coats. The comtesse was wearing a tweed suit and high heels; her daughter was dressed in loose cotton garments. The comtesse—with one arm out of her coat and her mouth open to tell her daughter, for the third time that hour, that she looked like a *clochard*—stopped to stare at Amadea's handbag.

"Hermès!" she cried cryptically. "Madame Sabadie, who is here?"

"No one, madame," Céleste assured her, "only *madame la marquise*, and her new companion."

"But her companion doesn't have an Hermès handbag?" demanded the comtesse suspiciously.

"I wouldn't know," faltered Céleste.

"Perhaps it's imitation," suggested the daughter soothingly.

"Imitation!" snapped the comtesse, an angry furrow appearing on her creased brow. "I know the difference, *moi*." And she scowled for a moment at this mystery of a handbag, before allowing herself to be ushered into the salon.

Conversation during the meal proceeded fitfully. The comtesse did not approve of domestic employees who sported expensive handbags. She couldn't afford one herself. She sat and dipped a toast finger into her soft-boiled egg and munched and brooded on the unfairness of fate.

"Who is she?" she demanded of her friend, jerking her head infinitesimally in Amadea's direction.

Amadea was talking to Madame Rolle, who was striving to be pleasant, but was somewhat distracted by the forbidding presence of her mother. Indeed, once the comtesse had broken off in the middle of a sentence and snapped at her daughter, "Marie-Laure, you're slouching!"

Marie-Laure had straightened up at once. Amadea, to cover the awkwardness, had made some comment about the other's Tintin watch. (What memories that brought back of her French childhood!) Oh yes, said Madame Rolle, she was a great fan. And they talked with animation for a few moments of Tintin and Capitaine Haddock and Milou.

The comtesse cut across their conversation. "I am told that you have degrees?" she said to Amadea, "from America?"

Amadea admitted that it was so.

"It's easier to get degrees in America," said the comtesse disagreeably.

"No doubt," Amadea agreed equably. The marquise gave her a look that was half a wink and distracted the comtesse with gossip about mutual acquaintances. The talk flowed freely for a time, until suddenly the comtesse exclaimed: "Oh, *mais,* I was forgetting what I wanted to tell you! It's about Catherine de Ravenel! Imagine what she's done now!"

"I have a scandalous relation," the marquise was beginning to explain to Amadea, "Fortunately not close—She's...

Amadea raised her head, cleared a slight catch in her throat, and finished for her, "My mother."

The effect was a moment of petrifaction. Then the comtesse coughed and said, "Ah, then you can give us her latest news. It's so long since I've seen her." She addressed herself to her plate.

Amadea shook her head. She had had no contact at all with her mother for ages. In the first years after her mother left, a postcard had come occasionally, once or twice a birthday card, and then silence. Amadea had written after her father's death, but there had been no reply. She had to assume her mother was not interested. Her mother had never been maternal, and a grown-up daughter would perhaps be an embarrassment.

The marquise regarded Amadea with raised eyebrows and said, "I believe she's in Los Angeles now. She's become rather well known as an interior decorator. But you knew that, of course?"

Amadea nodded.

"She is also a connection of sorts," the marquise continued. "My great-grandmother was a Ravenel. You didn't know?"

Amadea shook her head.

"So we are distant cousins, my dear. I am very glad. Come and kiss me."

Amadea complied, and then sat down, feeling stunned. "It seems such an extraordinary coincidence."

The comtesse regarded her with more interest than she had previously exhibited. "Not really. If you had come into any of our families the chances are there would have been a connection somewhere. We're very interbred." She warmed to Amadea.

Blood was obviously better than behavior in her eyes, thought Amadea wryly.

The furrow disappeared from the comtesse's brow. The handbag was all right.

*

Amadea, delighting in the company of the marquise, in the fields and trees, in her little house with its view of the hills, in her daily walks to the village, and in feeling, for almost the first time in her life, that someone took an interest in her, was happy: Cautiously happy, because experience told her one mustn't expect too much, but still, happy and growing in confidence.

6

For Raymond, however, time dragged. For many years, since his wife and son left, in fact, life had not seemed more than only very moderately worthwhile to him. Now it was a positive weariness and burden. He had no work these days. He could not sell his eggs or goat's milk, and the thug told the two or three people who came up the drive looking for him that he had gone to a retirement home, or that he was visiting his son, or any lie that would send them away. People were not curious: no one asked questions or looked disbelieving. Raymond stayed in the house then, as the thug had promised to break his nose if he showed himself, and he believed him.

There was something animal-like and impenetrable about the younger man. Raymond had learned that his name was Thierry, and that was all. They did not talk. The thug's silent presence was almost more unnerving to Raymond than his son's voluble insistence. But he recognized that this was psychological warfare and he resigned himself to endurance. The situation was lasting a long time, but it could not continue into eternity. Occasionally Thierry went into town and brought back food, which they ate without cooking, as neither considered it his job to make meals for the other. At least, thought Raymond philosophically, as he munched on his fourteenth meal of cold cuts and baguette, he wasn't paying for it.

*

Sylvie Fanel spent the periods between customers, which were long outside of rush times, in staring out the bakery windows. Not that there was much to see: her uncle loading or unloading the delivery van; various old men who spent their days sitting on benches; an occasional cat or stray dog sniffing the gutters; the cars of tourists passing slowly through, the drivers peering right and left and then turning the corner, never to be seen again. There was no one of any interest in Maugrebis. Her aunt, looking over her shoulder at a man descending from a jeep, had said, "that's M. d'Alembert, the one from the *manoir*," and had craned her neck at the man until he disappeared into a shop. Sylvie had seen only a man of advanced age—35 *at least*—in the wrong sort of clothes. It was different though when Thierry first coasted down the street on his motorcycle. Sylvie had been slouched against the window frame, thumbs hooked in jeans pockets, debating the advisability of a nose ring. Her mother and aunt would hate it—that was three points in its favor. But then again, it might get infected—that was gruesome. And then Thierry had rolled into sight, and parked his motorcycle and come into the shop, filling the doorway with shoulders and black leather, and asked for two *baguettes*, and after that the pivot of all her ideas was whether he would come again and whether he would speak to her, and did he like nose rings at all?

Thierry couldn't stay long in the village: Just the time to come roaring down the highway, coast down the main street, pick up some groceries, and roar away again. Raymond might escape in his absence, but, after all, where would he go? If he left his home he would be destitute. Still, it wouldn't do to leave him time to get in touch with the neighbors, supposing he knew any of them.

So although Thierry was aware that Sylvie would have liked to keep him talking—she had even followed him from the shop and admired his motorcycle and expressed a preference for tattoos—and he was not insensible to her charms, still, he preferred to get back.

Not that there was anything to do when he got there.

There was no conversation to be had with Thierry, Raymond had rapidly discovered. He wouldn't talk about ideas, or politics—"All politicians are dogs," period, silence—or books, or films, or even the weather. And he didn't discuss his past life or his future prospects; he just existed. Raymond had found out only—it was one of the few things Thierry told him— that Thierry had been in prison, and that Bruno, Hugo's partner, had given him his first real job. Bruno paid well and Thierry wanted to please him.

That didn't mean that Thierry liked work, though. He had watched Raymond spade his garden and care for his chickens and prune his trees and had stood silently, aimlessly watching, ignoring any suggestions that he might himself pick up a shovel, etc. They had sat for day after rainy day in the house, Raymond reading and Thierry, strongly disconcerted to find that there was no television, no computer, no CD player, nothing, had sat motionless for hours, staring into empty space.

Raymond had nothing against Thierry. He knew Thierry had nothing personal against him either, except perhaps the dislike many young people seemed to have for the elderly—as if they were a different species. Yet the man's blankness was hard to bear. Raymond felt a desire to shake him up, to get a response, any response. Any sort of talk would be better than this mutual isolation.

So one morning, after they had come in from milking the goats—or rather Raymond had milked the goats and Thierry had stood to one side, and only when he thought Raymond wasn't watching had he bent down and played with the smallest kid—Raymond had launched on his favorite speculation. "Tell me, Thierry, what do you think would have happened here in Languedoc if the Cathars had been able to beat off the Crusaders?"

Thierry looked up briefly, grunted, and said without interest, "Who're they? Your local soccer team?"

"Soccer team!?" Raymond felt a moment of outrage. Really, the fellow was stupid enough to eat hay! But after all, he reflected, maybe it was just a lack of education, of exposure. A man who liked baby goats couldn't be *all* bad. Couldn't be as bad as his own son anyway, he thought bitterly.

"No," said Raymond aloud, sitting up and speaking with enthusiasm, "better, much better. Soccer players?—people rushing around after a ball and thinking it matters; but the Cathars had beliefs, beliefs worth dying for. Can you imagine being willing to die for your beliefs? Being willing to walk singing to the cordwood stacked around a pole, waiting for you and a match?"

"Dunno," said Thierry. He crossed his arms, splayed out his legs, and leaned his head back against the wall. Time passed more quickly if one went into real mental hibernation.

"Do you know that your beliefs—well, that is, that Christian beliefs—about heaven and hell, angels, the last judgment, the coming of the Messiah, the devil, the final resurrection, all derive from Zoroastrianism? And that Zoroastrianism lasted, in one form or another, for 20 centuries, and that most of Languedoc was at one time imbued with the ideas of the Cathars, who were the spiritual inheritors of that dualist belief system?"

No answer. Well, maybe that *was* getting in a little deep. He got carried away so quickly. Better keep it simple, tell him a story, as if he were one of his old students whom he was trying to interest in the past.

"Have you ever heard of Montségur?"

"Who's he?"

"A fortress. On a very high mountain, a steep and rocky mountain, almost perpendicular, practically inaccessible. In the year 1244, five hundred Cathar faithful took refuge there against the crusaders, sent by the Pope and King Louis IX to exterminate their heresy. They held out for ten months, against an army of 1,500, until in the end, when a party of Basques made it up the tower rock and was bombarding them, they were forced to surrender. They were given the choice: to recant or die. Two weeks later, on the 16th of March, 200 believers, led by a young girl, Esclarmonde de Péreille, walked to their funeral pyre at the foot of the mountain...Sad, eh? And yet one has to admire them."

Thierry did not respond. Raymond tried again. "Is there anything, Thierry, more important to you than your own measly existence? Anything that really matters to you?"

Raymond looked at Thierry. He was motionless, apparently asleep. That was enough for one day. Tomorrow he'd give him another dose of history. After all, he was a captive audience, thought Raymond with something approaching glee, and the first returning spark of interest in life. He believed in the power of words, in the ability of stories to change patterns of behavior, just as people could influence others for good or evil by their own behavior. That he himself might influence Thierry—he hadn't a hope, he considered, old drunkard that he was. But he could show him what was best through others. What should he tell him tomorrow?

7

Lucien paced down the broad corridor of a Paris bank, between the gilt and mirrors. His business over, his mind turned to the telephone conversation he'd recently had with his grandmother. So Mademoiselle Heyward was a cousin of sorts. That was curious. The way she kept recurring to his mind was curious too. He decided he was glad of the relation: he could talk to her, maybe even take her out for a meal, and it would seem like the natural courtesy paid to a cousin. Lucien was a man who was kind to everyone. He was kind to men by training and good nature, to older women by training and congeniality, and to younger women by predilection. But he knew that young women—and older ones too, sometimes—were susceptible, and he knew that when one was well-to-do, tolerably good-looking, and charming, then one had to be careful or people started liking one too much. He didn't want any complications, but there was no reason he shouldn't ask his cousin to have dinner with him.

He came out of the building and settled into the back of a waiting taxi. He had been working hard lately, and perhaps, he considered, his social life in Paris was among his more onerous duties. There were those tedious cocktail parties to attend, where large numbers of people milled awkwardly about for two hours covertly eyeing each others' clothes, and where he would circulate, talking to those who looked most uncomfortable, because he knew no one else would; and formal dinner parties, from whose preparation even practiced hostesses emerged exhausted and anxious, having put their reputation on the line again: will this affair pass or fail? He thought, almost with longing, of the quiet simplicity and, and...What was the word he was looking for? ...Yes, the companionableness, of his grandmother's retreat.

*

Amadea's acquaintance with Lucien had been increasing, but only through the intermediary of his grandmother, and by accident as it were. Sent one day for a book, any book, she had brought back a collection of Shakespeare plays. Madame's English was very good, good enough even for Shakespeare, but she had waved the book away.

"No, no," she said, "I agree with Frederick the Great, who called them the 'abominable plays of Shakespeare,' and 'only worthy of Canadian savages.' It is Lucien who likes Shakespeare. He has a great knowledge of English literature. You haven't noticed? Ah, no, you would not yet, but you will get to know him better."

So Amadea knew that Lucien liked literature, and that he believed in mediation for resolving conflicts, and that he frequently travelled for his work, and that his family had a house in Paris and were involved in a great deal of charitable work, but nothing at all about his wife. Where was she, Amadea wondered? He must not spend much time with her, she thought, but perhaps it was one of those long-distance marriages, like her parents' had been. She did not ask Madame, even now that she knew they were relations. It would have seemed too personal, too intrusive. There had been wedding photos in a family album—Lucien and a beautiful woman in the sub-fusc clothing of a civil ceremony—but the marquise had quickly skipped over them, without comment.

*

A few days later, an airplane, flying in from Amsterdam, set Lucien down in Toulouse, and in two hours more he was crossing the gravel drive of his grandmother's *manoir*. Amadea was leaving the house. She checked at sight of him. How handsome he was, she thought. Not in a conventional style but...but why was she thinking such thoughts?

He traversed the stretch between them, stopped, and shook hands solemnly, as the French do daily with all their acquaintance. It was on the tip of his tongue to say something about their new-found relationship, but for some reason he said nothing. Maybe he was wondering why she was blushing. She wondered if she should say something to him or just pass on. There were days when she could speak naturally to him and days when his perfections intimidated her. And now she didn't know if he was glad or sorry of the connection. However, she had to say something or it would seem impolite.

"Er. How is Paris?" she said, looking at his shoes. What a stupid thing to say.

"Thank you. Much as usual, I believe. Failing in health, but likely to survive. I came from Amsterdam."

"Oh." She edged slowly around him.

"You will not ask me how is Amsterdam?"

"It seems so stupid."

"Amsterdam is stupid?"

"Yes. No. I don't know. Goodbye." She hurried away and he stared after her for a moment before going into the *manoir*.

Amadea reached home. Guilhabert was waiting for her. She put her arms around his neck and he leaned his head against her. It was very comforting. Guilhabert didn't care if she was a fool.

The next time they met was in the village. It was Saturday afternoon, and the streets were fairly empty. Amadea had bought some provisions which she swung in a bag as she sauntered up the main street, enjoying the sunshine and vaguely window-shopping. A man stumbled out of an alley ahead of her. Two passers-by side-stepped him neatly and walked on as he reeled and fell to the pavement. Amadea approached him: a man of sixty in tolerable working clothes, reeking of alcohol, and bleeding from a small cut on his head. He sprawled in the gutter, trying to sit up. If he had been lying quietly on the sidewalk, Amadea would no doubt have passed him by, as she had passed many such persons in Paris, with only a pitying look, but she couldn't pass someone who was struggling to get out of the street. She bent down to him. Her idea had been to help him sit on the curb and to ask if she could call anyone for help. But the drunkard had other ideas. He grasped her around the neck and staggered to his feet as she tried to escape. Enveloped in alcoholic fumes and more body contact than she had ever experienced, she fought down a strong desire to push him brusquely away, to kick his shins. They revolved clumsily.

"Let go!" Amadea cried.

"Help!" bawled the drunk.

A car braked sharply; a door slammed. Hands were releasing the drunk's arms, removing his dead weight. Gasping a little, and pushing her hair out of her eyes, Amadea saw that her rescuer was Lucien.

"*Cousine*, I am disconsolate. You dance in the street, and I am not invited."

Amadea blushed. "I couldn't just leave him."

"I know. You have a tender heart. Are you all right?"

She nodded. He continued, "I'll take him home. I know where he lives. It's past your house, so I can give you a ride too, if you're going that way." He began guiding his unwieldy burden toward the jeep. "It's not the first time I've taken him home. I tell him he should try marijuana—so much less harmful, but he refuses. He's a traditionalist." He buckled the traditionalist into the back seat, where he slumped against the window, and held the front door open for Amadea.

They bumped along the cobbles. Amadea, emboldened perhaps by the relief of escape, ventured, "I would have thought you were a traditionalist too?"

"In matters of intoxication?"

"No, in general, I mean."

He dropped his bantering tone and answered her seriously. "Yes and no. It always amazes me that humanity is very willing to throw off what was good in the past—in music, or art, or architecture, for instance—in preference for what is 'new' or 'original,' but inferior, and on the other hand, it clings with tenacity to its old evils: the self-interest of individual nations over the good of the whole; might making right—mass murder is traditional and continues in our day. The protests of the few against the inertia of the majority—that is traditional too. So, yes and no. Have I answered your question?" He glanced at her, wondering how she would answer him.

"Yes," said Amadea eagerly, "that is how I feel too..." And so they continued in this vein, until, too soon, they drew up before her house. Guilhabert was bouncing and whining at the end of his chain in enthusiastic greeting. The drunk raised his head and stared blearily at the dog.

"That dog—those dogs—look like the Noble's...My old friend, poor friend, he wanted to drink with me but my wife wouldn't let me, poor me..."

Amadea exchanged looks with Lucien. They tried to question the man, but he had lapsed back into a stupor and nothing more could be got from him.

Lucien was still at the *manoir* the following Monday morning. It was the hour at which Madame drank chocolate and she and Amadea were in the dining room. Lucien stepped into the room, wearing his overcoat. He kissed his grandmother goodbye and was leaving, but in the doorway he turned and with a fine show of gravity, said, "Grand-mère, I feel I should inform you, that our cousin was observed embracing M. Bordan in the street on Sunday. It was about one o'clock, *rue de l'Eglise*. He was drunk, of course."

"Was she?"

"No, she didn't appear to be."

"There's no accounting for tastes."

"As you say, Grand-mère." He gave a little bow—"Mademoiselle"—and closed the door with a grin.

Amadea felt her color rising, and played with the handle of her cup. Then she remembered something and said abruptly:

"Madame, do you know with whom M. Bordan drinks?"

The marquise raised her eyebrows at Amadea, looking at her over her glasses, "I do not."

"I just thought you might, because M. Bordan—is that his name? —said he was a 'nobleman.' He said this man had a dog like Guilhabert and I thought perhaps it is he who has lost him."

"Ring the bell. Yves will know."

Céleste appeared first, then Yves. M. Bordan drank with anyone who would buy him a drink, said Yves, with the righteous distaste of a man whose own limit was three glasses of wine with dinner.

"But someone who is, or is called, noble?"

Well, there was Trencavel. He was sometimes called "*Le Noble*" because he was very, very...Yves drew himself up exaggeratedly straight like a man giving himself airs. "And because of his name."

The marquise added for Amadea's benefit, "The early counts of Foix were Trencavels. It was a large clan, and the name is not unusual."

This man lived back in the woods and rarely came down to the village. He had the old Lobocôte property, Yves said, speaking to Madame. But yes, Yves had seen him drinking with Bordan: not falling-down-drunk, no, but definitely—Yves twisted his hand in front of his nose in the gesture meaning one's had too much to drink. His attitude suggested he wouldn't have anything to do with the likes of Trencavel.

"Would he have a telephone?"

Yves checked. No, not listed. "Typical of the likes of him."

Amadea felt the injustice but refrained from comment. "Could you tell me how to get to wherever he lives?" she asked.

Madame said wickedly, "Amadea has a taste for drunkards."

Yves shrugged expressionlessly as he sketched a map on a piece of paper. "*A chacun son goût.*"

8

Realizing that hungry men thought only of food, Raymond began to cook again. He broke a large quantity of eggs into a bowl, added diced potatoes, pepper, and salt, stirred it together, and tipped it into a frying pan. When the omelet was done he divided it in two, slid the smaller part onto a plate for himself, and set the much larger portion down before Thierry.

Thierry, who had been watching these preparations from under his lashes, looked up in some surprise and suspicion. What did he think? thought Raymond, that I was going to eat it all in front of him? Out loud he said, "Go on. Eat it. I'm not a Borgia."

"What's being bourgeois got to do with anything?"

Raymond sighed. "The Borgias were Italians. They poisoned people. But this food's not poisoned."

Thierry fell on his food with fork and thumbs and Raymond ate his own meal and pondered. He did up the dishes and night settled in. It was black outside and completely quiet; indoors there was only the light from a single bare bulb hanging down over the little table. There was silence inside and out. The two men might have been alone on the planet. They were at each other's mercy. Raymond got up and began to hunt for a book. There wasn't much room for a book to get lost in that tiny house and before long he pulled it out from under his bed, cobwebby and with bent pages: Froissart's *Chronicles*. He slapped the dust off against his leg and brought it back to his chair opposite Thierry.

He opened the pages, found his place, and began an introduction in his professorial tone, "Yesterday we spoke of people who were willing to die for their beliefs. Today we'll speak about what I, personally, consider to be worth more: people who were willing to die for other people. In the year 1346, King Edward of England was besieging Calais. The fighting had been fierce on Saturday, but by Sunday the English were victorious..."

Thierry broke in on him, "Not that again! Can't you just be quiet?"

Raymond scowled at him. "I can read in my own house at least, can't I? I'm free, am I not? You don't have to listen." I didn't ask you to come here, he added to himself, but since you're here you can listen.

Thierry shrugged. "*Bof*, do as you like."

Raymond read. He knew that Thierry couldn't help but hear: whether he was listening or not, he couldn't tell. But after all, one couldn't expect miracles. Maybe some of it would penetrate...

"'When Edward was assured that there was no appearance of the French collecting another army, he sent to have the number and rank of the dead examined. This business was entrusted to Lord Reginald Cobham and Lord Stafford, assisted by three heralds to examine the arms, and two secretaries to write down the names. They passed the whole day upon the field of battle, and made a very circumstantial account of all they saw: according to their report it appeared that 80 banners, the bodies of 11 princes, 1,200 knights, and about 30,000 common men were found dead on the field. After this very successful engagement...."

Raymond broke off his reading and glanced at Thierry to see if there was any reaction.

No reaction. "'After this *very successful* engagement...'" went on Raymond, "'We must now leave King Edward and his army before Calais, and turn our attention to what was being done in Scotland. King David had summoned his Parliament at Perth, and finding that England was very much drained of its forces by foreign service, determined upon an invasion. He made his preparations, but not so secretly as to prevent the news coming to the Queen of England, who, in her husband's absence, bravely undertook to defend the kingdom. She got together all the forces she was able, and marching to Newcastle, gave the Scots battle at a place called Neville's Cross, where she took King David prisoner. The capture of the King gave to the Queen of England a decided superiority over her enemies; they retired, and when she had sufficiently provided for the defence of the cities of York and Durham, as well as for the borders generally, she herself set out for London; and shortly after, having confined her royal prisoner in the Tower, joined the King, her husband, at Calais."

"The siege of Calais lasted a long time, during which many noble feats of arms and adventures happened. On several occasions the King of France attempted to raise the siege, but Edward had so guarded the passes that he could not possibly approach the town. His fleet defended the shore, and the Earl of Derby, with a sufficient force of men-at-arms and archers, kept watch at the bridge of Nieullet, by which alone the French army could enter so as to come near the town. The people of Calais all this time suffered very greatly from want of food; and when they found that there were no hopes of succor, they entreated the governor to surrender the place, upon condition that their lives were spared. Edward, at first, was unwilling to accept anything but an unconditional surrender of all the inhabitants to his will; at the remonstrance of Sir Walter Manny, however, he agreed to have placed at his absolute disposal six only of the principal citizens, who were to come out to him with their heads and feet bare, and with ropes around their necks, and the keys of the town and castle in their hands; upon this being complied with the rest were to receive his pardon. After some hesitation, six citizens were found ready to purchase the freedom of their fellow-sufferers upon these hard terms.'"

"Perhaps," added Raymond to Thierry, "you have seen Rodin's statue of the Burghers of Calais? Or a picture of it?"

Thierry made an imperceptible shake of his head, shrugged his shoulders.

"No? Well, never mind, it's a poor statue to commemorate a moment of heroism. Where were we? Yes... They left the town in the way appointed by the King, who received them with angry looks, and ordered their heads to be struck off without delay; all who were present entreated him to have mercy, but he replied that the Calesians had done him so much damage, and put him to so much expense, that it was proper they should suffer for it; and without doubt these six citizens would have been beheaded had not the Queen, on her knees and with tears in her eyes, entreated him to spare them. "Ah, gentle sir," she said, "since I have crossed the sea with great danger to see you, I have never asked one favor; now I most humbly ask as a gift, for the sake of the Son of the blessed Mary, and for your love to me, that you will be merciful to these six men." The King looked at her for some time in silence, and then said, "Ah, lady, I wish you had been anywhere else but here; you have entreated me in such a manner that I cannot refuse you; I therefore give them to you to do as you please with them." The Queen conducted the six citizens to her apartments, and had the halters taken from round their necks, after which she newly clothed them and served them with a plentiful dinner; she then presented each with six nobles, and had them escorted out of the camp in safety.'... And that, Thierry, is how to be magnanimous to one's prisoners."

Thierry got up and went outside.

*

Hugo must have forgotten about them, thought Thierry a couple of weeks later, and Bruno too. It had been ages now and there had been no sign of life from either of them. He had tried calling many times on his cell phone, but Bruno didn't answer at all, and Hugo just told him he was very busy, that he was in England, or in Ireland, etc., but that he'd be along soon. Thierry began to feel nervous. Suppose he were just left here?

In his unease he followed Raymond about, and had unbent to the degree that one day he agreed to toss grain to the chickens. He liked the way they came running and crowded about him when he shook the feed canister.

"Why do they pick on that dark one?" he asked Raymond, watching the speckled hens jabbing at one of their number.

Raymond looked up, almost startled. It was practically the first sign of curiosity Thierry had shown about anything and the longest sentence he'd heard from him. "It's called xenophobia. Chickens are like people. Bird-brained. They don't like anyone different."

Thierry grunted, but it was impossible for Raymond to know what he thought.

"You could feed the goats," he said, and rather to his surprise, Thierry agreed.

"You could spade that end of the garden," said Raymond a while later, but at that Thierry turned and went back into the house.

*

It was warm the next Saturday, the hounds of spring having been well and truly on winter's traces all week, and the earth now, freed from the grip of cold, loosened to the rising sun and breathed forth hope.

Amadea put on a light skirt and sandals and with a sweater over her shoulders set out to find M. Trencavel's farmstead. Her own hound—or was it M. Trencavel's hound?—trotted beside her, occasionally turning his jack-o-lantern face up to hers enquiringly and sometimes ambling on ahead to explore the bushes.

Yves, when he discovered that Amadea was serious about visiting 'Le Noble,' had rather to her surprise offered to run her over there in the jeep, but as she preferred to walk he had explained to her carefully how to follow the landmarks: the ridge of this hill, that fence line, the track through these woods. She was unlikely to meet anyone. It was too early in the year for tourists, and the inhabitants of these parts were hardworking people. Around the farms someone might be out mending a fence or digging a garden, but it was seldom that anyone took a bottle of wine, a loaf of bread, and went singing into the wilderness here. Amadea and Guilhabert left the road and strolled along a path bordered with bright young grass, below mists of new green leaves on limes and beeches.

Amadea drank in the day. What was Lucien doing on such a beautiful day, she wondered. He had called her 'cousin.' He almost *was* her cousin. Would she ever meet his wife? Surely that was inevitable someday?

*

Lucien, engaged in the dreary and acrimonious intricacies of a case he was judging, noted the sunshine beyond the blinds of the conference room, and turned his attention back to his job. One of the contenders was nervously playing 'snakes' on his cell phone while various lawyers outdid themselves in verbal theatrics and tens of millions of euros hung in the balance. What, Lucien wondered with part of his mind, was Amadea doing on such a day?

*

Amadea broke off a stem of last year's hay and swung it as she walked. She had grown used to country walks since her arrival here. She did not even start at the sight of brown cows in a meadow turning inquiringly towards her. Soon the cows and fences were left behind and the terrain became less inhabited and wilder. A climb, a descent—the earth was multicolored here, beige and rose and deep clay red—and they came out on a road where Yves had said they would. Amadea felt mildly triumphant. The next road should be Trencavel's drive. They turned into it, but now Guilhabert began to behave strangely: he acted eager, pricked his ears, wagged his tail, then walked forward hesitantly and turned round several times as if to go back. His tail was tucked under a little and his ears drooped. Amadea hooked her fingers under his collar and he followed her obediently but with obvious reluctance. Amadea, to whom unease was easily communicable, felt suddenly nervous as well. The narrow dirt road was overhung with low forest growth and the center was grown up in weeds and long grass. Only the occasional broken branch and the ruts of a motorcycle and some larger vehicle showed that it was still in use. The way dipped into trees, then out again, climbing all the while. Then before them in a clearing was a small and ancient-looking house, with outbuildings, an orchard, and the remnants of last year's garden, partly turned over. There was a chicken coop and a small herd of goats in a pasture. A large utility vehicle stood incongruously filling the foreground, its modernity out of place in that setting. Guilhabert whined deep in his throat. Amadea tightened her grip on his collar as he broke into a volley of barking. A man was emerging from the house and he did not look friendly. He was grasping a length of firewood and he gave Amadea a cold stare.

"Who are you and what do you want here?" he asked sharply.

This couldn't be M. Trencavel, Amadea thought. This was a man in his mid-thirties, of the type that in America would once have been called a "yuppy." His bearing was self-confident and his clothes indicated a good source of income. His surliness was not the rudeness of a man who didn't know better, but worse, the deliberate rudeness of a man who did.

"I'm sorry to bother you," Amadea stammered, "I was looking for M. Trencavel, but I must have the wrong house." She turned her attention to the dog, who was twisting her wrist with his squirming, and who was, frighteningly, growling at the man.

"Who are you? And what do you want with him?" The man stepped hastily behind his vehicle. "You hang onto that dog, or it'll be the end of him."

"I live near the village. I thought this might be his dog," gasped Amadea, trying to pull Guilhabert back a few steps. "This *is* his house, then?"

"I've never seen that dog before—but if I see him running loose around here, I'll shoot him. As to my father, he's gone to a retirement home in St-Bertrand de Bigorre. Now, take yourself off—go on, this is private property."

Amadea turned to go, pulling the dog after her. It was then that she noticed, beyond the SUV, that there was a large dog house next to the shed. A very large dog house, empty. She stopped a second, staring at it. The man waved his hand angrily at her. "Go on, get off, and don't come around here again!"

Guilhabert began to bark again. Amadea, with an accelerated heartbeat, put both hands on his collar and dragged him away down the drive.

Hugo went back into the house. Neither Thierry nor Raymond made any comment. Hugo was already in a bad mood. His father was not being any more cooperative than before, and he felt an odd change in the manners of Bruno's thug. His neutrality was too neutral, somehow. Hugo didn't feel he was one hundred percent on his side; still, he had called Bruno and Bruno had assured him that Thierry would do as he was told. Did he want to try using force on his father, or what? Hugo said no, not yet, but he wasn't happy.

*

Amadea wasn't used to being shouted at. Heart swelling with indignation, she walked rapidly homewards. It was much, much further in this direction. Her thoughts were in turmoil. On the one hand, she felt certain that she had been lied to. Guilhabert *was* M. Trencavel's dog. Probably the unpleasant son had dumped the father in an institution and then dumped the dog along the roadside. People did these things, she knew. But on the other hand, she thought, maybe it was just her imagination again. Maybe M. Trencavel was ill and couldn't be cared for at home. Maybe it wasn't his dog. Maybe Guilhabert had growled at the son just because he sensed he was a bad character—and so he was, she thought.

She had barely got in when Céleste rang to ask if she would come sit with Madame, as she, Céleste, needed to go out for a time. So Amadea spent the afternoon at the *manoir*, reading the newspapers to Madame, and eating the macaroons that Céleste had provided, and feeling calmed and comforted by a setting where no out spoke angrily and old people weren't sent to institutions. Here there was peace and order and pleasantness.

But of course, she considered, the d'Alemberts and the marquise's family were rich, and that made everything very much easier. However, Trencavel's son didn't exactly look poverty stricken, and she was certain that Lucien would never discard a family member, no matter how poor he was. It must be a considerable sacrifice for him to be continually leaving his own wife and home to stay with his grandmother, and yet he did it.

She related her adventures to Madame, who was suitably and soothingly indignant on her behalf. "What will Lucien say?" she finished. It was on the tip of

Amadea's tongue to say, "Don't tell Lucien," but then she was silent, not understanding the source of her own reluctance.

What to do with the dog was now a real problem. And yet when Céleste had come back and Amadea had walked home alone through the gathering dusk, it was pleasant to find Guilhabert waiting for her, to take him off his chain and bring him into the house with her. She curled up on the sofa and he curled up at her feet. She had never had an animal before. She had never asked her parents for one as a child, it had been so patently impossible. She knew that in the days before her mother left there had been permanent homes, that she had gone to a day school run by nuns for a time; but when she looked back at her childhood it seemed to her an existence made up of continual moves. Her early years she remembered as a series of identical hotel rooms: different cities but the same sheets, same soap, same anonymity. She had sat alone with a book while her father and mother went about their various businesses. Sometimes at lunch or dinner she would be taken down, carefully dressed, to the hotel restaurants, but usually she had eaten off a tray brought by room service. "Don't forget the tip," Maman had said, slipping on her high-heeled shoes and tossing her long hair as she went out in the evening. "You can watch television if you like," Dad had said, as he hurriedly knotted his tie in the morning. A pet would never have fit into that world. And then there had been the boarding schools. Perhaps that was why, she mused, she had never developed into the fully formed, rounded, and mature personality that she admired, like Madame, or Lucien.

No, she mustn't be always thinking about Lucien: he was married, after all. Think about Guilhabert, about how nice it was, since it seemed unavoidable, to have a companion. She reached down and petted the dog and he rolled his eyes up at her. She had the candy she'd saved for dessert, and she had a book she'd borrowed from the *manoir*. A pet and a book and a bar of chocolate—what more could one want? As a child she'd had only a book; she was coming up in the world.

9

At Raymond's the two men were alone again, Hugo having departed shortly after Amadea's visit. It was nearly dinnertime. Raymond rose, opened a cupboard, took out a pot, two pots, was searching for a jar of tomato paste...

"I hope you're not going to start reading after dinner," said Thierry disagreeably, having found Hugo's visit unsettling.

Raymond stiffened, his back to the young man. Then he slammed the pots back into the cupboard and left the house. Thierry rose and followed him, but when he saw that Raymond had only opened the door to the cellar, he came back in and sprawled out in his chair again. Raymond hunted in the darker corners of his cellar. Somewhere there was—aha! There it was. It had been there how long? Three years, probably. He pulled out the large and dusty jar and carried it upstairs. He slapped two plates down on the table and set the jar between them. "Dinner is served," he said to Thierry.

Thierry came to the table slowly. He had gotten used to Raymond's warm meals. He regarded the jar suspiciously.

"What's that?"

"Dinner. People who don't know anything, who won't learn anything, are like animals. You don't think

I'm going to cook for an animal, do you?" He opened the jar. The scent of rotting cabbage was overpowering, almost unbearable.

"Oh, faugh!" cried Thierry, rising and backing away. Raymond scooped out a large portion and dumped it on his plate. "There's nothing else," he said, with satisfaction, "and the stores are closed in the village now."

Thierry digested this unpalatable fact in an angry silence, then, reluctantly, with wrinkled nose, he sat down and stuck a fork gingerly into the mass.

"The wages of ignorance are sauerkraut," said Raymond.

*

On Thursday, Yves entered the drawing-room shortly before Amadea was to leave. M. Lucien had called and was asking if mademoiselle would mind waiting till he arrived?

What could he want? Amadea wondered rather apprehensively. She didn't think she was going to be fired again; she felt quite sure Madame liked her. There had been that scrap of conversation overheard, before she had known of their cousinhood: She had just left to go home, but had stopped beyond the door to struggle with a jammed zipper, when she heard Madame saying, "That's the girl you should have married, Lucien," and his answer, "But Grand-mère, she's much too..." Amadea had hurriedly abandoned the zipper and bolted away, ears and cheeks burning. And then the torture: too *what?* It had kept her awake tossing about for several nights.

Now, here was the front door opening, the sound of voices. Lucien was entering the room, greeting his grandmother, turning to her, Amadea.

"Mademoiselle, you are a woman of mysteries— a mystery-monger, shall we say?"

Amadea blushed slightly. She was always blushing slightly when Lucien was around.

"What is this my grandmother tells me? That some wretch chased you off when you went to ask about Trencavel? That he told you his father had gone to a retirement home in St-Bertrand de Bigorre?"

Amadea nodded. "Yes. I suppose I shouldn't have gone up the drive; it *was* private property...but I really thought the dog might belong to him."

"You have no need to justify yourself. He must be a real cad to have been rude to *you*."

This was said with enough warmth that Amadea glanced up at him in surprise. But she supposed she must have imagined it, because he was saying, quite casually, to his grandmother, "I have a curiosity to know if the dog really does belong to Trencavel. I thought I'd take him over to Bordan to see if he can identify him. Tonight's a good night; he might be sober. If you are agreeable, mademoiselle? And would like to come along?"

Soon they were grinding slowly over the gravel to the main road. Guilhabert sat grinning and panting on the back seat, his head brushing the car's ceiling. Then there was smooth highway. The jeep's lights cut through the gathering darkness in front of them. Lucien's hands on the wheel were long and capable-looking. Amadea took her eyes off them and stared out the window. They had driven for some way in silence, before Lucien said quietly, "I am very grateful to you.

You are so good for my grandmother. You give her something to think about."

Amadea felt a surge of pleasure and stammered, "I'm so glad..." Then, not knowing what to say, she fell silent. But after a while she added, "You surprise me in a way. I mean, your grandmother always seems to me so very self-possessed and cheerful..."

Lucien shrugged, "Yes, but we are social creatures, we humans; we all need companions. And my grandmother has always been accustomed to a great deal of company, and of intellectual stimulation. We— her family—were quite worried when she decided to move back here, three years ago, but she was determined. This was my grandfather's favorite residence, and at one time I think it used to bore my grandmother to come here, although she never told him so. Now he's gone, I think she feels it's a kind of homage to his memory to live here. Or perhaps she feels closer to him in this place."

Amadea said hesitantly, "Was it a happy marriage?" She believed in marriage, as the best of possible alternatives, but she had little acquaintance with happy ones.

"Oh yes, *very*. Happy marriages are rather the rule in my family."

"*Really?*" She stared at him with such astonishment that he smiled and added wryly, "With one or two exceptions." He changed the subject.

They had turned off the highway onto a country road, and shortly the jeep pulled up before a small farmhouse. A chained dog set up a racket that was answered by Guilhabert's thunderous bass in their ears. The door of the farmhouse opened and a woman appeared in the light. Lucien got out and greeted her. "My cousin," he introduced Amadea. She glowed with pleasure. They passed into the house through a narrow hall. Their hostess was a tired-looking, gray-haired woman wearing a striped tee and a flowered skirt. She ushered them into a tiny sitting room, where they sat on the edge of an uncomfortable sofa while she fluttered about. Her husband would be right in, right away, if they wanted to speak to him—

"No hurry at all," said Lucien politely.

—but it was so seldom that she got him to do any work, that she hated to stop him now, and it was so very kind, so very kind of M. d'Alembert to have brought him home last week. This drinking was the worst; they'd have been well off if it weren't for that, and the children wouldn't stay home on account of it, but went off to work in Montpellier—Jacques did, that is, and Jean went to Toulouse, but she'd see if Pascal were through...She disappeared. A clock on the mantel tic-tocked from behind a pile of photographs. The room smelled of must and apples, and the floor sagged. A stomping and cleaning of feet and Pascal Bordan appeared, sober, and greeted them with great bonhomie, throwing up his arms, "My friends, welcome, welcome." Pascal greeted everyone that way. He was a man with overflowing sympathy: he loved his friends, his neighbors, his neighbors' wives, his own wife, his bottle, and his cows. He beamed at Lucien and Amadea, unabashed by their last meeting.

They explained their errand.

"A dog?" Well, he'd have to see the dog. But it was strange about Trencavel. He'd been up at his house a time ago and a strange man—black leather jacket, tattoos—had told him he was taking care of the place for a while. Gone to an old-people's home? That was strange. Man was perfectly hale—hale as he was, and not at all the type to be happy there...he'd never go to one himself, prefer to fall down dead in a ditch any day. ("Someday you will," murmured his wife, with resigned affection.)

They had left the house and were approaching the jeep. Guilhabert was invisible, lying on the seat, but he rose suddenly with his hideous baying bark. Pascal jumped backwards in surprise, slipped, and knocked into Amadea, sending her staggering to her knees on the damp earth.

Lucien helped her up and studied her face for a second. "You're not hurt, are you?"

Amadea bit her lip and shook her head. No, it was just that she always managed to feel like something out of a slapstick movie in his presence. Pascal picked himself up off the ground, loud in oaths and apologies. Under cover of his noise, Lucien said to Amadea: "I'm afraid we're giving you a bad idea of French men. We're not all brutes, all the time."

Amadea stuttered, "No, I think French men are charming. That is, some of them, some of the time."

Lucien gave her an amused look.

Pascal was peering into the car as he brushed himself off. "Oh yes, that's Trencavel's dog. No doubt about it. Awfully proud of him, he is. Always says he has the ugliest dog in Ariège, and that's true. You wouldn't want to meet that character on a dark night, would you?" (Amadea and Lucien exchanged glances: hers saying "you see?" and his saying "you're right"). "He'll be happy to get him back—but no, you say he's gone to a home. That is strange, very strange."

"But why would the son say he didn't know the dog?" asked Amadea as they drove home. "Maybe that's why Guilhabert acted so strangely when we went to M. Trencavel's. Maybe the son chased him off after his father left?"

"I don't know," said Lucien, answering her first question. "Perhaps he simply didn't want to be bothered with him. I'll try to get in touch with Trencavel at the home and see what he wants done with him." He stopped the jeep in front of her house. "You haven't had dinner yet, I'm sure, and neither have I. May I invite you...? You can leave the dog though," he added, as Guilhabert thrust his jowly face between them.

Amadea ran inside to change. And then, in her pine-scented attic, as she peeled off her muddy clothes—quickly, don't want to keep him waiting—it occurred to her again: he's married. She took a pair of nylons out of a drawer, slowly. Would his wife mind? But then, of course, she was being foolish; he was just being friendly to a relation—that was all, nothing more. The French thought a lot of family relations, even if, in this case, it was only a connection in the fifth degree or something. Or maybe he was just being courteous to his grandmother's employee. ("The test of a gentleman is his courtesy to those who can be of no possible use to him.") They would probably just run down to the local bistro for something simple. It was all right, surely. She took out her best dress—it was cream-colored, a bit light for the season—but she knew she looked well in it. Though, naturally, it didn't matter if she looked well or not, she reminded herself as she ran a brush rapidly through her hair.

They did not, as she expected, stop at the local bistro. In fact, they headed towards the highway. She looked a question at him.

"There's a good restaurant in Foix," he said. And it's a long drive, he added to himself.

Oh, she thought to herself, aren't there any good restaurants in Maugrebis or Valzères or one of the other nearby towns? He must be very particular to drive so far for a meal. She glanced at him, but he had his eyes on the road. Dark eyes, dark hair, good shoulders, a good mind—she was intensely aware of his presence, and the drive did not seem long at all.

They drove into Foix and stopped in a medieval-looking street. Soon they were in a small, well-filled restaurant where the waiters treated them with more consideration than Amadea had encountered in a year. Lucien asked them to bring something a vegetarian could eat, and instead of fainting, they had bowed and murmured something affirmative and shortly returned with the most wonderful meal.

This meal, however, was wasted on Amadea: a bloody beefsteak would have passed unnoticed. She had not yet reached the age of preferring food to love, or thinking a meal more interesting than a man. Her attention was entirely concentrated on her dinner partner. Lucien had talked fluently and charmingly through the first two courses, and then Amadea, because he asked the right questions, and listened with such flattering interest, found herself talking too. They had talked of books, and politics, and the law, and slowly devolved onto personal matters. Lucien asked her how she found France, as a returning Frenchwoman. Had there been any culture shock?

And she told him the things that had struck her most were small: like learning that the center of Arthurian legend was not Wales but what is now Paimpont in Brittany, "and maybe that's correct," she added.

("Probably," he agreed.) Or like differences in table manners, she said, making an effort not to look in the direction of a group of businessmen seated beside them, who, with their napkins tucked into their shirts, were chewing open-mouthed and sopping their bread in their plates. "But after all, it doesn't really matter if forks are put down on the right or the left, does it?" she added. ("Not the least in the world, as long as one does it properly," he agreed.) Or like learning that three-quarters of married Frenchwomen had committed adultery, and finding it odd, but...

"But, er, happiness is constructed in many ways?" Lucien finished for her.

"Ye-es," Amadea faltered, "although how can they bear all the lying?"

"Sharpens the wits?" suggested Lucien.

"Well, maybe. But if it makes them happy why are they all so gloomy? Do you know that the French take more tranquilizers than any other nation?" She stopped. Perhaps she was offending him? she asked.

"Deeply," he answered, assuming an air of wounded dignity. "So your opinion is that the French are a nation of melancholic adulterers with bad table manners. Hmm. What is it the English say? Yes, I remember. *Eh bé,* mademoiselle, the same to you with knobs on."

Amadea laughed. Lucien grinned at her.

"So you will not be staying in France then?"

"Oh, yes. I love France."

And after that they had laughed a great deal and sometimes talked seriously about important topics like inequality—"I love my grandmother," said Lucien, "but there shouldn't be marquises"—and the hours had leapt past over the dinner and the dessert and the cups of coffee. It was late, very late, when they reached Maugrebis again, and Lucien stopped the jeep before Amadea's house.

Suddenly silent, they walked together to the door. On the doorstep Amadea said goodbye, very formally, and thank-you-for-the-lovely-evening, very stiffly. Lucien stood watching her while she felt for the door knob with one hand. Guilhabert was whining on the other side. Amadea did not look up but she felt Lucien's gaze upon her. Why didn't he leave? He was two feet away. She could have reached out and touched him. She was scrabbling at the handle, pushing, but it wouldn't open.

"Amadea." It was the first time he had used her first name. His voice was low and gentle. Why wouldn't the door open?

"Amadea—the door's locked."

"Oh."

He took the key from her, unlocked the door, and pushed it open.

"Sweet dreams." And then he was gone.

It was two in the morning. Amadea went into her living room, kicked off her shoes, and sat down by the table, propping her feet on another chair. She was shivering but she didn't notice it. She sat immoveable, staring unseeing out the window while the black turned to gray, the birds came, and then the day. When the sun had appeared over the farthest hill she made herself a cup of coffee mechanically, and then left it on the table, while she stretched out on the sofa. A little oblivion would be welcome. She slept till it was time to go to Madame.

10

"You are pale, my dear," said the marquise. "You were out late last night." So Lucien had told her, Amadea, thought. So it was all right then. "Or is it that I keep you too much indoors? Come, we will go sit in the arbor; the weather is very warm today. Ask Yves to get the chair cushions out."

The arbor was a small way from the house. There was a table and wicker chairs under brick columns with trellis work above and between. It would be covered in vines later, no doubt, and make a nice haven from the heat of summer, but now the leaves were small, and the sun came through nicely. There was beige gravel under foot and on a path leading between hedges one could see a small fountain set as a focal point. There were no flowers here, only hedges and symmetry.

As if answering Amadea's thought, the marquise said, "My husband planned this garden. It was his hobby. But he wouldn't have flowers—they were all relegated to the cutting garden. He said I was the only flower he wanted here. Ah well, I'm not much of a flower anymore," she added with a little laugh.

Amadea said impulsively, "But you're still beautiful."

"Thank you, my dear," but she waved the compliment away with a thin hand. "It does not matter now. Now I could have flowers, but I will not for him. Ah, how he loved me. More than I deserved, I'm sure. He had a loving and loyal heart—like Lucien."

Amadea, with downcast eyes, picked up the prayer book they had brought out and opened it. "Shall I begin?" she said rather coldly.

The older woman looked at her young companion and smiled. She continued, "I worry about Lucien. He is not very happy. One would not think it, because he is always joking, but that is our national habit, you know. He is too sensitive and Caroline was not good for him."

"Caroline?"

"His wife. She seemed like a good choice at first: beautiful, well read, of course, and of good family, but—she became a supporter of Le Pen. So sad. One couldn't possibly *love* a Le Penist, could one?"

"No," said Amadea faintly, "No, I suppose not."

"Lucien's views are modern," continued the older woman, her eyes wandering over the *manoir*. "He thinks we have too much; we are too privileged. He says that even our virtues have no virtue, as we give up nothing that makes a difference to us. What do you think?"

"The world is badly arranged; it should be redone," said Amadea.

"You are both right, but I am too old, too old, or perhaps too self-loving, to change..." There was a moment of silence and then the marquise added wryly, "Amadea, my dear, this is where you are supposed to contradict me; you are failing in your duties."

What is it to me? thought Amadea, who was uncharacteristically not paying attention and whose mind was still fixed on the politics of Lucien's wife rather than on Madame. If he married this Caroline, he must have loved her. Surely I don't want him to be unhappy? So why this feeling of satisfaction? Ashamed, she bent over the page. Then, in spite of herself, she had to ask, "Where does she live?"

"Who?"

"His—um, 'Caroline'?"

"Oh, in Paris."

Amadea swallowed and began to read from the prayer book: "*Heureux ceux dont les iniquités sont effacées et dont les péchés sont pardonnés. Heureux l'homme à qui le Seigneur n'impute point de péché, et dont l'esprit est exempt de dissimulation.*"

*

Raymond was reading from Chateaubriand, about the rowdy companion of the author's youth, who later, as part of the Loyalist forces during the Revolution, behaved heroically: "'He was taken at the affair of Quiberon; the action had concluded, but the English continued to bombard the Republican army; Gesril threw himself into the water, swam to the vessels, told the English to cease firing, and announced to them the misfortune and capitulation of the *emigrés*. They wanted to save him: they threw him a rope and pleaded with him to come on board. 'I am a prisoner on parole,' he cried to them from amongst the waves, and he swam back to land. He was shot with Sombreuil and his companions.' Well? Do you understand? He risked his life to save his comrades, and then refused to save himself, because he'd given his word to his enemies that he would not escape. Here was a man who considered keeping his word more important than his life. What do you think?"

Thierry didn't say anything. He wouldn't offer an opinion or make a comment or even say, "That was a good story." Raymond gritted his teeth in irritation.

"You don't want to know anything?"

"No."

"You don't want to think?"

"No."

"Do you know what happens to people like you?"

"What?"

"They end up believing things that aren't true."

Thierry wasn't interested. He yawned and scratched and stubbed out his cigarettes in Raymond's enameled mug. Silence and boredom. Silence and boredom. Silence and boredom. Raymond, his newly discovered mission to educate this lumpish youngster frustrated, fell to thoughts of revenge. Then he had an idea. It was a brilliant idea, he decided, turning it over in his mind and laughing inwardly. He leaned slightly towards Thierry.

"Do you even know why my son wants to get hold of this land?"

Thierry shrugged. "Wants to develop it, I guess. Sell it. I dunno. You should give in. Save everyone a lot of trouble. And me, I could get out of this *foutu* hole."

"It's not a hole, it's a hillside!" Here it was again. Raymond gritted his teeth. Could no one see the beauty of his property? And then, he had to admit to himself that Hugo had seen it: that was why he expected to be able to sell it. Or perhaps Hugo was simply certain he could sell anything.

Raymond began again patiently the following evening.

"So he didn't tell you anything," Raymond nodded his head thoughtfully, making it a statement, not a question.

Thierry smoked for a while. "Tell me what?"

Raymond hesitated, picked up a book. "Me, I'd have thought you could be trusted. But Hugo doesn't trust anyone. Maybe he's right. I shouldn't have said anything."

"Like what?"

Raymond pretended to read.

Thierry pretended to lose interest. But presently he got up and walked back and forth to the window. He stopped in front of Raymond. "Tell me what? What didn't he tell me?"

Raymond lifted his head.

"I shouldn't have said anything. Even Bruno doesn't know. That makes it more difficult, see? Forget it. Don't tell Hugo I said anything, please, I beg of you." He feigned worry. "He has such a temper when it comes to money..."

"What do you mean?"

"But it's not something one should tell. That's why he didn't want anyone coming around, right?" Raymond sighed. "I'd like to tell you, because you could help, and Hugo's wasting time. I know his business is important—and he always thinks a bird in the hand is worth more—but this is important too. And if he weren't so greedy we could share...No, I don't know if I ought to..."

Thierry, losing patience, reached out and gathered up a fistful of Raymond's shirt front in a muscular hand.

"Tell me or I'll..."

"...tear my shirt." Raymond completed for him calmly. "And I only have two others. Let go."

Thierry let go. Raymond smoothed the wrinkled flannel with a hand that was tremulous and work-worn, and smiled at his jailor.

"Perhaps it would be best."

Really, thought Raymond, Thierry was, in the Midi phrase, as stupid as a suitcase without handles.

"Listen. In the days when..."

"Oh, not more history!"

"That's where it all begins. You can listen or not."

"Well, go ahead then."

"This is a story that occurred in October, in 1391, and it concerns the Count of Foix."

"Why do they always have to be counts?"

"Excellent, Thierry, excellent observation! History should include all people, you're right. But this story is, unfortunately, about a count and his sons...Now the Count of Foix loved hunting, and he is reported to have kept upwards of 1,600 hounds for the purpose..."

"*Eh bé.*"

"*Oui.* But one night, when he had obviously over-exerted himself during the chase, he rose from the table to wash his hands, stuck one finger in the water, and dropped down dead. There was great anguish amongst his sons and followers, of course, but they kept the important things in mind. The castle of Orthez needed to be secured at once, before its inheritance was disputed. So listen, I'll read the rest of it to you: 'The knights seeing (the Count of Foix's natural son) Evan lamenting and wringing his hands, said to him, "Evan, the business is over. You have lost your lord and father. We know that he loved you in preference to all others. Take care of yourself. Mount your horse; ride and gain possession of Orthez, and the treasures within it, before anyone knows of our lord's death." Sir Evan made them a low reverence, and replied, "Gentlemen, I return you many thanks for the friendship you now show me, and I trust I shall not forget it; but tell me what are my lord's tokens, or I shall not gain admittance into the castle." "You say true," said the knights; "take them." The tokens were a small golden ring the count wore on his finger, and a little knife with which he sometimes cut his meat at table. These were the tokens the porter of the castle at Orthez was acquainted with, and had he not seen them he would never have opened the gate. Sir Evan left the inn at Rion with only two servants, and rode in haste to Orthez, where nothing was known of the count's death. He spoke to no one as he passed through the streets, and in coming to the castle the porter asked, "Where is my lord?" "At Rion," answered the knight, "and he has sent me to seek for some things that are in his chamber. Look, here are his tokens, his ring and his knife." The porter knew them well, and at once admitted Evan, who having passed the gate said to the porter, "Thou art a dead man if thou obey me not." The porter, in alarm, asked the cause. "My lord and father is dead," said the knight, "and I wish to gain possession of his treasure before anyone knows of it." Sir Evan knew well where his treasure was deposited; but he had three pairs of strong doors to open, and with separate keys, before he could gain admittance, and these keys he could not find."'

"'Now it happened, after he left Rion, that the chaplain of the count, Sir Nicholas de l'Escalle, found a little steel key hanging to a piece of silk, which the count wore over his shirt, and recognized it to be the key to the doors of the room that contained a small steel casket, in which…'"

"Well," said Raymond, "I'll summarize the rest: …in which the chief treasures of the count were always kept. There were priceless jewels—rubies, diamonds, and gold. Quickly Sir Nicholas made his plan…and 'hastened…to the castle…'"

"'…it was known at Orthez that the Count de Foix was dead. This was very afflicting news, for he was greatly beloved by all ranks. The whole town was in motion: some said, "We saw Sir Evan ride up the town toward the castle, he seemed much distressed; without doubt, what we heard is true." As the men of Orthez were thus conversing, Sir Nicholas came up, to whom they said, "Sir Nicholas, how fares my lord? They tell us he is dead; is it true?" "No," replied the chaplain, "he is not dead, but most dangerously ill, and I am come to seek for something that may do him good." On saying this he passed on to the castle. The townsmen, however, began to suspect that the count was dead, and resolved to keep watch at the castle, and send privately to Rion to ascertain the truth of the case. Sir Evan de Foix soon found what the townsmen were about, and that the death of the count was known; he said, therefore, to the chaplain, "Sir Nicholas, I have failed in my attempt; I must humble myself to these men, for force will be of no avail." Sir Evan then went to a tower near the gate, which had a window looking over the bridge to a square where the townsmen were assembled, and having opened the window, he'… spoke to them, and while he was doing so, the false chaplain, Sir Nicholas, quickly opened the doors to the treasure room and extracted the metal box. He hid it under his clothing, relocked the doors, and while Sir Evan was engaged still with the townspeople, departed the castle. He knew he had one safe asylum, and that was the fortress at Lobocôte.—That, Thierry, is what my land—this land all around you—is called: 'Lobocôte.' You can ask anyone. The building was on the hill over there, oh, half a kilometer from here. The name comes from the Occitan word for 'mountain'—'*loba*' which has often been transformed over the centuries..."

"But forget the name—go on with the story!" expostulated Thierry.

"My throat is too dry to continue. I absolutely need something to drink."

"Go on," said Thierry.

"Can't," said Raymond.

"Well, I don't believe any of it anyway. I know what you're leading up to. It's all a bunch of *conneries*."

Raymond nodded. "That's what Hugo thought at first. But now—you've seen for yourself how upset and excited he is. He wants rights to the land before he starts excavating. He's afraid I'll cut him out—him, my own son. He's judging by how he'd behave himself in such a situation. What do you think he keeps coming here for? For land in the back of beyond that no one wants anyway? He could get land elsewhere."

"Not free, he couldn't," said Thierry, showing an irritating burst of shrewdness.

Raymond hastily changed tack. "But if it were just the land, don't you think I'd be glad enough to sell? I'm getting old—I won't be able to live here alone forever. It'll all be Hugo's someday anyway."

This argument told on Thierry. True, he didn't like Hugo, or Hugo's type. But he recognized that

Hugo had money. Hugo had power, and brains, and charisma. If Hugo believed something was in his interest it very probably was. And that being the case, what was more likely than that he should intend to cut Thierry out? Wasn't his type always cut out? So he reasoned, or perhaps only felt, and he turned to Raymond and said again, "Go on."

Raymond leaned back. "I'd really, really like a drink; I really need one—it's been weeks." He hated the pleading note in his voice, but he couldn't quite keep it out.

"Tell me the rest and I'll think about going to get you something."

Raymond shook his head and closed his eyes. "I need it first."

Thierry reached out to shake the old man, but changed his mind. "Okay, okay. You can come with me. We'll take the motorcycle and run into Valzères. We'll buy some booze and come back. I can't leave you here."

And so ten minutes later Raymond was clinging to the back of the motorcycle and wondering if even a drink were worth it and whether it were better to die by axe blows or splattered all over the highway. The road shot past at such a speed that even breathing was difficult. And then there were different colored lights and cars on all sides, their shiny metal sliding inches past his knees as the motorcycle canted at a crazy angle, slaloming around them, and then there was a marked decrease in speed, a coasting turn, and the motor was switched off. The world ceased revolving and, oh bliss, they were stationary and here was the liquor store.

"And so," Raymond continued, when they were back in his house again, "'Evan opened the window, and said, "Good people of Orthez, I know well why you are thus assembled and sorrowful. You have good cause for it, and I entreat you most earnestly not to be displeased if I have hastened to take possession of this castle, for I mean nothing but what is just. I shall open the gates for your free admittance; I never thought of closing them against you." The chief among the townsmen answered Sir Evan, "You have well spoken, and we are satisfied. It is our intention that you keep this castle, and all that is within it. Should the Viscount de Chatelbon, your cousin, who is heir to the territory of Bearn, and the nearest relation of our late lord, claim anything belonging to this castle we will strenuously defend you and your brother Sir Gracien in your rights.'" And so Evan, though he never found the treasure, was secure of the castle, and his brother married the chief townsman's daughter—*voilà* Thierry—and they all lived there into happy old age. But Sir Nicholas the priest made all haste to reach his relatives at Lobocôte, and came here at night after a strenuous journey. He was shown to a chamber to sleep, and thought that all was safe and the treasure his. But during the night a storm came up, lightening flashed and thunder rolled. A bolt struck the western tower, the timbers kindled, and soon the roofs and beams of the entire castle were burning. Sir Nicholas, sleeping hard after his long journey, was woken at the last moment by the shouting of the guards and the running of the servants. He barely had time to rip up his soutane and tie it into a rope and climb down before the entire structure was in flames. And then it was that he remembered: he had left the treasure box in his room. So Sir Nicholas stood

outside in his skin, wringing his hands, lifting his boot-
less cries to heaven, generally bewailing the perversities
of fate, and not at all able to say—'I've left my treasure
chest inside!' The castle collapsed into a heap of rubble,
and the disconsolate priest followed the rest of the
household to another lodging...And you might think
that was the end, but no...There, the next night, he has
a nightmare in which he sees the tortures of Dante's
Inferno awaiting him. He wakes and spends the rest of
the night wondering whether he will be confined to the
fourth circle of the slope of hell for avarice, or sent to
the icebound regions of Cocytus, the very pit, for
treachery. He rises in the morning a changed man. He
repents, is sure the fire was a judgment upon him, and
sends a letter of confession to his superior, the abbé de
Laissoublie, who, being a conscientious but not very
clear-thinking man, one imagines, was in a quandary..."

"A what?" said Thierry.

"Between Scylla and Charybdis, between a rock
and a hard place...What to do with this information? He
received it as a confession, he considers. If he informs
the rightful owner of the treasure, it will be a betrayal in
his turn, for the priest's theft will be known. It will also
reflect ill on the Order. The man, one supposes, dillies,
and dallies, time passes, the abbé gets carried off by an
attack of ague, and the letter lies amongst the records of
the abbey, forgotten for centuries..."

Raymond changed tone. "And it was not until I
was doing research on a quite different matter—I was a
history professor, you know," he added, dropping his
eyes modestly, "that I stumbled across the records in a
dusty vault of the Bibliothèque Nationale. I was doing
research on the Cathars of the area, but you can imagine that the name attracted my attention...."

Thierry, looking more attentive than he had intended to look, listened with his mouth slightly agog. Raymond, the former professor, came to an end.

"So it's here?" asked Thierry, eyes kindled, "really here?" But then his native caution, or years of hard knocks and no expectations, resurfaced. It could be true, but probably it wasn't. Maybe it was all some sort of trick. Raymond was in a fix, and when people were in a tight spot they would do or say anything—and then later they left you in the lurch, tossed you aside. On the other hand, Hugo was after something, no doubt about it. Envy and jealousy tipped the scale. If Hugo was so upset with Raymond there was probably a reason besides just the land. One wouldn't fight with one's own father over just land, would one? He wouldn't have, anyway. Raymond, seeing the hesitation on Thierry's face, handed him a book.

"The beginnings are in here," he said, "the rest I had to piece together from old documents. Hugo has them now, or I'd show them to you."

Thierry grunted. He took the book and held it awkwardly. Raymond wondered for a second if Thierry could even read. But the younger man opened the book and began slowly—when was the last time he had read anything?—to decipher the text. Fortunately, he started with the introduction, which was in the modern language. What will he do when he comes to the medieval French? Raymond wondered. Well, he'd leave the boy to it. He had the bottle to finish. He picked it up, and was arrested by the sight of Thierry's shaven head bent over a book. Maybe the young man could be saved, regenerated, educated. The idea amused him. And tomorrow he was going to get some free labor. Life was almost interesting again. And he had the bottle. He had held off getting drunk until he finished the story, but now there was no reason to hold off any longer. He drained his glass.

But here, to his surprise, Thierry dropped the book on the table, reached out a lightning hand, and snatched the bottle away. "You don't need that. If you get drunk you won't be able to show me the site tomorrow. Go to bed!"

Raymond gasped and glared. "Give it back!"

The Thug's teacher, indeed! How dared he! Who was the authority here?

"Give it back!" Raymond made a snatch for it, but, being half gone already, missed. Thierry, without a moment's hesitation, lobbed the bottle through the small window above the table. There was a tinkling crash of glass and the frame swung smashed and empty. Raymond looked out the window. The bottle had broken and the alcohol, its fumes pungent in the night air, was soaking into the grass.

"You can't do that!" Raymond exclaimed with a gasp.

"Yes, I can," said Thierry calmly. "I'm stronger than you, so I can do what I want." He picked up the book again, fumbled with the pages, and went back to his reading.

Raymond, with an air of injured dignity and hatred in his heart, stripped off his clothes and lay down in bed.

In the morning, Raymond was sober and Thierry, having read with considerable difficulty half a dozen pages, was tentatively in a mood to believe. It would be easier than having to read the book himself. Besides, even if there was a niggling doubt at the back of his mind, searching for treasure made a break from the boredom.

He followed Raymond up a path that cut into the woods from a meadow beyond the house. The goats were grazing here and they bleated at Raymond as he went past, then stared curiously after their master as he disappeared into the undergrowth with the other man after him. The two men walked amongst the trees, pushing back occasional branches. The path led out of the hollow in which Raymond's house nestled and then went up and up. Raymond, who walked this way often, climbed easily, in spite of his age, but Thierry began to pant.

"Where are you taking me?"

The climb was unusual for him, city born, from the flattish land around Paris. He stumbled frequently.

"Soon," said Raymond, and walked away and on up. And then the ground leveled and they stepped through tall firs into a clearing. Ahead of them lay a meadow, then came an area covered in young growth and bushes, and beyond that was a breathtaking view of the valley on one side, with the deep blue hills beyond, and on the other, snow-capped mountains jutting into the clear sky. Even Thierry was struck and stood staring for a moment into the distance. There was a movement and a flapping sound, as of something fleeing in the tall grass, then silence.

"Capercaillies," said Raymond.

"What are those?"

"Ghosts," said Raymond, tongue in cheek.

Thierry made a snorting noise.

"It's there," said Raymond, pointing toward the undergrowth.

"But there's nothing there," said Thierry, disappointed and looking sharply at Raymond, whose jocular mood this morning displeased him.

"Well, I told you there wasn't. It burned, remember. But it's there beneath that undergrowth. And look, over there, do you see that faint line across the hill?"

Thierry squinted into the distance.

"That's the old road—been there since Roman times. That's the way the priest came, under cover of night. It was horrible for him. He had borrowed a horse, as his old mule wouldn't do for such a trip, but he wasn't a good rider. He came fast, fearful of pursuit. On the downward slope his horse got away with him, took the bit in its teeth—bolted in fact. He lost his stirrups, dropped a rein, hung onto the treasure box with one hand and the horse's mane with the other. And so he came, headlong downhill, gravel flying out from under the horse's hooves, and he was crying "*Saint Éloi, Saint Éloi, au secours!*"

"Why Saint Éloi?"

"He's the patron saint of riders of bad horses."

"You're making that up," said Thierry suspiciously.

"No, no—it's in the account. It's these little touches that give the story its verisimilitude, you know. Come on down, you'll see where the rock from the walls has fallen. And there are deep holes where the cellars were, so be careful you don't fall in. That's another reason we can't use a bulldozer."

"What's the first reason?" asked Thierry.

"You don't want your treasure chest containing first-class, grade-A, museum-quality medieval artifacts turned into a metal pancake, do you?"

"Guess not," said Thierry, eyeing the site with some trepidation. They walked across the meadow and into the brush. There, faintly, were the remains of a large stone building. It was impossible, to the untrained eye, to tell if it had been a castle, or a manor house, or even a large barn. That it had fallen quite some time previous was obvious. The beams and floors had rotted or burned almost entirely away and all that remained were heaps of rubble, hidden in places under humus, and deep holes half covered with fallen branches. Raymond had cleared some of the young growth off years ago, and had picked away at the trees since, for firewood. He handed Thierry the axe.

"The first thing, before we can start sifting through the dirt, will be to clear the trees."

Thierry began hacking. Raymond instructed him to cut the wood neatly—here was a saw—and stack it in a pile. Thierry almost rebelled at that.

"Why?" he growled, "Let's just chop it down and toss it aside."

"Yes," said Raymond, "but if anyone comes along this has to look like a wood-cutting operation, not an archaeological dig, right?"

"Oh, right," agreed Thierry. He chopped away in silence. Raymond worked too and a pile of wood grew.

"And you'll have to move those rocks: they can be stacked neatly over there. And any tiles you find—over there." Raymond sat on a rock and watched his helper work. "Now who's the strong one," he thought. Thierry was panting from the unaccustomed exercise and he stumbled occasionally. He had abandoned his leather jacket and his gray tee-shirt was black with sweat. "The meek shall inherit the earth and the strong shall carry stones. Brains *are* better than brawn," mused Raymond.

"Why are you just sitting there?" Thierry asked, scowling.

"Weak heart," said Raymond, surprised at his own facility with falsehood, "and I have all the other work to do—I have to conserve my strength. But I'll go down and make some dinner for us. You come along in another hour."

Thierry hesitated, then grunted his agreement. Raymond knew that as soon as he disappeared Thierry was going to sit down and rest. He would have to make some excuse to keep the boy away from the site in the afternoon. Too much work at once would discourage him, and Raymond wanted a steady worker.

11

Amadea did not see Lucien for some days after their evening out. Having found herself lingering in the evening, dawdling down the drive—perhaps that was the sound of the jeep?—she made a conscious effort to leave earlier. But one afternoon, not long after she came home, she heard the sound of the jeep outside her house. Guilhabert, recognizing a friend, did not bark. There was a scrunching of gravel, knocks. Lucien stood on the doorstep.

Amadea rushed to open the door, stepped out slowly, pulled the door shut behind her, and stood tongue-tied, while he saluted her. Then, recovering a little, she asked, "Does your grandmother need me?"

"No, no, she's fine. I came to fill you in on our dog mystery."

Amadea raised her eyes to his questioningly.

"Yes. The mystery is that there is no retirement home in St-Bertrand de Bigorre, none at all. Nor is there an alcohol rehabilitation center, or anything of a social care nature of any sort. Are you sure you heard correctly?"

How stupid of me! thought Amadea. Why was she always making stupid mistakes? She stammered, "I thought it was there, but obviously, I must have made a mistake, I must have misheard, I'm so very sorry to have given additional trouble, so stupid of me."

"Yes. And I won't forgive you unless you come out and have a drink with me. It's *l'heure de l'apéritif*, or what someone—Morand, maybe?—called 'the evening prayer of the French.'"

"I don't usually take an aperitif," said Amadea uncertainly.

"Never mind. You can drink orange juice. Even coca-cola. Anything that will prevent you from saying 'take an aperitif.'"

"Why?"

"Oh, it's one of those things, like with the forks, or not saying *messieurs-dames*. What sort of company did you keep at that English Institute? It's a good thing you left there. They were obviously beneath you."

"No—I was fired for being dull and for thinking poetry a good learning tool."

"You see. I told you they were beneath you. '*O poésie, perle des trésors!*' My English teacher made us learn scads of poetry—is that the word, 'scads?'"

"Maybe," said Amadea, with doubt on her face.

"And tomorrow we will go over and ask the young Trencavel where the old Trencavel is, agreed?"

"Yes. On foot?"

"Euh..." It was Lucien's turn to be taken aback, but he recovered quickly. "Certainly, on foot."

Amadea was embarrassed. "I didn't mean we had to go on foot."

"It's all right. I do indeed feel a sudden desire to commune with nature." He struck an attitude. "*Viens! Respire avec moi l'air embaumé de rose*'—and all that."

"It's too early for roses," said Amadea shyly, "there are lots of nettles, though."

He grinned at her. "Come on. I need that drink."

Evening was beginning as they drove away through the lengthening light of spring, and morning was not too far away again when they returned. Amadea ascended to her attic like a weightless sprite and fell into bed. There was something she should urgently think about, she knew, but instead, she remembered something Lucien had said, and giggling, she laid her head on the pillow and was instantly asleep.

When she awoke it was bright daylight. She hadn't overslept, surely? She sat up abruptly. Lucien was coming. He mustn't find her in bed, in her nightgown. She fumbled for her wristwatch. No, she still had time. She dressed hurriedly, ate breakfast quickly, took care of her minor household chores, tied up the dog— "sorry, Guilhie, not this time, good dog"—and set out to meet Lucien at the top of the shortcut. He came walking up the hill between the cedars. He saw her standing at the head of the path and raised a hand in greeting. Her heart skipped a beat and she raised a tentative hand in return. Yes, now she remembered what she had to think about. He was married.

But he gave her no time to think about it. He took up their talk where it had broken off the night before, and one topic led to another as they followed the trail across the hills.

Guilhabert stood with pricked ears at the end of his chain and watched, with growing anxiety, as his mistress walked away with a man: She wasn't going away with *him* was she? She wasn't going for a walk with a *man*, was she? That man was all right but surely she

wouldn't choose *him* as a companion over himself,
Guilhabert, the finest dog in the Pyrenees? Guilhabert let
out a loud exasperated whine. But the two figures were
retreating. Why, they were going right away! Without
him! It was unbelievable, inconceivable, oh, bad, bad,
judgment! Guilhabert bit at his chain and the whine
rose to a howl. They were ignoring him; their backs
were disappearing round the bend. They were gone.
Guilhabert sighed noisily and lay down in disgust.

Amadea trod lightly, the hem of her pale cotton
dress catching occasionally on the branches of low-
growing bushes. A plum tree along the way was in blos-
som. Lucien, watching her bend down a spray to admire it, decided he was really very glad he'd come out.
The plum tree was very pretty. So was Amadea, very.
The quickening of his heartbeat, those sudden intakes
of breath, rather surprised him. He was too experienced
not to know what it meant, but he chose to ignore it, to
put it down to the fresh air, or the altitude, or anything
else. They went on. Soon the way became steeper.

"I'm afraid it gets steeper here," Amadea said,
turning to him. "But I'm forgetting you know these
parts better than I do...I feel guilty for having inveigled
you into this long walk. I'm sure it wasn't really what
you'd intended." She hopped over a little trickle of water that ran down the hill into a ditch.

He followed her. "Yes. How guilty shall I make
you feel? No, I am not in favor of exercise, or of sports.
Men have only a certain amount of energy and—let us
use the scientific term—testosterone. You agree? You
are silent. I take that for agreement. Now, there are several ways of expending this energy, testosterone, etc.
One can make war—a time-honored tradition, but we'll

waive that, of course. One can make love. Or one can run about the block, hit balls over nets, pump heavy weights up and down in a gym. Americans like to do these things. The French much less. That's why we're better lovers."

The path was precipitous here, so Amadea gave her attention to it so as not to look at him. Yet when they had scrambled the rest of the way to the crest of the hill it was she who was out of breath, panting and puffing, while he was cool and unconcerned, his breathing apparently as even as ever.

Amadea sat down on a rock and tried to catch her breath.

"*Oui*," he said, "I see you share my feelings about exercise. I'm so glad we see alike."

Amadea, who was not going to aver that she preferred love to exercise, or vice versa, stared at the white peaks of the mountains rising abruptly to the south, and said nothing. Lucien looked down at her.

"*Bon*. You have the gift of silence. Very wise. But not very French."

"There's still snow," said Amadea, waving toward the mountains.

"'There is the snow of yesteryear'—that's what everyone says in the mountains—'and of all our yesteryears down to the last syllable of recorded time'...but I am talking nonsense, and have been for some time. Will you forgive me?"

Amadea nodded and they continued, talking placidly of Ronsard and Shakespeare and EU agricultural policies and not at all of anything delicate, but Amadea felt suddenly subdued, and Lucien felt he'd made a mistake.

Clouds had been drifting across the sun as they walked and by the time they reached Trencavel's turn-off the first drops of rain were beginning to fall.

"It's here," said Amadea, rather pleased with herself for having managed to find her way again. "But that wasn't there before." She pointed to a chain that someone had stretched across the road. A hand-lettered sign on a piece of cardboard had been tied to it—"Private Property. Trespassers will be Persecuted."

(Thierry, showing Raymond the sign he had made, had been disconcerted to see the older man collapse with laughter. "What's wrong?" he had demanded, staring at his sign. "Nothing, nothing at all," Raymond had said, "It's very appropriate.")

"The younger Trencavel's work, I assume," said Lucien. "A man who knows Guilhabert de Castres and Latin wouldn't make that mistake."

"Maybe we shouldn't..." said Amadea.

Lucien shrugged. "We have business here." He strode purposefully towards the chain, but before he reached it a motorcycle roared into the drive from behind them. Amadea moved uneasily off the road, while Lucien turned to meet the cyclist, who stopped and cut his motor. The man removed his helmet. He was not the man Amadea had seen before, not the yuppy-type son, but a man in a dark jacket: your ordinary-thug-type of man, Amadea thought. He didn't look welcoming either, though, and he spoke in an odd growling voice. Lucien, with calm politeness, managed to extract the information that the two Trencavels, father and son, had gone away for a family vacation, and that he—the motorcyclist—was looking after the place in the meantime. He didn't know anything about any dog, and it was private property—See? There was a sign—so they'd better keep off in the future, or they'd have him to deal with, right?

Amadea ventured tentatively, "But M. Trencavel said his father had gone to a retirement home?"

Thierry was momentarily taken aback, but the appropriate response came to him: "No. You misunderstood. He had to go to one of those alcohol rehab places. He drinks, you know."

"Where could I get in touch with him?" Lucien asked. "You must have a contact number."

"No. I told you. Trencavel drinks. He doesn't think about things like phone numbers."

"All right. Where could I reach the younger Trencavel?"

"He drinks too," snapped Thierry, losing patience. "You just keep away from here, right? We're not interested in any dogs." He started the motorcycle. The noise put an end to all conversation and he guided the machine around the stretched chain and disappeared up the drive.

Lucien and Amadea were left standing in the road. The rain was starting to fall thicker. Lucien looked at Amadea's crestfallen face and raised his hands. "All this is very strange, but at the moment—I'm suddenly tired of the Trencavels: father, son, and motorcyclist. Let's get out of the rain." He guided Amadea under the sparse protection of a newly fledged lime tree. "Now, I think it would be best to call Yves, and ask him to pick us up. Do you agree?"

Amadea nodded. The rain intensified while Lucien searched his pockets for his cell phone.

"On the other hand," he said, after a slight pause—it was not usual for him to forget things—"a walk in the rain will no doubt be very refreshing. Do you agree?"

"I'm sorry," said Amadea, shivering.

Lucien stepped in front of her. "Amadea, I have three favors to ask. First, you must take my jacket"—he stripped it off and held it out to her. She took it reluctantly. "Second, you must stop saying you're sorry. And third, I wish you would stop looking sad."

Amadea looked up at him. He stepped back rather hastily. "Let's go."

They walked side by side in silence as the rain lashed at them and Lucien considered with some amusement how it was that he found himself striding damply across country, with water trickling down his neck, while he worried about a homeless dog, the whereabouts of a complete stranger, and the moods of a young woman so sensitive that she could be depressed all afternoon by the mere mention of...well, anyway, it was a good thing he was going to be away in the next weeks.

12

The stack of firewood was growing rapidly in Raymond's woodshed. He brought a load down with him every time he visited the site and he had persuaded Thierry to do likewise. The rain had interrupted Thierry's labor, but now, after a day and a half of confinement, he paced back and forth impatiently in the little house, and at last said he was going out, rain or no rain.

Raymond shrugged, "Suit yourself. But don't fall into any cellar hole."

Thierry snorted and went out. He was gaining in condition rapidly and had soon climbed the hill and was swinging his axe with abandon. Raymond said they could start digging soon. The small rain wet the handle of the axe and it slid under his hands a little, but he paid no attention to it, nor to the slickness of the earth under his feet. He was working toward one of the cellar holes. It was beyond those bushes. The rain had stopped now and the mist, rolling up the hill, had obscured the hole and the valley below and the mountains beyond. He was alone here, more alone than he had ever been. He might have been the only man left in the world, but he did not stop to indulge in flights of philosophy or imagination, he just hacked away. Warmed by his work, he took off his jacket and hung it on a tree limb. The roots of the sapling he was working on refused, stubbornly, to give way. Trencavel had said he had to get the roots out, too. He circled the tree stump, chopping. That should do it. He inserted the axe under the stump and pried. It came loose and he reached down and picked it up, shaking the earth off. He stepped back a step or two to survey the patch he'd just cleared. Oh, yes, he'd meant to get rid of that bush there; he'd just take a swing at it now. He stepped back and the ground gave way beneath him, and he was falling backwards, falling, and the axe was falling above him. Instinctively, as he tumbled to the bottom of the hole, he rolled himself into a ball and the axe bounced off a projection above him and skimmed over his head. A sickening jolt and the world stopped spinning and he opened his eyes. He was still alive. He sat up gingerly. No, nothing was broken. His head hurt and there were painful areas when he moved, but he'd been hurt worse before, many times. He rose. He'd just climb out and he wouldn't tell Raymond about his fall.

Once standing, however, he found that the smooth brick sides of the cellar rose above his head, except on one side where the wall had crumbled, but there the earth overhung the hole: it was that overhang that had broken and cushioned his fall. He had brought down with him an avalanche of dirt and detritus. On the other sides the earth gave no purchase for a man of his weight. The occasional root or twig came away in his hand. He was trapped. Raymond would find him here. He'd look like a fool. He tried jumping at the walls, searching anywhere for a hand or toe hold, but his head hurt and he soon gave up. He was a fool, he thought bitterly. Suppose Raymond took his opportunity and left, went clear away in his absence, then where would he, Thierry, be? He'd lose his job. Oh, but Raymond wouldn't leave, because there was this treasure to be found. Or was there? No, he was a triple-dyed idiot. He sat down against a pile of rubble and rested his head in his hands. If there wasn't any treasure, then Raymond had been tricking him. He had wondered sometimes if he wasn't being hoaxed; Raymond's attitude had seemed so—so not very serious. Money made people serious. Raymond—if Raymond had made it up then he wouldn't come looking for him. Why should he? He would seize his chance and run away. Raymond would leave him here. And that being the case, what were the chances that anyone else would come along and pull him out? Ah, but he had his cell phone! No, it was in the pocket of his jacket, hanging from a tree limb. He shouted at the top of his lungs, "Trencavel! Raymond! Help! Anyone!" But his bellows were met by silence. The mist lay thick all around. He would starve to death here and only his bones would be found.

"TRENCAVEL!" No answer. No, no one would come. He was a fool, a fool to have trusted the old man. "*Ohé*, Trencavel!" Thierry banged with his fist on the bricks. The 'benign indifference of the universe,' vaunted by Camus, did not comfort him a bit. The mist hung gray and still above him, the undergrowth motionless, the air quiet. Dusk had come unnoticed while he worked; now it was nearly dark. Controlling his rising panic with difficulty, Thierry crouched on his heels to wait.

Raymond, when Thierry had departed, had considered his options. He could make a run for it. Pity the battery was dead in his old *deux-chevaux*, and the bicycle didn't have brakes, but he could nobble Thierry's motorcycle and get away. Go to...Ah, that was the question, though. Where would he go? If he went to the police and told them about Thierry, they would come out here. They'd find the boy cutting firewood. He would look all innocence and say he'd been hired to do just that—Thierry had brains enough for that kind of defense. The police would think that he, Raymond, was just a crazy old man, and they would go away, or, worse, they'd go away and then send social workers to check up on him, to suggest that he should be put away in a home. No, when one was old, one was too vulnerable—one couldn't ask for help. He would wait and see what happened. Things were bound to resolve themselves on their own. He would wait for Thierry to come back.

But Thierry didn't come back. Obviously the boy was taking a liking to work. The afternoon passed, dusk came, and Raymond started to consider what to make for dinner. Thierry would be hungry. He was a satisfying person to cook for: he ate with great appetite whatever—well, bar the sauerkraut—was put before him. It made Raymond feel that he was a great chef, even though he knew he was only a rather middling one. Still, there was nothing like encouragement to make one better. Let's see. They'd had enough egg dishes for a while; goat's cheese ditto. He still had some dried mushrooms left. Perhaps a mushroom stew? And afterwards, he had a good story for Thierry. The boy didn't even protest about having to listen these days. He was actually rather pleased with him.

But it was getting late; Thierry should have been back by now. The stew was ready, and it wasn't bad, if he did say so himself, thought Raymond, tasting it again. Time passed. Really, Thierry should have been back. Where could the boy be? From slight curiosity, Raymond progressed by stages to real anxiety. Thierry should have been back. He couldn't be working in this darkness. Suppose the fool had cut himself with the axe, or chopped a tree down on himself, or fallen in a cellar hole? Raymond walked from the window to the door, the window to the door. He stepped out into the yard and peered in the direction Thierry would come. Well, what was it to him if Thierry came or not? Let the devil take him. He went indoors and sat down, then rose again. Well, what did he care? What did he care, he kept asking himself, as he shrugged on his old jacket, took up a lantern, and went out into the evening.

He stumped up the hill, moving more rapidly as the deepening shadows and the silence increased his unease. "*Ohé*! Thierry!" he called as he approached the clearing, "*Ohé*!"

And faintly, a call came back, "Raymond! *Ici!* In the hole!"

In the cellar hole! *Bien sûr*, Thierry was in the hole. Hadn't he, Raymond, thought that was where he would be? The young fool, Raymond muttered to himself, surprised at the depth of his own relief. Of course, he told himself, it was just that if the idiot had really been injured it would have been very tedious: he had no telephone; he would have had to run for help, a long way. He worked his way carefully to the edge of the cellar and lifted the lantern so that it lit the cavity. Thierry stood there, looking foolish and relieved and scowling to hide the fact. He waited for Raymond to say something taunting, something cutting. If the old man did, he'd punch his lights out when he got up.

"Soup's getting cold," said Raymond, and then, gruffly, "You're not hurt, are you?"

Thierry, surprised, shook his head. He couldn't remember the last time anyone had cared whether he were hurt or not.

"I brought a rope," said Raymond. "Wait while I tie it to something. You'll have to climb out yourself. I can't pull you up on my own."

A short time later, Thierry, considerably muddied, stood beside Raymond. Neither man said anything. Raymond untied the rope and together they slipped and skidded down the hill.

13

The next time Amadea saw 'the Thug,' as she thought of him—although he was probably a perfectly respectable fellow, she told herself, and those semi-shaven heads were fashionable among all sorts—was in the bakery. She found the shop empty except for the Thug and the Niece, who both looked up at her in some displeasure when she came in. Obviously, she was interrupting something. The Niece, in fact, rolled her eyes. Humbly, Amadea asked for a loaf, paid, and departed as rapidly as she could, thinking they wished to be alone; but to her surprise the Thug followed her to the door. She walked up the street, feeling that he was watching her. She told herself that she was just imagining it. She turned into the cobbled side street and half way along looked back. He was behind her. Well, after all, if he was going to M. Trencavel's it might be his way too; although why had he left the motorcycle in front of the bakery? She turned onto the highway, not looking back. It would seem so odd if she kept looking back; it would seem as if she thought he were following her. He should have turned in the other direction on the main road. Here was the gravel drive leading past her house. She quickened her step. Don't look back; he isn't there. And yet, and yet, surely the gravel was scrunching behind her? She walked faster. She wanted to run, but surely it would look absurd? Why should she run even if he were behind her? She had no reason at all to be afraid of him. He had every right to walk this way if he chose. That he might want to murder her in the woods—imagination run wild! And if she really thought so, why didn't she run? Or look behind? She was within sight of her house. There was Guilhabert, barking a greeting at the end of his chain. If she could just reach the dog. She was walking so fast she had passed the woods in no time. She looked back. A figure in a leather coat turned and went back down the hill. Panting from the rapid climb and shaking slightly, she untied the dog, took him into the house, and locked the door. But after all, she thought, reason returning as her sense of security increased, perhaps he simply mistook the road, or maybe he just wanted to see where this road led, just as she too had been wandering round, exploring the neighborhood.

*

"I followed that girl," said Thierry to Raymond, as he dropped a bag of groceries beside the sink. "I know where she lives."

"What girl?" asked Raymond in astonishment.

"That one who keeps snooping around."

"*Who* keeps snooping around? What are you talking about? What have you been taking?"

"Haven't been taking anything," grumbled Thierry. "The one who came here with that dog, the one Hugo chased away, the one who came here again with that man. It looks suspicious to me."

"She's got my dog," said Raymond, and then added, "Don't you go following people—you'll get into trouble."

"Well, let her give the dog back and stay away," said Thierry, addressing himself to the easier part of the speech, "I don't believe she comes about the dog. Why didn't she come in a car then? I think she comes to look around. Maybe she knows something. Maybe there's some connection between you and her. Maybe she's looking for something too—you know what."

Raymond didn't know what to answer to this. He tackled the easier part. "I'm afraid to take the dog back. Hugo doesn't like him, and he's threatened to kill him."

Thierry grunted. Hugo, yes, they'd been forgetting about Hugo lately, but obviously he was going to show up again sometime and then what? Thierry couldn't help feeling that somehow his relationship with his prisoner had changed and that everything had become very much more difficult. Raymond, too, was reminded of his son. The atmosphere in the little house, which of late had become almost convivial, deteriorated into a depressed silence.

*

Lucien, seated behind his desk in Paris, was also keeping the younger Trencavel in the back of his mind. "Jean-Pierre," he called his secretary, scarcely lifting his head from the papers he was reading. A thin young man with a face like a perky terrier stuck his head around the door. "Find for me the number or address of a certain Trencavel, age thirty to fortyish, first name unknown, according to rumor living in Bordeaux, possibly engaged in the real estate trade. Father's name is Raymond."

Jean-Pierre the efficient appeared a little later with a list of possible Trencavels. Lucien took the list.

He'd have to do some sleuthing when he had time, he supposed. He was surprised no one in Maugrebis seemed to know much of anything about either Trencavel, father or son. The father was truly an outsider, or all the details of his life would have been public knowledge. Lucien had a vague uneasiness that something might be wrong with him, and he couldn't quite look away and pretend it wasn't his affair, even though he thought most probably he would be going to a lot of bother about nothing. He sighed, tossed the list onto a pile of papers, and went on with his work.

Hugo Trencavel, looking up as the glass door of his office opened, was impressed by the client who entered. He summed up the cost of his wardrobe in a glance that ran quickly from the man's head to his feet. But more than the man's clothing, it was his poise that impressed Hugo. He decided to get rid of the not-very-promising customers on hand fast, so he could give the newcomer the attention he obviously deserved.

"So we were wondering," said the young Englishman seated before Hugo's desk, in very tentative French, "if there might be anything a little cheaper for sale, something that needed renovation, perhaps?"

"No," said Hugo, changing tone abruptly with his interlocutors. "No. All the houses in this area are completely renovated."

The Englishman and his wife stared.

"Well, perhaps, that is...All of them?" stuttered the man.

"All of them. From Bordeaux to Montpellier."

Lucien, seeing that Hugo was becoming short with the man he'd no doubt, a moment before, been buttering up, made a deprecating gesture, and sank patiently into a chair. He could wait.

Hugo couldn't though. He got rid of his customers with promises to call soon, as soon as he heard anything, as soon as time should have taken its toll on any house in the area, etc, ushered them to the door, and turned with a crocodile smile on his new client.

Snob, Lucien commented to himself without rancor, but he composedly informed Hugo that he was interested in buying a piece of land: a specific piece of land. In fact, he believed it was a piece of land belonging to M. Trencavel's father, but he was unable to get in contact with the man. Perhaps M. Trencavel could help him?

"Ah-euh," said Hugo, his smile vanishing like chalk beneath an eraser. Here was a dilemma. He really didn't want anyone speaking to his father. On the other hand, a buyer like M. d'Alembert appeared to be—he turned Lucien's card over in his fingers—was an opportunity not to be ignored. Perhaps it would be better to sell outright, rather than subdivide? When Raymond agreed, of course; Raymond would agree soon. But no, the only reason anyone with money would be interested in the land would be because he intended to do exactly what he, Hugo, wanted to do, that is, subdivide. Hugo made up his mind. He handed the card back and retreated behind his desk. "My father, monsieur, isn't interested in selling, I'm afraid. I could show you some other parcels of land in the area, but I doubt they'd suit you." Hugo's tone was dismissive. He just wanted to get rid of the man now. He hesitated, then spoke coldly and clearly, "and I suggest, monsieur, that you don't bother my father. He's not in his right mind anymore, you know."

"Where could I find him?" asked Lucien.

"Monsieur, his whereabouts can be of no interest to you. He's not competent to act and were you to inveigle him into selling I should be forced to seek legal action, monsieur. I've no desire to offend, but I think it as well that I should forewarn you, monsieur."

Well, thought Lucien, undismayed by his dismissal and finding himself back on the street, he hadn't learned anything except that the man was as unpleasant a character as he had expected; and that the man, or his employee in Maugrebis, was a liar. Lucien had made discreet inquiries at a shop across the street and found that M. Trencavel had been at work all this week and the one preceding it, and not, ergo, on vacation with his father at all. And there the trail of Trencavel senior ended. Lucien debated how much prying he should do, and decided, in the lack of any other evidence of wrong-doing, that there was really nothing to justify it. Still, it bothered him...

14

Amadea had more reason for wandering about the neighborhood now as the evening light was lasting longer and she did not dawdle about the *manoir*. That hour of the aperitif together and the walk the next day—they had squelched home in almost complete silence, but somehow she did not feel it had separated them. He had given her his hand over the slippery bits. She had had no reason not to take it. And why should he not come in while she was sitting with his grandmother? Just a day or two later he had done so; they had talked of M. Trencavel, of her Latin studies, of the classic she was reading.

"Do you never read anything modern?" he had asked her.

She had said that the harshness of too many modern novels depressed her and that books had to be moral or they weren't worthwhile. Lucien and his grandmother had raised objections, and she had said ingenuously, "Well, perhaps you, who are so much closer to perfection, don't need any help, but I feel I need constant bucking up. And where should I get it if not from books?"

"Amadea, you are droll," Lucien had said, in echo of his grandmother.

However, when she remembered this exchange, and many other such exchanges, she felt it hard to justify her own behavior. Obviously, the books weren't doing enough for her. She could not hide from herself that she sat at the *manoir* every day in tense expectation: would he come or wouldn't he? And as the evening approached, if the marquise had not said definitely, "We won't be seeing Lucien tonight," then her ears were attuned to every noise from outside and her heartbeat increased and her throat felt dry. Would he come or wouldn't he?

He was a married man, she tried to remind herself constantly, *married*, and if she had an excuse she would force herself, sometimes, to get up and leave early.

So she had time for exploring. To take the dog for a long brisk walk—on occasion almost running—didn't change anything, but it filled up the time and gave an outlet to strained nerves.

Now, for a week, all her time would be free. The marquise was going visiting. She would pass through Paris and go on to spend some days with her sister-in-law. Amadea would not be needed. Lucien's father had arrived one day in a three-piece suit and a chauffeur-driven car: something large and shiny and venerable. He was a heavy-set man with some remnants of good looks and Lucien's air of quiet confidence. He had greeted Amadea charmingly as a long-lost relation, but he had obviously been in a hurry to get off.

Yves and the chauffeur, an elderly man, had brought down a heap of brown leather luggage, speaking to each other with exaggerated politeness and ill-concealed impatience: "Allow *me*, monsieur"; "After *you*, monsieur." The suitcases had gone in the trunk. ("It will be scratched, monsieur,") and onto the roof ("It will fall off, monsieur.") Amadea had placed the medicine case beside the marquise as she sat in the backseat with her hands resting on her cane.

"Thank you, my dear. Virtue is its own reward. I'm sure..." But she did not finish her sentence. She murmured to her driver and the car moved off.

Amadea stood on the steps of the *manoir* and watched the marquise's white head in the gray car until it disappeared from sight. She felt desolate and alone. She would not be needed for a week. She could spend her time as she pleased. She would not see Lucien for over a week: a week, seven days, one hundred and sixty-eight hours—an eternity.

*

"Lucien," said the marquise to her grandson, as they sat together in the small salon of the Paris house, "are you dallying with my companion?"

Lucien and his grandmother were the best of friends. He couldn't remember when was the last time he'd felt annoyed with her. Perhaps when he was nine or ten and she had interfered in some scheme of his. Now he felt distinctly nettled. But politeness was a habit not to be overcome by feeling.

"Do you want me to?" he answered with a smile.

The marquise beat a hasty retreat, and contented herself with observing mildly that Amadea was a nice girl.

"I wouldn't dally," said Lucien, to tease her a little, "with any other."

*

The next morning Amadea woke late and lay in bed, trying hard to enjoy the warmth and laziness of a free day. She lay in bed and tried and tried. A bee buzzed about the attic. Impossible to go back to sleep. She would not see Lucien for a week. She kicked off the covers, dressed, and took her breakfast outside to a little wooden table that stood on the *manoir* side of the Cow Shed. It was a beautiful morning, really. The air was full of scents, the sky cloudless. The birds, intoxicated by spring, kept up animated conversations on all sides. Guilhabert, seated beside her, took his gaze off her breakfast, and rolled expectant eyes in a smiling face toward her. She gave him her last piece of baguette. "Yes, we'll go for a walk. Come along." She put a sweater and a sandwich in a small knapsack and they set off.

She walked in the direction she had walked with Lucien, and he accompanied her again in imagination. Here they had walked side by side; and there he had sprung upon a rock, thrown his arms wide dramatically, and declaimed: "Drink deep or taste not the Pyrenean spring."

"No," she had said uncertainly, "I don't think you've got that quite right, somehow," and he had laughed. It had bothered her all the next day. What was the word? Ah, yes, 'Pierian.'

And here they had passed some cows—those same cows that were in the meadow again, now become hallowed cows by association with Lucien—and she had quoted that bit by Stevenson on the friendly cow. And he had said that that was very nice but the French didn't write poems about cows. "Oh, yes," she had contradicted him, "even Victor Hugo has a poem about a cow, and the poet Dupont says he'd rather lose his wife than his beautiful oxen." He said it was delightful to discover she was an expert on bovine verse, and that she should have invited him on a country walk sooner...And sometimes, of course, they had talked of more serious things. She relived his words and looks and gestures as she hiked. Here, where she was scrambling up this incline, he had given her his hand.

Trencavel's house was down below, in that valley over there. She would give it a wide berth. Guilhabert pricked his ears in that direction and looked inquiringly at her. They turned and followed the ridge in the other direction. When they had gone quite some ways, Amadea decided to rest. She sat on a lichenous rock, surveyed the mountains and the valley, and ate her sandwich. It was not lunch time, but she had been walking for a good while and thought it would be better to turn back soon. She gave the last bites to the dog and got up to go. But there, behind her, through the trees: Was it a wall? Or perhaps just a cliff of rock? Calling to Guilhabert, she decided the sandwich had given her energy to explore that far—providing, of course, it didn't turn out to be the back of someone's outhouse or cow barn. She climbed steadily upwards through the increasing undergrowth. The trees were fairly thick here, then thinned as the land went steeply up. She turned to the side where the incline was less sharp and burst panting into a little clearing. Guilhabert, rushing past her, leapt towards a man seated on a pile of rocks. The man rose at sight of them. Amadea stopped short. Guilhabert was leaping in ecstasy around the man, groveling at his feet, whining and licking his hands.

The man bent and stroked the dog, speaking to him. He was a man in his early seventies, perhaps more; his hair was thin and gray and his face lined, but he was wiry and fit-looking. His bearing, when he straightened from the dog, was upright and dignified. He was wearing a torn and dirty tee shirt, and his pants, held on by a piece of rope, were filthy, but he looked, somehow, unlike a laborer. He came toward Amadea.

"Who are you?" His tone was harsh, but there was a softening element of curiosity in it. It struck her then who he must be, of course.

"He's your dog, isn't he? He must be." She dove to the heart of the matter. "I live over there," she waved a vague hand, "and I found him a month or two ago. M. Bordan said he might be yours, and I came twice to your house, but you weren't home...I'm so glad I've found you..." she ended rather uncertainly, as he didn't seem exactly delighted.

"No, he's not my dog," said Raymond, pushing the dog away from him, not wanting to have to explain matters, not knowing how to explain matters.

"He certainly *thinks* he's your dog," said Amadea timidly.

"You're mistaken, mademoiselle. It is a bizarre instance of love at first sight," said Raymond, with a hint of amusement in his voice, "he'll get over it."

Amadea stared at him in disbelief. Raymond relented. "Or, yes, he was my dog. But I cannot keep him now." He stared away from her, into the distance. "My son doesn't like dogs. Or not this dog, anyway. He is better off away from me at the moment. It is like that. If you could keep him for a while, I don't know how long—some days, or weeks?—then I would be very grateful. I know I have no right to ask a favor of you, a stranger, but it would be a great kindness. He's a good dog."

"Yes," said Amadea, "all right. But when can I bring him back?"

"When you can't keep him any more. Now, please," the tone was still harsh, but there was a note almost of pleading under it. "Take him now, and go away—before...before anyone finds you here. Please." What must she think of him? Raymond wondered. But it didn't matter. The important thing was that she left before Thierry came back.

Amadea reached for Guilhabert's collar and fumbled with his leash. Twigs snapped in the woods; someone was coming. Raymond became urgent. "Mademoiselle, please. This is private property and if you are found here it could be very unpleasant. Take the dog and go!"

The Thug stepped into the clearing a hundred yards above them. Amadea recognized him even at that distance. Thierry shifted his grip on the handle of his large axe and came trotting rapidly down towards them. Amadea didn't wait, but pulling hard on Guilhabert's leash, plunged back down the hillside, the rocks rolling out from beneath her feet, till she was in the undergrowth again, and then continued rapidly on downhill. The dog came reluctantly, looking back occasionally and barking. Behind them Amadea could hear the two men's voices raised in argument. She and the dog rushed down the hill in no time and reached the rock where she had eaten her sandwich. She paused there to draw breath and to listen. No one seemed to be following them. She relaxed a little, and, still trying to regain her breath and shaking somewhat, proceeded at a quick walk, almost running.

Well, one good thing: She could tell Lucien she had seen M. Trencavel and that he was alive and well and digging stones, or whatever he had been doing. There wasn't any need to fear he'd been murdered—or, no, that's what *she* had vaguely imagined; Lucien, no doubt, had been more rational. And, she added to herself, she could simply tell the marquise; there was no need to speak to Lucien directly. Yes, that would be best.

So she was stuck with the dog. Poor Guilhie. She rested her hand lightly on his back as they walked. How could she take him away with her? Because now that leaving had suddenly become very difficult, she realized it was what had been at the back of her mind. She realized that she had, at some time recently, subconsciously decided that she would leave when she had settled about Guilhabert. She had vaguely imagined that M. Trencavel would reappear and want him back, and then she could go away. It had been a good pretext for not making plans, for allowing the days to pass without taking any action. Because she knew that she should go away. She did not know whether virtue was really its own reward, but she was certain that getting involved with a married man was wrong.

These unpleasant thoughts distracted her from her recent disagreeable experience. She hurried home through the lovely afternoon without seeing any of its beauty.

15

The next day the weather changed. Mist hung over the valley; higher there was a little wind and a nip in the air. Amadea shivered as she went about her household chores. Thoughts of Lucien and thoughts of her impending departure were occasionally intersected by the thought of the Thug rushing down the hill, axe in hand, and the memory of M. Trencavel urging her to leave.

She walked to the village for supplies. Stepping unsuspecting into the bakery, she found herself once again facing the Thug. He was leaning a bulky forearm on the counter, talking to Sylvie. Their twin gazes pinned her with almost equal hostility. What is the proper etiquette on meeting a person who, at a previous meeting, has waved a weapon at one? Pretend one doesn't see him? Put one's nose in the air? He was staring at her. She said 'good-day' to him civilly, collected her loaf (Sylvie slapped it down hard beside the cash register) and departed with a polite '*merci*' and '*au revoir*'.

At home she set herself to energetic house-cleaning. She vigorously mopped a spotless floor and dusted a dust-free mantel. Now there was nothing more to clean, yet she had to keep busy. She stared into the fireplace. Perhaps she could start a fire: a fire would be very cozy. True, she had never built a fire, but how difficult could it be? There was a stack of firewood in an adjacent lean-to. She fetched an armful of small logs, and piled them one on top of the other in the fireplace. Guilhie, thinking perhaps it was a game, or perhaps with an intuitive grasp of her abilities, pushed past her and pawed at the wood. Afraid he would get burned, she took him outside and tied him up; then she came in again and held a match to the logs. Nothing happened. The wood wouldn't burn; she only singed her fingers. She got a stack of old newspapers and plopped them down by the wood. She crumpled up a sheet and lit it. It burst into flames, and as she hastily tossed it toward the wood, she became aware that Guilhabert was barking. Intent on her fire-building, she had not heard anyone approaching. Someone was knocking. Who could it be? Lucien? Her heart began to race. Let it be Lucien. Oh, please, not Lucien. She stood up quickly, pushing back her hair. She was wearing her housecleaning clothes...oh, but no, Lucien wasn't coming this week. Feeling both relieved and disappointed, she crossed to the door and pulled it wide.

The Thug stood there. He wasn't smiling and somehow he was inside the door and shutting it before she had time to wish she hadn't opened it. She was staring into his black leather chest, caught between the man and the wall of the entry.

"Er...*bonjour*, monsieur," she said, quivering. What had he come for?

"*Bonjour*," he grunted. And then, without preamble: "What have you been hanging around Trencavel's property for? I told you to stay away."

"I'm very sorry," she said, trying to speak calmly, "I did come to M. Trencavel's to ask about the dog, but now I know he doesn't want him, I won't do it again." But why did it matter? she wondered vaguely.

"Your secret is safe with me," she added, in an ill-advised attempt to joke, to keep the conversation light.

"Secret!" he exploded. Obviously she had said the wrong thing. "Secret? What do you know about any secret?"

"I-I-I don't anything about a secret. I-I-I was j-j-joking." She stuttered as she stared at him wide-eyed. What was he hiding there? Drugs or guns or something? She didn't want to know.

He took a step closer. Amadea felt panic rising. There was no escaping him, and no escaping either, the threat in his attitude. He hissed at her: "Take care you..." And then he broke off, stared around, sniffed, and in quite a different tone said, "Something's burning!"

"*Oh!*" Amadea darted past him into the living room. It was full of smoke. Flames shot up mantel high from the pile of newspapers. The floor was kindling. She rushed across the room and grabbed a cushion off the sofa and began whacking at the flames, fighting off the smoke with her free hand. The Thug joined in, thumping with the other cushion and stamping energetically on the floor, where the fire flickered, died, and sprang up again. Amadea's cushion came apart and filled the room with feathers, but still she beat with it. The fire was out. No—there!—the Thug stomped vigorously. This time it was really out.

"That's it, I think," said the Thug. He crossed to the window, undid the catch, and pushed it open. Amadea stumbled over to it and stood there coughing

as the feathers drifted down behind them and the
smoke began to dissipate a little.

"Um...er...thank you very much," she said to the
Thug. She wasn't afraid of him anymore. He wasn't going to harm her now: You don't harm someone whom
you have just helped put out a fire. "It would have
burned down but for you."

"No problem." He smiled. It was an unprac-
ticed smile, but a very nice one, in spite of a scar on one
cheek. He was quite young, she realized suddenly,
younger even than herself by a year or two.

"Would you like a cup of coffee?" She asked
impulsively.

"Na. I don't drink that stuff. It's bad for you."

Amadea stared at him. "Tea?" she suggested,
tentatively.

"Okay."

She made the tea, set the cup in front of him,
and sat at the table opposite. He poured four teaspoons
of sugar into his drink and stirred it noisily while the
wind blew the last of the smoke away. He eyed her and
his mood seemed to grow dark again. He gazed mood-
ily out the window at the *manoir*.

"Is that where your boyfriend lives?"

"I don't have a boyfriend."

"That rich idiot."

"He's not an idiot!" Amadea retorted rather
hotly.

"All rich people are idiots."

Amadea thought it would be better to change
the subject. Did he like the area? she asked, guessing by
his accent that he was, like herself, a stranger here.

"Na," he answered; he didn't know that he liked
all this greenery everywhere. He'd been hired to chop

down trees. He liked that all right, but otherwise—boringest place he'd ever been. He was from Paris. Oh, well, true, the *banlieue*, but even if one had to stay in the *banlieue*, one could always go—he was going to say, one could always go *Beur*-bashing—but he was rather enjoying being the hero of the day; he didn't want this girl to think less of him, and somehow he didn't think she'd like the idea of bashing people.—"Go to the movies," he finished.

She was going to ask him what movies he liked, but he, following a train of thought of his own, which led from the persecution of *Beurs* to the persecution of black chickens, said suddenly, "Do you know that speckled chickens pick on other ones? It's really weird. You know, if you watch animals, you see lots of strange things...Goats now, goats aren't like that. I like goats better. They all get along fine. And the little ones are very friendly....You know, I said it was really boring here? But that wasn't quite true. I mean, sometimes it is boring, very boring, but at other times, I don't know, sometimes it makes a person think. Perhaps I wouldn't mind being a farmer..."

Amadea murmured "ah" and "really?" and didn't feel she was quite capturing everything he meant to convey. Here, however, was a graspable concept. "I've always thought farming a good occupation," she said.

"Yes. Well....Trencavel's got a lot of land," he said as if to himself. Then, remembering why he had come, he added, with a sharp look at her, "*Do* you know anything about it?"

"About what?" asked Amadea wide-eyed and with such patent innocence that he believed her.

"Okay. So that's okay then."

What's okay? wondered Amadea, but she said nothing, and they talked of other things. A car was coming down the road, its tires crunching on the gravel. The Thug rose and zipped his jacket up six inches and then down six inches, preparatory to leaving. His eye fell on the *History of Languedoc* that she had borrowed from the marquise.

"So you like history?" he asked. "Me too."

Amadea must have looked her surprise because he was continuing, "Oh sure. Those guys in Calais, Montségur, Gaston Fébus, Cinq-Mars...You know all this?"

They became aware that someone was knocking on the open door, and Amadea knew, even before he called "Amadea?" that it was Lucien. And in the same instant she wished desperately that it was anyone else— even a cohort of the Thug's. She went toward the door. Lucien came into the room. The Thug stepped around him, tossed an *au revoir* over his shoulder to Amadea, and left. Lucien turned to watch him leave and then looked at Amadea, then around the room, with its blackened floor and ashes and feathers.

"You see," said Lucien slowly, "I knew you were a witch. The fire was necessary, I suppose, to put a spell on that fellow. He seems much tamed. I am also under a spell. That's why I came."

Amadea missed the import of most of this speech. She only knew that she was turning crimson, and that she began to babble. "I was trying to burn the house down and he came to help me...I mean, I was trying to light a fire and he—in the fireplace I mean, and he came, and then the fire caught—but not in the fireplace—and he helped me put it out."

"I see—I think. I'm glad you're all right."

Amadea reached for the broom and began sweeping together the debris. The floorboards were blackened for several square feet around.

"I'll pay for it, of course," she said miserably, feeling deeply, deeply culpable.

He didn't answer that for a moment, seeming lost in thought, then he roused himself and said, "Don't worry about it. I'll send Yves over to repair it." He added, "I didn't know you knew that fellow."

"I don't. He came to threaten me, I think."

He looked at the two cups on the table. "*Ah oui?* What was he threatening you about?"

Amadea, twisting her hands around the broom handle and not looking at him, answered his unspoken question first. "No, the tea came later, after he helped me put out the fire. He said I was to stay away from the Trencavel place."

"*Ça, par exemple.* I thought he told us that already."

So she recounted her adventure of the day before, making it brief partly because she had to admit she had been so silly as to lose her way and had gone stumbling about where she had no business being, and because it seemed, today, unreal, and in Lucien's presence even the Thug's menacing behavior and her own fear faded away and became immaterial.

"And he seemed to think I knew about some 'secret,' but I think I convinced him that I don't."

"Stranger and stranger," was Lucien's only comment when she had finished her short recital, but he stood looking thoughtful. She stood looking at his shoes. She loved his shoes. She loved him.

She ventured, "I'm surprised to see you here. I thought you wouldn't be back till next week."

He said, "I came ..." and then hesitated. If he finished with "to see you," the die was cast. There were so many ways to finish such a sentence: I came to check on the house, I came to take care of some business...

Amadea waited with a feeling, of intense pleasure and dismay, that it was on the tip of his tongue to say "to see you," but no, he was saying—

"To see about some things, and...to invite you out to dinner, if you would like?"

Amadea looked down, relief and disappointment written all over her face. She turned away and stood looking out the window, playing with a splinter on the sill.

He put his head on one side. "It is such a difficult decision? Going to dinner or not?"

Yes, it was a horrible decision. And he knew and she knew that it was hardly just a matter of satisfying evening nutritional needs in each other's company. But what were principles for if one didn't stick to them?

"No thank you," she mumbled.

Because, because—she beat hastily about her mind for a polite excuse. He knew as well as she that she had nothing else to do. She could tell he was startled. Maybe no one had ever turned him down before.

He was standing silently, watching her, waiting for some explanation. She had none to make. She could not look at him. She was in love with him and he was married.

His silence was unnerving. She said huskily, "I don't mean to offend you."

"You do not offend me," he replied instantly and gallantly. "You startle me a little, I confess. No doubt it is good for me to be startled. It is perhaps the crux of our relationship: you were sent by the fates to

startle and exercise me. *Eh bé. 'Tu trembles, carcasse'*—
that's a quote. Shall I light the fire before I go or should
I leave instantly and never darken your doorstep, etc?"

What to answer to that? Yes or no, either would
sound churlish, Amadea thought, still not looking at
him.

"Difficult, eh? I'll light it for you, if you'll allow
me." He moved about, went out to the woodshed,
opened the damper, knelt by the fireplace, and soon a
fire was burning nicely in the grate. He knelt beside it,
watching the flames flicker and grow. Amadea stayed by
the window. She had read enough French literature to
be wary. She knew that she could trust neither him nor
herself. Lots of French men—and women too, apparently—had these flexible ideas about the bonds of marriage.

She was extremely beautiful, he thought—
growing more so every time he saw her—and she was
dismissing him. Why? he wondered. "I am not Valmont," he said to the fire.

"No," said Amadea, in acute embarrassment,
because it was precisely that arch-seducer she was keeping in mind. That's what Valmont said too, she reminded herself.

Lucien sighed, "But perhaps you will say that
that's what Valmont said. Ah well." He rose. He actually felt embarrassed. "When the fire burns down, add
another log. *Au revoir.*"

"Thank you," she whispered, "goodbye."

*

Lucien, having just arrived at the *manoir*, was
leaving again. He had a train to catch at 5:00. He
wanted Amadea to move down to the *manoir* and that

was only possible if he left. So, having dispatched Yves and given instructions to Céleste, he carried his small bag out to the jeep, debating with himself. Would a visit to Trencavel and his henchman be of any use or not? Trencavel senior was, by Amadea's evidence, sound in body, at least. There was no need to worry about him. But the more he thought about it, the more he worried about Amadea herself. They—Trencavel junior and senior and the young man and perhaps others—were obviously up to something, presumably something illicit or they wouldn't be so defensive, and it seemed they were afraid Amadea knew something. Or perhaps, he reflected, remembering the two cups on the table, the young man was simply attracted to Amadea. A not very surprising development, really, he thought wryly. Having seen her that day in the rain, the man had, on the next sighting, come running down the hill out of pleasure, and had then come to visit her, dropping hints of some secret for the purpose of impressing her. But no, that didn't explain Trencavel junior's belligerence, or Trencavel senior's fear, or the motorcycle man's previous hostility.

The jeep rolled down the drive, onto the highway, and soon it was turning into Trencavel's road. A little talk with these people might after all be beneficial, he had decided. He would tell them that he and Amadea had no interest in whatever they were up to. He would also let them understand that he knew all about it, while Amadea knew nothing. He would not need to mention the police; they would make the connection themselves. The jeep bumped along Trencavel's drive. If it occurred to him that an unarmed man bearding hostile men with a secret might be in some danger, it did not deflect him. He was one of those men whose capacity for fear was not well developed, and besides, he had professional knowledge of "how to do things with words" and get people to agree.

But no one was home. With a feeling of anticlimax he banged on the door and halloo-ed round the yard. Except for a few chickens pecking about in a pen and a young goat clambering around the yard, all appeared deserted. A large garden had been prepared for planting and an open shed was chock full of new-sawn wood, but neither woodsman nor gardener appeared. The hills were silent round about. The motorcycle was gone. Lucien went back to his vehicle, pulled out a pad of paper, wrote several lines, and left the letter in the crack of the door.

Then, feeling uneasy and telling himself he was being irrational, he pointed the jeep toward Toulouse. He had done what he could. Amadea would be safe at the *manoir*. Now he had other affairs; he had, in fact, all those affairs he had put on hold in order to come back to Maugrebis. His was a well-disciplined mind and ordinarily it did what he wanted it to. Today it seemed willfully intent on sliding away from important matters to his last conversation with Amadea. He found himself pressing down harder, harder, on the gas pedal, and resolutely released it. He could not apply the balm of speed to a wounded ego. Besides, although neither his pride nor his principles would allow him to take unfair advantage, he thought in his heart that Amadea would be unlikely to resist him if he were determined to carry his point. He knew she liked him. He knew she liked him a lot. So why had she turned him down? A car appeared in front of him; he changed lanes automatically and flashed past it. It diminished so rapidly in his rearview mirror that he looked down at his speedometer, and then, startled, shifted his foot to the brake, and brought his speed down 10, 20, 30 kilometers.

*

Raymond, coming down from the hillside with an armload of tiles, cursed: That rascally young goat was always getting loose. He'd have to tell Thierry to mend the fence again, or the kid would have to be tethered. What had it eaten? It had what looked like bits of paper sticking out of its mouth. Providing it wasn't his book on Gnosticism! He chased the kid round the yard. But no, it was just a piece of paper.

Thus are the best laid plans of mice and men sometimes eaten by goats.

16

Amadea, after Lucien left, huddled by the fire and cried and cried. She was still crying when a knock came at the door. Hastily she scrubbed away her tears, blew her nose. Did she have time to run bathe her face before she opened the door? It must be Lucien. Oh, why was the mirror upstairs? The knocking grew to a thunderous hail of blows. Lucien wouldn't knock like that. Maybe it was the Thug again and she couldn't face him now. She burst into tears once more. The knocking continued, so she had no choice but to creep over to the door.

"Wh-who is it?"

"Sabadie. Open up."

Amadea opened the door. Yves, carrying a tool box, stepped past her into the room. He had no eyes for her tearstained face; he was looking at the charred floor.

"Burning the house down, eh?" he said to her, looking at the fireplace. "Tsk." He crossed to the burned spot. "*Aïe.*"

Amadea blushed and blushed. Yves circled the blackened area with his hands on his hips, surveying the damage and shaking his head. At last he raised his hands as if to say, "What can one do with fools like this?" and, taking a crowbar from his box, began to lever up the boards. Bent over his work he said to Amadea, "You're to stay at the *manoir* for a while. M. Lucien said so. He's left himself."

Amadea protested. Yves repeated, "M. Lucien said so." Amadea shook her head; she didn't see the need.

"It was the will of M. Lucien," said Yves doggedly, as one might say, "the will of heaven," and clinched the matter by adding that his wife had prepared a room. Amadea might have resisted the will of Lucien, etc., but she was far too considerate to ignore another woman's housekeeping preparations. She wavered.

"And Guilhie?"

Yves regarded with disfavor the large black head snuffling in his tool box. "You'd better take him with you. He won't be any help to me." (In fact, M. Lucien had said she was to bring the dog, but it sounded more satisfying to Yves as his own largesse.)

Amadea put some things in a bag, and, calling the dog, set out for the *manoir*. Her beautiful *manoir*. No, not hers, she reminded herself; she was only an employee here, a servant, and she would shortly be leaving. She passed under the cedars, over the gravel, pulled open the heavy front door that was always unlocked during the day, and stepped across the hall to the kitchen. She put her head around the door. Céleste was there, briskly rolling out pastry. She looked up at Amadea's entrance.

"Ah. There you are. *La pauvre*. What a thing to happen!"

"Yes. It was very stupid of me. M. Sabadie said I was to come here."

"Yes. M. Lucien wanted it, and besides you will be in Yves' way there, you know."

"I am sorry to have caused extra work for your husband."

Céleste shrugged. "Gets him out of the house." She gave Amadea a conspiratorial look. "Don't say I said so though...Eh, he likes you. He hardly complained at all." She continued with her cooking, rolling a sheet of pastry out thin as thin. Amadea watched her. Here, for almost the first time in her life, were people who liked her: Madame, Céleste, even Yves.

She asked if she could help. Céleste answered rather too hastily, "No, no, you sit right there." She pointed to a kitchen chair. Amadea understood. They knew her competence in practical affairs was severely limited—nil even—but it didn't seem to matter. Here for the first time she had found acceptance. Now she would have to go away, wouldn't she? She *should* go away, to get away from Lucien, but if she went, she would be jobless again and shortly penniless. If she stayed—but how could she stay? And so it went, round and round.

She chatted with Céleste till the oven door closed on a large pan. Then, "Come" said the house-keeper, "I'll show you the room I got ready." She led the way upstairs. Guilhabert, fortified by quite a lot of scraps, padded beside the two women, looking about with curiosity. Most of the rooms in the house were shut up. Of the upstairs, Amadea had seen only Madame's bedroom, with its *lit à la polonaise,* and her Roman-sized bath.

The room Céleste opened for her was a large one, looking forward across the meadow. It had oak paneling and an immense bed with carved bed posts and embroidered hangings. Amadea stared.

"Here?"

"Don't you like it?" Céleste faltered. Amadea noted the ironed sheets, the bedclothes tucked in with mathematical neatness, the piled pillowcases with eyelet lace, the bouquet of flowers.

"It's beautiful. I'm afraid I've put you to a lot of work, too."

"It's a beautiful room, isn't it?" said Céleste, adding with a frank tactlessness not intended to hurt, "It's not the room the companions are usually given. But M. Lucien said you were to have the best."

Amadea felt a surge of pleasure and relief. So he wasn't angry then.

"You being a relation, I suppose, and Madame being so fond of you..."

"They're very kind," said Amadea.

"Oh yes," said Céleste, as if that explained everything. She went back to her work.

Amadea went over and sat on the bed. Guilhie, unimpressed by grandeur or 'blanched linen, smooth and laundered,' jumped up beside her and made himself comfortable. She pushed him off gently.

If she left, where would she go? What about Guilhabert? Perhaps she could stay and everything would be as it had been: she would read to Madame, and they would laugh and talk; she would leave always the instant *he* came, or before if she could, and if she loved him from afar, whom did it hurt? And yet she knew it was impossible. She would wait till Madame came back and ask if she knew of someone else in need of a companion or care-giver. She would not tell her *why* she wanted to leave—that would be too embarrassing, but Madame would guess anyway.

When Amadea came down to the kitchen the next morning, Yves was already gone and Céleste was on her knees, cleaning cupboards. Amadea asked if there was anything she could do to help with the housework, but Céleste assured her that Marie, who helped with the cleaning, would be along shortly. Then, glancing at Amadea's disappointed face, she added, "Well, since you like to walk—and if you're going in to the village—there's a list–oh, there—of things you could pick up..." Amadea seized on the idea eagerly.

In the village she filled Céleste's string bag with various vegetables, two eggplants, oranges, a lemon, a box of tea: everything on the list. Then she stood in the street considering, while Guilhie beside her observed the passers-by with a genially patrician air and a slowly waving tail. She didn't want to go back yet; she felt uncomfortable at the *manoir*. She vaguely felt that her respectability was compromised by her own feelings and that she was in some way an impostor there now.

Well, she could go and sit on a bench by the church to while away the time. Or, there was the bistro halfway up the street. She could go there. She had to pass the bakery, and as she glanced cautiously through the windows—perhaps the Thug was there and she would just as soon not meet him—her eyes met those of the Niece. By the time she had taken the few steps that would carry her past the door, Sylvie had stepped outside and was hailing her. "Hey! *Ohé!*"

Amadea turned. Sylvie stood on the bakery step, cigarette dangling from her fingers and a ferocious scowl on her face.

"Thierry's mine, do you hear."

Amadea stared. "I-I beg your pardon?"

"He's my boyfriend." Sylvie threw down her cigarette and ground it out with a vicious toe.

"Oh," said Amadea, comprehension dawning: Thierry must be the Thug. "I assure you, I don't doubt it in the least." She felt a wild laugh rising in her throat and then she looked at Sylvie and it died away. She felt sorry for the girl: she was uncivil, but she was obviously suffering. "He's not interested in me, if that's what you think," Amadea added gently.

"He told me about going to your house," said Sylvie. "He says you're a real woman." There were tears in her eyes. "You don't look like a real woman to me, but what do I know, right?" She turned abruptly and went back into the bakery.

Amadea, full of pity, tried to follow her, but Benoit had appeared from the depths of his bakery, so she quietly closed the door again and departed.

Benoit regarded Sylvie, who was fumbling with another cigarette. "Your aunt'll be here in a few minutes," he said warningly. She shrugged. He pretended to be arranging the loaves in their racks. He felt for her in a mild way. She wasn't such a bad type at heart, really. She wasn't even a bad worker. She was just young: young and lonely and rudderless. He wanted to say something helpful, but it came out wrong. "Don't be unpleasant to that one, at least," he jerked his head in the direction of the door through which Amadea had just disappeared. "She's a nice girl, nice manners—you would do well to copy her." Sylvie made a sound between a growl and a shriek, ripped off her apron and left the bakery. Benoit stared after her in perplexity, then threw up his hands and went back to his baking. Compared to women, bread was beautifully predictable.

*

Amadea held the door of the bistro open for Guilhabert, while the proprietor looked up impassively. She went to sit on an uncomfortable iron chair by a tippy marble-topped table near the wall. She ordered a hot chocolate and sat staring into space while it congealed. Sylvie and Thierry—they were just one more reason why she should leave. Outside, people went by or stopped to tell one another what a fine day it was, and Amadea wondered how they could manage to look so cheerful. She tried to remind herself how lucky she was in so many ways; that other people had terrible, insoluble problems and she had none in comparison, etc....It didn't help.

At the sound of a motorcycle stopping nearby, she looked up from her introspection. A few moments later, Raymond Trencavel came through the door. He checked abruptly at sight of Amadea, so that Thierry, looming large behind him, first gave him an irritated push forward, then, catching sight of Amadea himself, grabbed his arm as if to retreat. But it was too late: Guilhabert, seeing his former master, had leapt up, nearly overturning the table, and was bounding about at the end of his leash while Amadea struggled to restrain him and keep her chocolate from spilling.

Raymond crossed to the dog. "Good dog, Guilhabert, quiet..." The dog settled into submissive wiggles.

"*Bonjour*, mademoiselle. You've been taking good care of him," he gestured at the dog. "I didn't have time to say so the other day, but thank you. He looks well."

Amadea raised her eyes from the contemplation of her own misery. Something prompted her to say, "And you? Are you well?"

Raymond hesitated, rather taken aback.

"He's fine, fine," said Thierry gruffly, standing foursquare and looking fierce. He was chewing gum furiously.

"*Bonjour,* monsieur," Amadea turned to him.

"*Salut.* How come you always look so sad? You look like your cat just died." Amadea shook her head. Thierry stood chewing, chewing. He didn't show any inclination to leave, and Raymond was waiting to take his cue from the younger man. Amadea, polite as ever, gestured to them to sit down. The *patron,* with his still impassive face hiding considerable curiosity, crossed to take their orders. Raymond sat petting the dog. Thierry sat chewing, chewing. Their drinks came. Thierry took his gum out and stuck it under the table.

Amadea, shocked, started unconsciously to say—"Nnn–"—then bit her tongue.

Thierry looked at her, startled.

"Why not?"

Amadea squirmed uncomfortably. "Well, it's not your table," she said apologetically.

He considered this a moment, then reached under the table, peeled off the wad of gum, and stuck it back in his mouth. Amadea shuddered and hoped he'd retrieved the right one. Raymond smiled to himself. Thierry's scowl deepened.

Conversation was difficult. Amadea was revolving a determination. She took a deep breath and said to Raymond, "Do you think you could find some-

one else to keep Guilhabert soon? I know I said I
would, but I wasn't thinking straight then. I've made up
my mind to leave—and I can't take him with me."

"Euh–oie..." Raymond bent over the dog, considering if he could take him home. True, Hugo hadn't
been around at all recently—but presumably he'd be
back, yes, surely he'd be back. However, maybe he
would come and leave again quickly like last time. He
could hide the dog for that period, perhaps. And
Thierry? Perhaps Thierry was an ally now? But Thierry
seemed strangely restless lately. So restless that today he
had downed tools and suggested this trip to the village.
It would have been unthinkable in the days after his
arrival; their relationship had become almost that of...of
what? Well, and yesterday, after Thierry had told him
about visiting the girl to warn her off, he had explained
all about the dog, and Thierry had been almost sympathetic. Still, there was no knowing what went on in that
head. He glanced across at the young man.

"You're going away?" said Thierry to Amadea,
as if this fact suggested some idea to him. "When?"

"Soon, I hope."

"Take the dog," Thierry said to Raymond. It
was he who gave the orders, decided everything. Raymond should remember that. He'd been forgetting too
much lately.

"And Hugo? What about Hugo?"

"Where's Hugo? I'm tired of waiting for Hugo."

"Oh, *moi*," said Raymond, "I can wait."

So Guilhabert would go home with Raymond.
Amadea, filled first with a sense of relief and freedom,
soon became aware of a growing feeling of loss. She
told herself firmly that it was for the best, and tried to
rouse herself. She was aware of the two men sitting be-

side her, the Thug rather crowding her at the small table.

"You're not cutting trees today?" she said to Thierry.

"Oh sure," Raymond answered for him, "Thierry's got lots of work to do."

Thierry speared Raymond with a glance over his glass. It was so black that Amadea looked from one man to the other in surprise. Raymond rose and went to the counter. Thierry, with an eye on his turned back, leaned towards Amadea and said quickly.

"Look. I want to ask you something..." He paused; asking seemed difficult. He leaned back in his chair and said, "Euh...what's your name?"

"Amadea Heyward."

"Pfui," he wrinkled his nose. "Is that an Arab name?" he asked suspiciously. Amadea toyed with the idea of saying "Yes," but after a second, said, "No, Amédée."

"Amédée. *Bon*. Listen. I have something to ask you..."

Amadea gazed at him in some alarm. "Ye-es?"

"You're going away right? Is it...do you...what I wanted to ask is..." he struggled for words, and missed his chance. Raymond was returning, a bulge in his pocket and a smile on his face.

Thierry swore.

"Yes," said Amadea politely, "What did you want to ask?"

"Yes, uh...do you like goats at all?"

Raymond rolled his eyes at the ceiling.

"Goats?" Amadea looked bewildered, but answered seriously. "I'm afraid I've never made the acquaintance of a single goat."

"I adore goats," said a high childish voice behind them. The three looked up. Sylvie disentangled a chair from its neighbors at an adjoining table and sat down with them uninvited.

"Ooh, nice dog. What's his name?" she asked Thierry.

Thierry shrugged, his eyes resting on his friend without seeing her.

"Guilhabert," answered Raymond.

"Weird name!"

Raymond rolled his eyes at the ceiling again. Thierry seemed sunk in his own thoughts. Amadea sat contemplating her empty future; nothing in the immediate present really impinged. Sylvie made one or two attempts to talk to Thierry, but without success. She fell silent. They all sat in silence. Inertia or some subconscious undercurrent of feeling kept them pinned to the café table.

"He isn't interested in me," thought Sylvie.

"So I'll have to go away," thought Amadea.

"I think what Raymond told me isn't true," thought Thierry.

Raymond regarded the three still juvenile faces growing longer and longer. "And these young people think they have problems," he thought. Suddenly he felt fine himself.

"Hey! Cheer up, everybody! *I'm* the one with the problem!"

Three pairs of eyes regarded him with distaste or disbelief. A tear splashed down Sylvie's cheek. Amadea, in sympathy, began to weep as well. Thierry rose hastily and stalked to the door. Raymond, with one backward look, undid his dog's leash from the table leg—"*adieu, mesdemoiselles*"—and abandoned ship.

Outside the bistro, there was a slight problem. Obviously Guilhabert couldn't ride on the motorcycle. Thierry realized he'd been hasty in telling Raymond to take him, but what did it matter, after all? Hugo wasn't coming; Bruno didn't answer his calls; Raymond—he was having his doubts about Raymond. He didn't know what to believe anymore. "You can walk alone," he said distractedly to the astonished Raymond, kicked the starter over and departed in a cloud of blue smoke.

Sometime after Raymond had reached home, on foot, with a delightedly happy dog, the motorcycle bounced up the drive and stopped before the house. "Well," said Raymond cheerfully to Thierry, as he crossed the yard with another armload of tiles, "where have you been? I've been back ages. *Au travail*—back to work...Ah yes, and you can bring down some more of these tiles when you come." Thierry stood watching Raymond as he puttered about the yard. "Well?" said Raymond, "well? Go on, go on, *allez, cherchez de la gloire dans la boue...De la gloire dans la boue*," he repeated the words to himself as he leaned a ladder against the house, enjoying the sound. What a wonderful language his language was, that even something like mud could sound so exalted: *de la boue*. Thierry, however, did not appear to share his enthusiasm. He remained standing, hands dangling, head thrust slightly forward, and eyes narrowed.

"Is it all true, your story about the treasure?" He demanded in a harsh voice. "I want you to tell me the truth."

"Truth," said Raymond, through a mouthful of tacks, "truth is many-sided, multi-faceted, a monster or a marvel, depending on circumstances. You want to be careful with truth."

Thierry, however, had learned something in living with Raymond, and did not allow himself to be immediately distracted or confused by ambiguous statements.

"Tell me—is it true?"

"Is what true?" Raymond climbed two rungs.

"About the treasure. Or are you just—is this all a hoax?"

Raymond went up another rung. "Thierry, Thierry, your suspicion wounds me...But I see you need proof. *Eh bé, bon.* Did you not see my dog?"

"What about him?"

"What color is he?"

"Black—so?"

"So do these facts not suggest anything to you? A black dog—found in the wilderness—oh, over there, just where we're digging?"

"What are you getting at?" Thierry growled.

"Do you not know that it's a long-accepted truth of folk wisdom that a black dog found in the wilderness has surely been sent by supernatural powers to lead those who are kind to him to treasure? *Alors,* I was very kind to him, so we should find it; but Hugo—*he* was cruel to the poor creature, so perhaps he's jiggered our hopes..."

"I don't believe any of that. How can you talk such nonsense?" Thierry spat the words out indignantly.

"Nonsense? Nonsense? A belief with the force of ages behind it, a belief sprung from centuries of tradition, a belief—listen, Thierry, this belief is an international belief and you can be sure that when something is believed in more than one country it must be true; I mean, it's not just one of your little local aberrations, is it? Well, do you know that they believe this too in

Germany? The truth of the matter is so well established that in Bavaria the word *Hund*, 'dog,' means 'hidden treasure,' as well. That's conclusive, isn't it? Oh, *absolument*, in my opinion. And furthermore...."

Thierry shifted from foot to foot. He didn't know how to tackle non-arguments like these, and Raymond's flood of words confused him.

"*Allez*. To work," said Raymond, prying out a broken roof tile. But Thierry went into the house, threw himself down on his back on Raymond's bed, and put his arm across his eyes. He didn't know what to believe.

Once, Raymond came in during the afternoon and looked at him, and his heart even contracted a little at the misery on the young face. Odd how fond of the boy he'd gotten. He almost wished...He turned abruptly and went back to his work.

Thierry lay there till evening. When Raymond called him rather sarcastically to eat— "Dinner is served, *monsieur*"—he came and ate silently, then snatched up his jacket, and left the house.

"Where are you going?" Raymond called after him, startled, and almost as if his departure concerned him. But Thierry didn't answer. There was the deafening roar of the motorcycle and then its diminishing wail in the distance. Raymond shrugged. He had his bottle, his lovely little bottle. He kissed Guilhabert, fed him the last of the dinner, and took him out and locked him for safekeeping in an outbuilding. Then he fed the goats and the chickens. And then he settled down to drink.

17

Amadea climbed wearily—one foot after another, one foot after another—back to the *manoir*. Nothing prevented her from leaving now and she could not pretend to herself that she had any other course. She would call Lucien. She didn't want to talk with him, but she would have to tell him he would need to find another companion for his grandmother. The thought of the marquise was rather fortifying; the marquise would not have got involved with a married man. She was coming back in a few days, and perhaps there would be time for Lucien to find someone before her return. If not, then she, Amadea, would have to wait. But they had got companions through an agency before and they could presumably do so again. Someone else would no doubt fill the position just as well or better than she had. Somehow, for all Amadea's generosity of spirit, the idea of her position being well filled, and Madame being well pleased with her replacement, was not comforting. And Lucien—would he take her replacement to dinner?

She came into the *manoir* kitchen and began to unpack the groceries.

"Mademoiselle, you are pale," said Céleste with concern.

"Yes. I have a headache. I think I'll go lay down for a while."

Céleste clucked over her and promised to bring her up a *tisane*, and Amadea was too downhearted to protest, but trailed wearily up the stone staircase and dropped onto her bed. After lying for a time face down, she raised herself up. Well, 'if it were done when tis done, then 'twere well/It were done quickly.' Once the call to Lucien was over, it would be definite and she could put her efforts toward the future. She smoothed out the damask coverlet of her bed and went to the heavy oak door. There was an odd commotion coming from the Sabadie's apartment beyond the kitchen. She wondered vaguely, as she came downstairs, why Céleste had not come with the *tisane*. Perhaps she and Yves were quarrelling.

The phone was in the hall. She reached for it, stood a moment clutching the receiver, and dialed Lucien's cell phone number. No answer. When one is steeled for a conversation it is unnerving to be cheated of it. By the telephone there was a list of other numbers, including one for the Paris house. She tried there. The phone was answered by a young-sounding voice whose owner said he was the housekeeper's son. He was trying hard to sound formal: He would be glad to take a message, and—no message?—and, oh, madame was? That is, with whom did he have the honor? She repeated her name but assured him it didn't matter, she would try later. She dialed the office number. It rang. She counted the rings and jumped when a man's voice answered. "Lucien?" she said eagerly.

"*Non. Excusez-moi madame,* regrettably, I am only his secretary."

"Oh." Amadea was taken aback. Was M. d'Alembert in?

No, but the secretary could take a message.

"Tell him...that it's Amadea," she said. "Um. At the *manoir*," (in case he knew any other Amadeas).

"Oooh?"

"If he could call back?"

"Amadea-at-the-*Manoir*, I shall tell him as soon as he comes in."

Amadea put down the phone, and stood blankly staring at the wall for a second. Céleste came bursting through the hall door.

"There you are! What do you think has happened!?"

"Lucien!" cried Amadea in fright.

Céleste didn't hear her, fortunately, caught up as she was in her own problem. "You'll never believe!" She pulled at her apron distractedly, explaining volubly. Her daughter and son-in-law had been involved in a traffic accident that morning and were in the hospital with four broken legs! Amadea followed Céleste into her apartment as she talked. Yves was stuffing clothing and toiletries into an elderly suitcase. Every item he put in, Celeste snatched out, folded, and returned to its place. Yves was also explaining. They were leaving at once, they said, because someone had to take care of the grandchildren. They were at a neighbor's for the instance.

"Where?" asked Amadea, trying to get some little bit of information out of the joint flow of words.

At a neighbor's—oh, a good woman, but they couldn't stay there, poor things, for long, and someone would have to care for Catherine and Pierre, and so they were leaving to care for them...

"Yes, but where?"

Oh, Toulouse. They were leaving for Toulouse at once, and it was providence that she was there and they could leave the *manoir*, otherwise it would have been difficult, but now, there would be no problem, thank heavens, and they'd be back when they could, and how very fortunate that Madame was away now, and so there was nothing to prevent them from going. The suitcase was overflowing. Céleste looked around for her purse. "Four legs!" she exclaimed, "it's incredible, *épouvantable*." Yves seemed almost subdued by this blow of fate. He snapped the bag shut. "Four!" he exclaimed in an awed tone, shaking his head, "one—that's normal; two—well, bad luck, but these things happen; three—*c'est un peu fort*; but *four!*" He swung the bag off the bed, snatched up his car keys, and they were gone.

Amadea wandered through the empty house. Her footsteps rang overloud on the marble and parquet floors, and were muffled on the carpets, where the quiet weighed and seemed unnatural. She went into the salon. Here she had first seen the marquise. She crossed to a window and stood looking at the meadow while inside the shadows deepened. Outside, the sun was declining, lying soft and silken on the limes across the lawn. The flock of peacocks rose one after another and flapped heavily up into the trees to roost. She hoped Yves had fed them before he left. Tomorrow she would have to search for their food. What else did Yves do at night? She supposed he locked up. She thought there was some sort of surveillance equipment that was turned on at night, but she had no idea how to operate it. Better to leave it be. If she touched it she'd probably have an alarm ringing all night. She went about the ground floor, checking the latches on the long windows and sliding the bolts on the doors. She didn't suppose anyone could get in now, should anyone want to get in, and surely she was quite safe here? But she wished she hadn't given Guilhie back. With the dog she could have faced the night with equanimity. Now she found herself constantly looking over her shoulder. The house seemed very empty and she was very alone. But it was only her imagination, she told herself, that made the house seem eerie now.

She fixed herself a sandwich for dinner and ate it rapidly, standing with her back against the wall, and went upstairs to her room, jumping as the wind blew a second-floor shutter against the wall with a bang. There was no lock on the door, unfortunately, but she wouldn't need it, certainly, she hoped. No, there would be no intruders. She had not worried about thieves entering the *manoir* while Yves and Céleste were there: why should she now? She wondered why Lucien didn't call, but, of course, she reminded herself, he was very busy, he would have other things to do. Maybe he was in Amsterdam again.

The hours passed. Nine o'clock, ten. She got into bed and tried to sleep. Eleven, eleven-thirty. The house was quiet no longer. It creaked and moaned as its timbers settled, and those little scurrying sounds or scratchings were probably just mice, she told herself, and believed it, because when, just as she was dropping off to sleep, the first sound of a footfall came on the staircase, she knew it instantly for what it was, and sat bolt upright in bed, gooseflesh rising and ears stretched. She slid quietly out from under the covers and stared about in the darkness for a place to hide. The footsteps came on, up the stairs, not particularly trying for quiet.

A hand felt along the wall, the steps continued, paused before the first bedroom door, the second. The next was Madame's room, then hers. Amadea dove under the bed.

A hand was on the door knob. The door squeaked open slowly and a hand rasped over the paneling. Amadea lay like a trapped rabbit. Maybe the thief would find there was nothing to take here and would go away. But she didn't believe it. Her heart raced and her knees trembled. The light sprang on. In the crack below the bedclothes she could see two black leather boots, much cracked and muddy. They crossed the room towards the bed. The bedclothes were flung back. Amadea stifled a scream.

"Amédée? Come out."

The Thug! Amadea crawled out with as much dignity as she could manage, but it is difficult to crawl from under a bed in a white cotton nightdress and look dignified.

"What are you doing here?" she demanded in exasperation, standing before him all atremble, and yet feeling, instinctively, that she was in no danger from him.

Thierry sat down heavily and unselfconsciously on her tousled bed and took out a package of cigarettes.

"What were *you* doing *there?*" he countered.

"I thought you were a thief or a murderer or I don't know what! What are you doing here? How did you get in?"

"Through the window."

"But I locked them all."

"You don't think those latches would keep anyone out, do you?"

"Well—what do you want?" Amadea asked, not sure she wished to find out.

"I have a question to ask you." Thierry lit his cigarette and waved the match in the air.

"A question! Well, but...but you can't break into someone's house in the middle of the night, just to ask a question!" Amadea expostulated.

"Well," said Thierry doggedly, "I did, so I can." He stared at his cigarette, held between thumb and forefinger. He added grudgingly, "I'd have been here before but my motorcycle broke down." (It had, in fact, first run out of gas, but he didn't feel she needed to know that.)

"How did you know I was here?"

"I heard in the village." (He had, in fact, gone to the bakery to make it up with Sylvie, but he didn't think she needed to know that, either.)

Yes, they knew everything in the village. The cleaning woman had passed it on to the bakery, Amadea supposed.

"...and since you're going away, I couldn't wait."

"What was the question?" Amadea asked, growing calm. He didn't seem violently or larcenously inclined. She even began to feel some curiosity.

"It's about...about..." Thierry took a deep puff of his cigarette and plunged on. "You know about history, right? So it's like this, see? I have to know if something is true or if it's just a lot of *idioties*...And you're the only one I know to ask..." (The only one who won't laugh at me, he added to himself, waiting to see if she would laugh). She didn't.

"Well," said Amadea, sitting down opposite him on a small chest. "I'll try."

Thierry hesitated again, then went on rapidly, "Raymond told me this story, see?" He repeated it to Amadea, almost word for word as he had heard it, from the stolen treasure chest on, and not forgetting Saint Éloi, or the Chevalier Gracien's marriage to the daughter of the townsman.

Outside the wind had increased; the sound of the trees soughing and an occasional spatter of rain hid all other noises. They might have been two people marooned alone on an island in a limitless sea, Amadea thought, as she led Thierry into the small sitting room that served as Lucien's study. She took down one book after another, including the history of Languedoc that she had just returned. She flipped the pages, reading here and there, or looking for references. Thierry looked over her shoulder or moved about behind her back. "Here's a mention of your Count of Foix, so we know he existed," said Amadea, "and here it says there was a problem with the succession....But I don't see anything further....and, of course, nothing about the theft of a chest. Of course, that doesn't mean it didn't happen, only that it's not mentioned here...Let's see. A book of chronicles? Pity you don't remember whose. Was it Froissart's maybe?"

Then several things happened at once. There was a rattling of the window lock, and a leg was extended over the sill. Amadea dropped the book and nearly screamed. The leg, in fine grey wool, was followed by a twill raincoat. Lucien slid into the room. Amadea had a flash of painfully intense awareness that she was dressed only in a flimsy nightgown, that she was prowling about Lucien's semi-private sanctuary, and that she was in the company of a man dressed in black leather. Thierry, seeing the look of agony cross her face, had a flash of painfully intense awareness that he was in someone else's house, in the middle of the night, and that he was undoubtedly about to be accused of breaking and entering. He didn't stop to think that Amadea would surely vouch for him; he lost his head entirely and in one swift movement pulled a switchblade out of his pocket, stepped behind Amadea, and grabbed her by the neck. The knife at her throat, Amadea froze, her eyes like saucers.

Lucien brushed the rain off his sleeves, said "Good-evening, mademoiselle, good-evening, monsieur" to them, and then added to Thierry, "If you really intend to do that, would you take her outside? There's no need to get blood on the carpet."

Thierry and Amadea stared at him in disbelief. A hostage who is worth less than a floor covering is not worth anything at all. Amadea twisted her head about and gave Thierry a hurt look. Thierry gave her neck a little jerk. It wasn't her fault, but he was annoyed.

Lucien continued, "On the other hand, I've been watching you through the window for some time, and I can tell that you're looking for something. Perhaps I could help?" He leaned against his desk, crossing his feet at the ankles. "I'm not going to call the police if that's what you're worried about."

"Maybe you already did," said Thierry suspiciously.

Lucien held his cell phone out to him. "Here. Check it. You'll see that the last twenty calls were all made to the *manoir*."

"But I didn't hear you!" exclaimed Amadea, almost forgetting everything else in this new agony.

"I suppose you were upstairs," said Lucien conversationally. "These walls are thick." He still held the phone in his outstretched arm.

At last Thierry shifted the knife, took the phone, and played with the buttons for a moment. Then he handed it back. "Yeah. Okay." He released Amadea and folded up the knife. Amadea rubbed her neck and moved away.

Lucien waited till she was on the other side of the room. "So what are you looking for?"

Thierry said to Amadea, "You tell him."

Amadea scowled at him and said nothing.

"All right," said Thierry, "I'm sorry. I'm sorry. But I didn't know what that guy was going to do. Okay?"

"Okay." said Amadea. "Well," she said to Lucien, "Um."

"He's going to laugh," said Thierry.

"I won't laugh," said Lucien.

"*Ah, je m'en fous*," said Thierry and sat down stolidly and took out another cigarette. Amadea, with somewhat more than the usual amount of stuttering and false starts, managed to outline the situation: Thierry cut wood for M. Trencavel—who was all right, she added in parentheses, and had taken the dog back—and M. Trencavel had told him this story and they, she and Thierry, were looking for evidence to support or refute it. Thierry listened to her account in silence, adding only an occasional expletive or explanation.

Lucien listened without interrupting, and then said, without the ghost of an outward smile, "No. It's only partially true. Evan did exist, and he was the favorite, but out-of-wedlock, son of the Count of Foix.

However, the story in the *Chronicles* is different. After his father's death, Evan went to take control of the castle, as you say, and there were difficulties involved. The priest did not steal a coffer containing valuables, though, but rather brought Evan the key to the treasury. The townspeople supported Evan's occupancy of the castle, but it was the Viscount of Chatelbon who succeeded the Count, after paying large sums to Evan and his brother. Nor did Gracien marry a commoner, but rather a daughter of the King of Castille. Nor did Evan die in happy old age, I'm sorry to say, but burned to death while committing a practical joke. I'm afraid someone's been playing a joke on you, too."

"Then I hope something awful happens to him too!" exclaimed Thierry vehemently. He thought for a moment, and then added, "And the dog? It's not true about the dog, either? About '*Hund*' meaning 'hidden treasure'?"

"What?" said Lucien. He thought a moment, and then went to the bookshelf, searching. He took down a tome on superstitions, flipped the pages, and read. "Yes, this appears to be the case. That is, it appears to be the case that people have believed in such a connection. But, you know, people have also believed in the past in a great many things that were not true: that the world was flat, for instance, or that cheese bred maggots. I'm afraid your M. Trencavel is either a bit confused, or he's been having you on."

Thierry said, "He's not confused. He did it on purpose. I'm going to kill him."

"No!" cried Amadea.

Lucien, taking him less seriously, said, "Where's your motorcycle? I didn't see it outside."

Thierry said sullenly, remembering that he had a long wet walk ahead of him, "It broke down. I left it in the woods where the highway meets the road."

Lucien said, "If you promise not to commit any crimes against this Trencavel, I'll give you a ride home. We can hook up a trailer and collect the cycle on the way." He crossed to the door and held it open. Thierry, not having been brought up to the *bataille de la porte*, walked through it without a pause, and Lucien turned to Amadea.

"Very fetching attire."

Amadea looked away.

He went on, "I'll be back in less than half an hour. Will you wait for me?"

She nodded imperceptibly and he disappeared.

*

When Thierry pushed his motorcycle the last yards into Raymond's yard, all was dark and still. He opened the front door and stepped inside. He had promised the man from the big house not to hurt Raymond, but he didn't let the promise weigh too much with him. If Raymond was in bed he was going to rouse him—and none too gently. But when he flicked on the light, the feeble rays of the single bulb showed him that Raymond was sitting at the table, asleep, with his head resting between his arms and his fingers still curled around a glass. Thierry swore. He had forgotten that Raymond would be drunk. On another day he wouldn't have minded, but today he wanted to talk to Raymond, shriek at him, slap him a time or two maybe, have it all out with him.

"You stupid, lying bastard!" he roared, "Wake up so I can talk to you!" No response. In irritation,

Thierry kicked hard at the legs of Raymond's chair, which splintered, and tipping sideways, dumped Raymond in a bundle on the floor. His head struck the floor, bounced up and lay motionless. There was a moment of tension before his heavy breathing assured Thierry that he was still alive. Thierry felt a little better. He raised his leg to kick the old man, but, some memory of a moment of friendliness perhaps interfering, he refrained, and turned instead in search of the bottle's remaining inch of alcohol. As he grabbed the bottle and tilted it to his lips, his eyes fell on a paper that fluttered over in the movement of air. It was a note. *"Thierry,"* it said, *"When you read this I shall be most deplorably drunk. One of us has to be responsible. I've decided it's you. Feed the animals in the morning and don't forget to milk Clorise. You've seen me do it. Yours, etc."*

Thierry swore again and sat down, staring at the piece of paper. Because, of course, he'd have to do it. That was the effect Raymond had had on him. He couldn't let the animals go hungry just because he was angry. He finished off the alcohol, stepped over Raymond's prostrate body, and went to bed, feeling that it was a heavy thing to be a responsible man.

18

The rain had stopped and the wind had died. Amadea took her Burberry from the hallway, went out into the blue air of approaching dawn, and sat on a stone bench on the terrace. Soon he would come. She shivered and pulled the coat tighter around herself. Her bare feet brushed the smooth, cool stones. The passing night held the scent of dew on conifers, of the earliest roses, and wisteria. Lucien would come and stand before her. She would rise; he would say her name in his beautiful voice. She would turn to him and his arms would go around her...It would be wonderful. It wouldn't, mustn't happen.

She had to get a grip on herself. "America! America! Confirm thy soul in self-control"—that's what the song said—self-control even when faced with a Frenchman. She shook her head impatiently. She was babbling, babbling to herself, when she needed to keep her mind clear. Yes, there was his car coming back. The lights came slowly toward the *manoir*, swung away to the right and disappeared. Amadea waited with her heart in her mouth. In a moment he would appear around the end of the house. She turned in that direction and stood waiting at full tension. He startled her by stepping onto the terrace from the drawing-room windows behind her. She spun around. He came towards her. "Amadea..."

It was exactly as she had imagined; she had only to wait till he reached her. She sat down abruptly and clasped her hands and knees together, not looking at him. He stood in front of her.

"I heard you called. I heard you were alone here. When you didn't answer my calls, I was worried and decided to come down." He had many more things he wanted to say to her. Her position was rather spoiling his scenario, but he was flexible and it wouldn't have mattered—only he was so soon brought up short.

"Thank you," said Amadea, "I'm so sorry to have given you trouble. I never dreamed you'd come here because...because..."

"Because of you?"

Oh, but this was awful. It was so exactly what she wanted to hear. Amadea clenched her fingers together and said in a stifled voice, "I only called to tell you I'm leaving."

"Leaving?" Lucien's face changed for a split second, then regained its humorous gravity.

"I suppose my grandmother has offended you? She *is* a tyrant."

"Certainly not!" Amadea looked up to meet his slightly mocking smile. She dropped her eyes again.

"That Yves *is* a rascal."

"No!"

"Hmm. Not my grandmother, not Yves. Presumably not Céleste, either. Oh—but it couldn't be myself?"

Amadea didn't answer; he bent forward slightly to try to see her face.

"*Bon*," he continued, "I admit, I'm not so very handsome, but then, one can't have everything, and I am so extremely charming, *n'est-ce pas?*"—he looked inquiringly at Amadea and she nodded, as if against her will—he went on, "so polished, so polite—surely you can't object to *me?*"

She didn't react. He sighed and turned to half sit on the parapet, crossing his ankles. "Maybe you can. Or maybe your sympathies only extend to stray dogs and underdogs."

Tears swam in Amadea's eyes. Lucien changed his tone.

"You're crying? Amadea, listen. I find you very *sympathique*, very lovely, and it's spring, a time when the start of a relationship seems fated, even imperative— and we could have a good time together. If you want to—excellent; if you don't want to—*tant pis.* There's no need to make a tragedy out of it, nor any need to leave..."

"I have to leave."

"But why? Do you think I have to be told 'no' more than twice, or, okay, three times?"

"I don't know," she blurted out, "but you're married and..."

"Married?" he said in a startled voice. Then smiling, as hope reappeared, he added, "Didn't my grandmother tell you? I've been divorced for years." He pushed away from the parapet and came rapidly towards her.

She bounded away. He stopped.

"But what? If the problem was my being married, and I'm not married, then...?" he left the sentence unfinished, a question mark hanging in the air.

"Then it's still wrong," said Amadea despairingly, "all wrong." She turned to leave.

Lucien stepped in front of her. "Why is it still wrong? If that was the obstacle and now it's removed—

where is the problem? I see none. I see that we are here, alone in a glorious dawn: you so very beautiful, and I, so not-altogether-repulsive; you are fate and I am nature..."

"No!" said Amadea, and moved farther away.

"*Bon,*" Lucien shrugged and went back to lean against the parapet again. He rather wondered at himself. He wouldn't have expected himself to be so persistent. But then, he'd never met much opposition before. He studied his shoes for a moment and then glanced at her.

"Don't look so terrified," he said in a half-pained, half-amused voice. "What do you think I am?"

"Sorry," said Amadea.

"Sorry, sorry," he repeated, "why don't you stop telling me you're sorry and explain to me why, since you obviously like me, you intend to leave?—You do like me?" He bent again to study her face. "Yes? No?"

"I don't want to talk about it," she said, biting her lip.

"I'll take that for a 'yes,'" he said. "Is it that you think my grandmother would object? She wouldn't, although we'd be discreet, of course. And if we should wish to continue for long, at the right time I will tell her: 'Grand-mère, your companion has become *my* companion. I will get you another one.'—She will be sorry to lose you, but she will find that very natural." Lucien had a certain qualm here, but he resolutely ignored it.

"Is that what happened to the others?" Amadea asked bitterly.

"What others?"

"The other companions."

"Oh, heavens no—nice women, of course, but no, horrors, no, perish the thought, you're the only one."

"But I don't want to have an affair with you!"

He regarded her without anger but with mild perplexity.

"Of course, mademoiselle. You like me, but not well enough to sleep with me. It is your right, mademoiselle."

Amadea knew she should go away then, but she found herself blurting out, despairingly, "No, you don't understand. I love you!"

Lucien sprang up. "Oh! *Mais, c'est fantastique!* I love you, too."

"No, you don't!" Amadea exclaimed, with the nearest approach to scorn he had ever heard in her voice. She continued in a shaking voice, "Before, I thought you were married. I thought you liked me and that if you hadn't been married, maybe...maybe..." She took a deep breath and went on rapidly, "I thought maybe if you had been free you might have loved me as I love you. But you're not married, you're free, and all you want from me is...is...in short, you *are* Valmont! But *I'm* not a victim!" And with that she turned, and with great dignity, walked into the house, walked through the salon, and bolted up the staircase.

She flung herself down on her bed and a deluge of shame and disappointment poured over her, and yet always in the back of her mind was the tiny, very tiny hope that he might come, and knock on her door, and yet make all right. But the hope grew more and more miniscule, till at last she abandoned it, and flailing about like a drowning swimmer, was overcome by a gulf of sorrow.

*

Lucien, when she left, sat motionless for a few moments on the parapet. Then he rose brusquely and strode into his sitting room. Somewhere he'd seen a packet of cigarettes; the thug must have left them—yes, there. He snatched up the packet, whacked it vigorously against his hand, extracted a cigarette, and lit it impatiently. He'd given up smoking years ago, but now he began to puff and inhale as if the cigarette were a respiratory drug. Well, he didn't need a love affair cluttering up his life anyway. He was a man with lots of other pleasures in his existence: lots of pleasures, lots and lots. He chain-smoked the pack as he strode back and forth, back and forth, then, crumpling up the packet, he tossed it aside, and went to fling himself on his bed in what was, for him, a truly bad temper.

*

So Amadea struggled with her grief until, in the morning, as nearly annihilated as a living young person can be, she rose, very hollow, and like a walking shadow crept down the quiet stairs. She paused for a moment in the hall; the sunlight came in through the salon door and lay in a bar across the ground. Somewhere he was sleeping. How did he look asleep? In her mind's eye she saw his dark hair on a white pillow, his laughing eyes closed. He would find her note when he awoke and be glad, after all, that she was gone. But she mustn't think about any of that now. She would collect her things from the Cow Shed; then she had a bus to catch. She pulled open the front door and slid noiselessly out. If only last night hadn't happened. She could have gone away with the warm feeling that here, at least, she had been liked and, and—*respected.* Her thoughts caught on the word and a lump rose in her throat. No, she mustn't think like that. He probably didn't even understand why she had turned him down. He wouldn't understand that she felt, like the Edwardian she resembled, that anything less than *all* was too little. Maybe she did value herself too highly—what difference did it make any way? Maybe she should turn back, run back, and tell him all right, okay, anything you want, so long as she could stay near him? She loved him. No. She mustn't think like that. Her self-respect was all she had to hang on to. She was not going to be taken on trial—or vice versa, use him that way either. If he loved her, let him show it. If he didn't, they were better apart. A slight feeling of resentment imparted enough warmth to carry her a hundred feet from the *manoir.* After that, her love exonerated him, and it was heavy work placing one foot in front of another. But it had to be done. One foot after the other. I, Amadea, the Incorruptible, will not give in. One foot after another, one day after another. No, the future was too empty to contemplate—better concentrate on the feet. And so, trudging wearily, she reached her home.

19

It was while Thierry was finishing his struggle with the goat Clorise the next morning that the SUV rolled into the yard. He looked up startled. Then he hastily dumped aside the milk and came out of the pen. Hugo waved a hand towards him and shouted, "What are you doing there?"

For nothing would Thierry have answered that he was milking a goat. "Nothing. Looking for mushrooms," he hollered back sarcastically. Hugo strode into the house. Thierry followed him.

Raymond still lay on the floor where he had fallen the night before, only Thierry had covered him with a blanket and slipped a pillow under his head. Hugo gave him a not too gentle kick. "*Ohé*. Wake up!"

No reaction.

"Don't kick him!" said Thierry, standing in the doorway.

"You shut up!" Hugo turned on him, "I'm not paying you to let him get pissed."

"You didn't say he shouldn't," said Thierry sullenly.

"Shut up!" Hugo shouted at him. He kicked his father hard.

Thierry didn't like to be shouted at, and he didn't like Hugo's kicking Raymond; and he was feeling foul anyway. He crossed the room and stood beside the little table. He considered picking up the empty bottle and hitting Hugo over the head with it; in fact his hand was tightening around the bottle, lifting it, when Raymond opened his eyes, and, seeing Thierry beyond his son's legs, muttered, "Don't."

Thierry put the bottle down again. Hugo never knew how close it had been, but he suspected something. He looked from Raymond to Thierry, trying to divine what had just passed between them, then gave it up. He pulled his father into a sitting position against the wall and considered him.

He had been against the use of force. He had been sure that he could get what he wanted by sheer psychological pressure. But every time he drove over here—and he was a busy man—his father was either unconscious or immoveable. Force would leave marks and bruises, and who knows? the old man might even die and then there would be inquiries. Besides, that sort of thing was Bruno's style; he didn't like it. Still, he was losing patience. No, no. There were better, more subtle ways of breaking him down. A week away would do him good.

"Where are you taking him?" Thierry asked, as he watched Hugo lift his father's arm and heave him up.

"To the car. Help me! Take his other arm."

Thierry hesitated.

"Who's paying you?" Hugo snapped at him, and Thierry came forward slowly and took Raymond's other arm. Even as a dead weight, he was easy for the two men to drag between them.

"Where are you taking him?" Thierry asked again, disquieted.

"Not paying you to ask questions," said Hugo, opening the back door of his SUV and then stepping aside to let Raymond tumble in. A little pushing and shoving and his knees jammed in at an uncomfortable angle, and the door could be slammed shut on him.

Hugo pulled a wad of bills out of his wallet and slapped it into Thierry's hand. "Bruno sends you these." He strode around to the driver's door. Thierry followed him.

"Where are you taking him?"

Hugo, sensing by the tone that his subordinate was about to turn rebellious, hastily started the engine, because, after all, if it came to a showdown, he wouldn't bet on his own chances.

Thierry laid a hand on the wheel through the open window. Hugo said grudgingly, "He's going for a rest cure. You can stay here till he comes back. Maybe a week." He started very slowly to let the car slide backwards. Thierry continued to stare at him, and Hugo added, "One would think you'd grown fond of him."

"Yeah. Maybe," Thierry grunted, "You're not going to hurt him?"

"Me? I'm going to make his fortune, that's all. What do you think I am—a criminal?" Hugo snapped impatiently.

Thierry stepped back and Hugo quickly accelerated backwards, spun the vehicle around and roared away.

Thierry turned and went towards the house. Inside, he sat down at the table. The bottle was empty. He hurled it across the room and it shattered against the wall. What to do now? To believe Hugo that Raymond would come to no harm? What was Hugo going to do with him? And if he did something and the police got involved? Who would be found living in Raymond's house? Maybe it was better to leave at once. But to go where?

He pulled the wad of bills out of his pocket and counted it. More than he'd expected. Bruno paid well. The job with Bruno was the first he'd ever had. Before, there had been lounging about the streets with other overgrown urchins; there had been purse-snatching and fights; breaking and entering; car thefts: six months in a reformatory, a year and a half in prison. He didn't want to go back. Bruno paid him well. He'd been able to buy the motorcycle. He'd had money in his pocket for the first time in his life, earned money. It made him feel different. And he was getting old—24 soon—it was time to settle down. So maybe it was better to stay. Probably it was okay. Hugo had said to stay. And where would he go if he left? And there was Sylvie...

Thinking only of himself and his own worries, he went outside. The hens were cackling. He hadn't fed them yet. He found their food and released them from their coop. He always like the way they came running around him when he held the feed can, as if he was a movie star and they were his fans. Today he hardly noticed them, yet it was while he was scattering grain that he began to think about Raymond: Raymond telling him about the chickens and the goats, Raymond trying to interest him in books, Raymond telling him stories. He had come to like those stories—in a way, that is, just a little. Raymond had come looking for him when he had fallen in the hole. He needn't have done that. Thierry wondered why he had. There had been nothing in it for him. And Raymond had cooked dinner for him. Lunch and dinner, every day. He hadn't had anything like that outside of prison. He wondered what Hugo was going to do with the old man. He thought about Hugo and he thought about Bruno, and the more he thought the more uneasy he became. He stopped scattering the grain and stood rooted to the spot, staring into space, his hand suspended over the pan of chicken feed. He had to admit it to himself: he liked Raymond. He liked him a lot. And Raymond was old, and vulnerable. And Bruno thought like a criminal and Hugo thought only of money.

Thierry flung aside the pan, leapt the small enclosure of the pen, and ran for his motorcycle, leaving behind a flurry of wings and squawking.

The motorcycle wouldn't start. Cursing, Thierry bounced vigorously up and down on the starter for several minutes before giving it up. Desperately he looked around. There was Raymond's old bicycle. It didn't have brakes, but he was in a hurry and wouldn't need brakes. Hugo was far ahead already, but he knew—he felt practically certain—where Hugo would take Raymond. He knew, anyway, where he would take someone he wanted to get rid of. He had to get help, because he had to have a car and he might have to deal with more than just Hugo. Damn that his motorcycle should choose this moment to behave like a motorcycle! He tore the tarp off the bicycle and pulled it out of the shed. It was rusty and ancient but appeared to work still. He jumped astride and, gritting his teeth at the grinding of the pedals, sped down the driveway.

*

Guilhabert, locked in his shed, was a dog with a grievance. He had heard the voices come and go, and the vehicles depart, and no one had come near him. He didn't like it. Here it was, plain morning, the light coming in though the small window, and he was still a prisoner. He was used to being locked up for periods, but this was too long. And everyone had gone away, he could tell. He stretched up to the window, but it was too high and too small. He sighed, shifted about uneasily, and began, without knowing why really, to dig a hole by the door. His powerful front paws tore up the hard earth and flung it away like a mechanical digger. Soon a large hole appeared and daylight showed under the door. The dog put his nose through and pushed, but his shoulders stuck. Not big enough. He resumed digging, and shortly found himself at liberty. He looked about. No one. He circled the yard, sniffing the ground. No one. He raised his head, gazed everywhere. The place was deserted: only the stupid chickens going about their usual pointless business and the stupid goats eating grass. They were of no use to him. He looked into the house. No one: but he could tell that Hugo had been there. Thoroughly ill at ease now, he trotted back and forth across the yard. Then, as if coming to a sudden decision, he plunged into the bushes and disappeared.

*

When Lucien woke and came downstairs it was in a much softened mood. A cup of strong coffee first and then he was going to have a talk with Amadea. His behavior last night had been...had been, well, certainly not successful. In all his longish career he had never before felt that he had hurt anyone, or not very much anyway; no, his vanity had never led him to believe that he had produced more than a three-weeks regret in anyone. He felt a twinge of irritation: Why couldn't Amadea be like that? Amadea, he sensed, was not going to be all right in a week or two. Well, if she was different, she was. He should have known it, should have been more careful. Now, he had to try to say something that would make things better. Although what could that be? An apology, first of all, he supposed. The French don't usually apologize, so she would understand the value of that...So thinking he came slowly down the stairs. But...what was that on the console in the entrance hall? A note, with his name on it? With a sinking heart he reached for it and opened it.

"*Monsieur*,"—so he was 'monsieur' now, Lucien thought wryly. Well, he deserved it.

"*Please make whatever explanations you think fit for me to your grandmother. When she returns to Paris, I will call to say goodbye and thank her for her kindness. I loved being her companion. But I am going away, as I told you I would. I hope you can find a replacement without too much difficulty. I am truly sorry for the inconvenience.*

Yours, Amadea"

That was all. Lucien was brave, even where women were concerned, but he experienced a moment of pleasant relief at the thought of the conversation avoided. But no, he couldn't leave it like that. He had to talk to her. He stood and ran his eye over the note again: "going away." Going where? The sudden thought that he might never see her again was unaccountably painful. He glanced at his watch. He'd slept later than usual, but not so very late. She'd go to the Cow Shed first, surely, and then...Surely she would still be there? He'd go and find her. But if she left before he arrived, how would he discover where she'd gone? Abandoning all thought of breakfast, Lucien crammed the note in his pocket. He opened the heavy front door briskly, stepped out into the sunshine, crossed the terrace with rapid strides, and was already breaking into a trot when he was brought up short by the sight of the Thug pumping madly towards him on an ancient bicycle.

Thierry's face was a curious blotched mixture of heated red and fear-induced pallor: the ride down the hill without brakes had exceeded any flirting with disaster he'd ever tried before. He pumped up to Lucien, who stood watching his arrival with mingled irritation and amazement, and then, as it struck him that it might concern Amadea—with a sudden leap of apprehension.

"Where is she?" he barked at Thierry, running forward and putting a hand out to steady the handlebars, as Thierry skidded the bike to a halt in a spatter of gravel.

"*She*? What?" gasped Thierry.

Lucien, comprehending at once that it was not a matter of Amadea in despair taking her life, or any of the other half-imagined possibilities that had sprung to mind, stepped back and regained his sang-froid.

"Never mind. What's up?"

"He's taken him!" said Thierry, struggling for breath.

"*He?* Who?"

"Raymond. Trencavel," Thierry managed, "Hugo—his son—he's taken him. I think he's going to...I don't know, I'm afraid he might...Maybe he'll harm him. I need"—gasp—"your help. I think I know where he will have taken him. My motorcycle's broken down, you know. Come on. We have to use your car. Maybe we can find them before anything happens."

"Have you called the police?" asked Lucien.

"No! No police!" exclaimed Thierry, "You call the police and I'm gone!"

On a bicycle? Lucien wondered, but the desperation in the other man's voice convinced him the Thug was serious. Thierry was almost begging. "Please. He's old. I think they're going to hurt him. The police won't do anything until it's too late anyway." (And what will they say about my part in it all? he added to himself.) Out loud, he added, "Please." He had never begged for anything in his life. Everything in his whole future, he felt, depended on Lucien's going.

Lucien stood a second weighing the situation, and at that moment he was struck by how everything—his whole future maybe—seemed to depend on his staying. But Trencavel was old and friendless. Lucien made up his mind. "Come on then," he said, and turning, the two men ran toward the jeep.

As the jeep hit its top speed a few moments later, Lucien turned to Thierry, "Now: Who are they? Who are you? And what is all this about?"

"It's a long story, and you won't like it," said Thierry gloomily. It wasn't, for a story, at all like the stories Raymond told. Why were the stories he got involved in always such stupid stories? Stupid. Really stupid.

"*Eh alors?*" prompted Lucien.

Thierry sighed noisily and nervously, looked out the window, and began.

Lucien listened, taking in the facts: Hugo wanting the land, Hugo in partnership with Bruno, Bruno sending Thierry to pressure Raymond, the growing friendship between Thierry and Raymond hinted at but skipped over. (Where did the treasure come into it? That too was skipped over, but Lucien was able to make his own deductions.) Hugo coming to take Raymond away...

Lucien listened with one part of his mind. One part of his mind felt anger and compassion for an old man being persecuted and now, perhaps, in danger, but some other part of his mind was thinking of Amadea. Maybe she was getting on a bus right now. She had said she loved him. Many other women had said they loved him. It was a phrase one threw about like confetti: it meant anything from "I find you fairly attractive tonight" to "I want to be your partner (until someone else takes my fancy)." It certainly hadn't meant much in the case of his ex-wife. They had come together in a *coup de foudre*, and drifted relentlessly in opposite directions thereafter. Their marriage after a year of cohabitation had been an attempt to bridge the rift. The divorce papers a year after that had made no dent in the emotional life of either party. From Amadea the words sounded serious.

"Hurry!" said Thierry.

"Amadea!" thought Lucien, but aloud he said, "This is as fast as it'll go. How long has it been since Hugo left?"

"Half an hour, maybe; I'm not sure."

"We'll never catch up, you know. We really should call the police—they'd get there faster." He didn't add what he thought—that if Hugo were really planning to do in his father, they'd be too late already.

"I think they'll try to make him change his mind first," said Thierry. That's what he'd do, anyway. "But if the police come, then they might lose their heads, and who knows what might happen." He knew something about *that*, too.

Lucien nodded, rather surprised to find Thierry capable of so much psychology, and concentrated on his driving.

20

Amadea, coming slowly to consciousness, felt something wet on her cheek. Someone was breathing in her ear. She opened her eyes a crack. Guilhabert the dog was regarding her with a questioning look. "A living dog is better than a dead lion." The words from Ecclesiastes swam into her mind. But who was dead? And where was she? She opened her eyes fully. Ah yes, she had fallen asleep on the sofa of the Cow Shed, and it was her love that was dead. Dead, but not gone; dead and she would carry her dead love around forever. Oh, why had last night happened? Why couldn't she just have gone away in the warm and confidence-inspiring belief that he would have loved her if he had been free? She sat up, and locking her arms about Guilhabert's neck, rested her head on his broad one. She had a bus to catch. She straightened up—and it was only then that it struck her: what was the dog doing here?

"Oh, Guilhie," she murmured, "I suppose you remembered me. It's very sweet of you, but I'll have to take you back." No, there was no alternative. She would have to take him back to M. Trencavel before she left. She rose, splashed some water over her face, closed the window the dog had opened, and tidied the house so that it would be all ready to leave when she got back.

Then, calling the dog, she set out, with a hollow heart and a determined step, to walk across the hills.

*

Hugo, speeding down the roadway with his father—not too fast though; don't want to be stopped by the police—reached for his cell phone and called Bruno. He told Bruno what he'd done. He couldn't wait forever, could he? After all, he'd been patient, hadn't he? He found he was justifying himself to Bruno—as if Bruno would care. But Bruno interrupted him: he had a better idea. Hugo listened with appreciation. That Bruno was clever, he had to admit it.

"Okay, okay. So I'll get rid of Raymond in Toulouse and meet you there."

"Raymond?" said Bruno.

"My father, I mean," Hugo corrected himself irritably. This was not the moment for remembering that Raymond was his father. He had to get off the rural route, fast; the *nationale* in the Toulouse direction would be better.

*

Lucien and Thierry were approaching Toulouse.

"Here, the next turning," said Thierry, his voice full of tension.

Lucien followed Thierry's directions, and before long pulled off the road. Here the jeep was hidden but they were within sight of a locked, chain-link gate. A large sign hanging on the gate said Bruno Bouchenet and Hugo Trencavel, SARL Construction. Inside were various metal warehouses and hangars protecting heavy equipment. Beyond were heaps of sand and gravel.

"There's a guard," said Thierry, "there's always a guard."

"Why there?" Lucien had asked him, and Thierry had answered, struggling to put vague ideas into words, "Because Hugo's just for show, you know? Bruno, he's the one who gets things done. If there's going to be any dirty work, it'll be Bruno who does it. They could drop him in cement. I saw that in a movie once."

"No," said Lucien, "they won't do that, because if it's a matter of inheritance, not having the body would be very inconvenient."

"Oh, right," agreed Thierry, somewhat relieved.

"What I would do in their place," Lucien said, "Would be to try and make it look like an accident. Let him drink and fall, say—which is why I think you're probably right about this being a good place for it. If that's really what you think they intend to do?" He looked inquiringly at Thierry.

"I don't know. I don't know," Thierry answered, "maybe not, but why did they take him then?"

Now here they were. "The heavy equipment will mostly be out for the day," said Thierry peering forwards, "Oh, *there*, in there, Bruno's car. He must be here."

"And Hugo's car?"

"No. It's a big utility vehicle. I don't see it."

"Listen," said Lucien, "You stay here, and stay out of sight. I'm going to look around. If I'm not back in fifteen minutes, you'd better call the police. You will do this?" Lucien looked hard at Thierry.

Thierry nodded.

Lucien got out of the car, removed his jacket, and made a run at the top of the fence. He jumped, caught the wire near the top, and vaulted over. Thierry looked after him in some surprise and admiration.

Lucien ran towards the hangar near where Bruno's car was parked. If Bruno, or Hugo, or both of them were working Raymond over somewhere, they'd choose one of the warehouses, he guessed. The first warehouse, however, was padlocked on the outside. He sidled around the edge of it, but there was no one in sight. The next building was an open hangar; he skirted it, then another warehouse. The main doors of this were also padlocked, but there was a small door on the side. He put his ear to it and listened. There was the faint sound of a telephone ringing inside, but nothing else. The ringing stopped as if answered. Lucien turned the handle of the door softly. It wasn't locked. He opened it carefully and stuck his head inside. He had a clear glimpse of a large hall containing much empty space and two small tractors. No Hugo, no one of Trencavel senior's description, or Bruno's. To his right was a windowed office space. A man, seated there with his back to the door, was talking on a phone. At the sound of the door opening he turned brusquely about. Lucien pulled the door shut again briskly and retreated around the end of the building, hoping he hadn't been seen.

Well, he now knew Raymond wasn't being held here. From this side of the warehouse he had a clear view of the yard. There was nothing, no one there amongst the piles of gravel and sand. The sound of the door alerted him to his own danger. He didn't think the guard could have seen his face, but he must have seen the door close and was coming to investigate.

Lucien rounded the far corner of the building rapidly, and a large Rottweiler-type dog rose from the ground with a bellow and raised a racket on seeing him. The dog was tied to a doghouse, but the guard would be there in a moment.

"Hey!" yelled someone.

Out of the corner of his eye, Lucien caught sight of a burly fellow armed with a heavy stick. The back fence was beyond the gravel pile. Lucien, deciding that prudence was the better part of valor, turned his back on the guard and ran. The decision was taken in a split second and the next he was speeding, legs pumping, toward the fence. Behind him he heard the man loosing the dog, siccing it on him. He heard the guard's yells, heard the dog's barks, high with anger and excitement, then silence as the dog too put its strength into running. What was the charm to stop mad dogs?— *Hax, pax, max?* He didn't think it would work: better just to run, run, run. *Dieu*, it must be right on his heels; he could hear it right behind him.

"Amadea," he thought irrelevantly, "Amadea, these things never happened to me before I met you." And then he didn't think anymore, but put all his effort into covering the last yards to the fence. Here it was. He jumped, and, not so neatly as the first time but with an adrenaline-inspired agility that astonished even himself, made it to the other side just as the dog hit the fence. The animal fell back, baying in rage, while Lucien, still going at a speed an Olympic sprinter would have admired, disappeared into the woods and brush surrounding the yard.

After a time he slowed, and sometime afterwards he stumbled across a lane, and then, coming to a walk, settling his clothes to rights, and struggling to get his breath back under control, he made his way back to where he'd left the car. Thierry was waiting anxiously.

"I was just about to call the police. Well, was Raymond there?"

"No," said Lucien, staunching the blood from where he'd cut his arm in getting over the fence.

"Oh," said Thierry, feeling relieved, and also a little deflated and ridiculous, because he'd been wrong, because there hadn't been any need for heroics.

"There's only a guard there. And a very vicious dog."

"A vicious dog?"

"Looked like a Rottweiler. The guard sicced it on me."

"Oh, that one. Na, he just makes a lot of noise. He wouldn't harm a flea."

"*Now* you tell me," said Lucien, with some amusement. "Anyway," he continued, "We now know that Raymond isn't being murdered here, so we're going to continue our investigations like civilized people, and drive up to the gate, and ask where Bruno or Hugo may be found."

"No!" said Thierry.

"Yes," said Lucien, whose breathing had by now returned to normal. He put on his suit jacket, smoothed his hair into its usual becoming disorder, and letting out the clutch, drove the jeep out of its hiding place and straight up to the gate. There was no bell, so he leaned his hand hard on the horn.

"What if he recognizes you?" said Thierry.

"He'll think he's mistaken," said Lucien. "You stay down."

Thierry crouched below the dashboard, while the guard, looking considerably perturbed, appeared around the edge of the warehouse and came towards them. He was still carrying the stick and approached the gate warily.

"*Bonjour*, monsieur," said Lucien, in a tone of polite neutrality, as he got out of the car and approached the gate as well, "I was hoping you could tell me how to get in touch with Bruno Bouchenet or Hugo Trencavel? I am a judge," (no need to tell him what kind), "and I have business with them. They don't seem to be answering their phones."

The guard looked Lucien over curiously, but after all, he'd only seen the trespasser from the back, and this man was surely too calm to have just been trespassing. Besides he said he was a judge, and judges didn't trespass. It couldn't be the same man. What could a judge be wanting with Bruno Bouchenet anyway, or Trencavel? This was worrisome.

Lucien regarded the man with friendly patience while he waited for an answer.

"I don't know anything about M. Trencavel," said the man, deciding to be civil. This man was part of the law-and-order establishment after all; one had better be careful. "M. Bouchenet, he left half an hour, an hour ago, maybe longer, with a bulldozer on a flatbed truck. I don't know where he was going. Bit unusual, his taking it himself, but then, Bouchenet, he always has..." he was going to say "various games going," but finished, "lots to do." He was no blabber-mouth, he reminded himself.

"Where was he going, if I may ask?" said Lucien, "Perhaps I could catch up with him on the site? I need to talk to him about a rather urgent matter."

"Sorry," said the man, "I don't know. I could try to call him for you, but if he's not answering there's not much point. What with the equipment going, he might not hear, you know. I'd keep trying."

Lucien nodded, said he'd do that, thanked the man politely, and retreated.

The man called after him, "You didn't see anyone snooping around here, did you? I just had someone trespassing here. The dog chased him clear over the fence."

Lucien raised his arms in a gesture of ignorance, and getting in the car, backed it briskly away from the gate and then, when the man's back was turned, spun it around and drove away. Thierry raised his head.

"What now?"

"No luck. The guard says your M. Bruno left an hour or so ago with a bulldozer on a flatbed truck. Unless you have any idea where he'd be going with it?"

"Raymond's!" exclaimed Thierry, an expression of anguish on his face. "He's going to Raymond's house.—Hurry! Maybe we can get there in time to stop him!"

"What?" said Lucien, "Stop them from what now?" But even as he spoke, his own imagination took the necessary leaps.

"I know because it was my idea," said Thierry miserably, "It was in the first days, when I'd just been sent there. I was really bored, you know?" he glanced at Lucien, as if hoping that being bored might make what he'd done all right, even though he suspected it wouldn't—"I was really bored, and that was be-fore...before..." Before Raymond fed him and talked to him and worried about him when he didn't come home, he meant, but these were too many and too nebulous thoughts to formulate. "Before I knew Raymond," he went on, "and, like I said, I was really bored. There's no television there even, you know?—so I called up Bruno and I told him: why don't they just put some pressure on the old guy?"

"Meaning?" said Lucien, with his eyes on the road.

"Never mind," said Thierry, with the sulkiness creeping back into his voice. He fell silent.

"*Et alors?*" prompted Lucien.

"Bruno said they didn't want to use force on the old guy yet, because that might finish badly. He said they were going to use psychological pressure. I said, 'what's psychological pressure?' and he laughed and said 'you are', meaning me, and then he hung up. So I let another day go by, and by then I'm ready to break the walls down in that tiny house I'm so bored—I mean, it was worse than prison, even—and so then I get this idea. Why don't they really break down the walls? Bulldoze the house? Then Raymond would have no place to go, no money; he'd have to agree to whatever they wanted, right?"

"There are laws," said Lucien neutrally.

"Oh, *ouais*, the law," said Thierry with a shrug. "You know how many shirts Raymond has? Three. And they all have holes in them."

"'*C'est moralement que j'ai mes élégances,*'" quoted Lucien, "I'd like to meet your M. Trencavel."

"Oh sure, Raymond knows a lot—I know that now—but how does he look? He looks like a guy who drinks. He does drink. Who's going to believe him? Me, I know something about the law..."

Lucien smiled inwardly, then admitted to himself that Thierry's viewpoint might have equal validity with his own.

"...I know who gets believed and who doesn't. Besides, the law means lawyers and lawyers cost money. Raymond hasn't got any money."

"Mm," said Lucien, "so you suggested your demolition project to Bruno. And what was his reaction?"

"He said it was a good idea, but that they were hoping it wouldn't come to that...and then he and Hugo, they got involved in something else—I don't know what, they always have things underway, you know? And for a long time they were out of touch. They wouldn't answer calls, or if they did, they'd just say they were busy and to stay put. So, I forgot about it, and then, I got to know Raymond..." his voice trailed off. He thought about Raymond's tricking him over the treasure chest. It didn't seem to matter at all now. Maybe some day he'd even think it was funny. What a lot of work the old man had got out of him.

"And now you're on Raymond's side?" Lucien finished for him.

Thierry nodded glumly.

"So at the moment we're assuming that Bruno is heading to bulldoze Raymond's house, and that Hugo is keeping Raymond out of the way in the meantime?"

Thierry nodded again, and shortly afterwards the jeep regained the highway and headed, at the top speed of its not very extensive capacity, back toward Maugrebis.

Now, there was nothing to do but drive. Lucien's thoughts turned again to Amadea. Or rather, he hadn't stopped thinking about her since he woke this morning, only he had been momentarily distracted at times by the train of events. Amadea. What was he going to do about her? And suppose he never saw her again? No, it was unthinkable that she should just disappear into the wild blue yonder without a word from him. He had to see her again to tell her...tell her what, exactly? And then what? And then she could disappear into the wild blue yonder?—Having received his gracious permission to do so, he thought, with growing irritation at himself. He was beginning to see Amadea's point. No one, in all his thirty-four years, had ever told him he was a cad before. It was only Amadea, who loved him, who might reasonably feel so. Because it was only with her, of all people, that he had behaved like a cad. He, who knew something about affairs of the heart, had started without a thought for the future. He had had no intention of marrying again any time soon. And yet he had seen her growing interest, had watched her face light up at his appearance, had seen all the signs of dawning love, and he had never once hinted to her—until it was too late—that he was only playing, just testing the waters, so to speak, just out for a little short-term pleasure, with the commitment put off until sometime in the future, "if things worked out." She was right: if that was the way he felt, then he didn't care for her, and she was right to go away. It was fortunate she had thought he was married; that had perhaps protected her a little. But it didn't make his own behavior any the better. He groaned a little between his teeth, and banged one fist lightly against the steering wheel. Tsk. It was enough to make one weary of life. He thought he'd swear off women for good.

Thierry glanced at him, startled. Strange, how much this man seemed to be taking Raymond's fate to heart. Well, he'd learned a lot about people in the last few months. People—Hugo and Bruno aside, of course—people were a lot better than he used to think.

21

Amadea picked her way between the growing grass and wildflowers. Bees hovered just at ankle level. She didn't notice them, nor the sun beating down as it climbed the sky. The feeling of weariness had dropped away from her after her sleep, and she felt now only light—empty and light as a feather, drained of all emotion. She proceeded across the countryside like a disembodied spirit, devoid of substance, devoid of thought. She had a task to do; she was doing it; that was all.

*

Guilhabert, as depressed as a dog can be, and empty also, followed her soberly. Really, what was the world coming to? he thought. First no Raymond, then no breakfast. He'd come and found this girl. He'd gone to his bowl, he'd placed a foot upon it, wagged his tail, rolled his eyes, and she'd ignored him! She hadn't understood at all, hadn't paid his pleas the least attention. People were incomprehensible. In fact, they were a lot worse than he used to think.

*

Bruno Bouchenet, carefully maneuvering a flatbed truck around a corner it was never meant to turn, began to curse. It had taken him much longer than he expected to get here, and now he was here, he was not sure he was on the right road, and he was not sure this road was practicable with the bulldozer loaded up behind. And that Hugo was out of reach. What was the point of a cell phone if one never answered the damn thing? He knew Hugo was just clicking the thing off automatically, without even looking at it.

The flatbed lurched as the offside tire went into the soft dirt and sank, sliding slightly to the side. Spinning the wheel round, heavy arms flying, he straightened the rig out and stepped on the gas. The wheels spun, mud flew, the engine shrieked, and then the wheels caught and the rig lurched forward. Half a meter—and he had to slam on the brake again because a fence post blocked the way. And then again, back a foot, forward, back—this time it was moving; this time it was really stuck—"*Putain de merde!*—St. Christopher help me!" Ah, there, that always worked! Brake now, back again, ah, *merde, merde*....And so on, round a quarter of the points of the compass, until he had arrived at last on the straight of the dirt road, with the rig sighing and quivering under him as its weight depressed the still soft earth of spring. He wiped the sweat off his brow with a greasy chamois-cloth rag. Then, looking down the road, he saw that it was blocked by a small herd of gray cows. He had knocked down a portion of the fence, and the cows pasturing in the field had ambled out to where the grass was greener, apparently unconcerned by the mechanical monster heaving to and fro in the lane.

Bon, he thought, first that turn, now these cows. *Bon*, a few blasts of the horn should get rid of them. He leaned on the horn: the cows looked round with mild alarm in their sloe eyes. On his rapid approach in the truck, they milled from side to side of the road but did not disperse. Then Bruno noticed that they were not only blocked in by fences along the lane, they were also unable to proceed forward. A cow tethered on the verge had tangled her rope around bushes in such a way as to form an effective road block. She, with her head wrapped close to an acacia branch, lowed pitifully.

Bruno opened the door and descended wrathfully from his cabin. But here the cows, thoroughly agitated by now and seemingly too frightened to consider that they might pass quietly out of the way, in single file, along the sides of the flatbed, decided that confrontation was the only solution. Bruno was met by a row of menacingly lowered horns and heavy breathing. He hopped rather quickly back into the cabin, and from its safety proceeded to anathematize cows as the stupidest beasts in creation.

At this point, however, a man appeared over the rise of the pasture and came, on not very steady legs, down toward the scene of battle. It was Raymond's neighbor, Pascal Bordan, and he was wearing a blue peasant smock and carrying a bottle of *plonk*. He hailed the rig and the rig's driver with upswept arms, "Goodday to you, monsieur. A beautiful..." he was going on conversationally, but Bruno cut him short:

"Are you the owner of these cows?"

"Which cows?" He answered, because only the tethered cow was his.

"Ah, you're drunk," snapped Bruno in rising irritation.

"I am," answered Pascal with dignity, swaying slightly as he cradled his bottle, "it's my métier."

"Well, make it your métier to get these cows out of the way! Go on!"

Pascal didn't move, but stood, apparently lost in thought.

"Go on!" shouted Bruno, beginning to lose his temper.

"But, go—where?" asked Pascal in wonder.

"Oh, go to the devil!"

"Monsieur," said Pascal, "you are not polite." He turned about, almost tripped over his own feet, put his nose in the air, and headed at a slow goose step back over the hill.

"Hey!" Bruno half-descended from the cab again. "Hey! Where are you going?"

"Monsieur, I am going to the devil. *Au revoir*, monsieur."

"Hey! Come back and move this *putain de vache!*"

Pascal turned back bristling. "Monsieur, I may be *soûl* but my cow is not *lou—lou* He struggled for the word "louche," then gave it up: "No one insults my cow!" Turning maudlin, he sobbed, "Maria, I'll defend you!" He draped himself across the front of the truck.

Bruno leapt from the cab. This was the limit! He couldn't waste all day like this. One good chop would plant the old guy.

But Pascal didn't wait for the one good chop. Swinging his bottle like a sword, he lunged at his adversary. Bruno swung his fist. Pascal dodged the blow and fenced with the bottle. Bruno, as the bottle brushed his chin, decided it was ridiculous to quarrel with a drunkard over a cow. He leapt away from Pascal and back into his cabin, slamming the door and locking it. Pascal beat on the door with his fist. Bruno was furious now. Bested by an old drunkard over a cow! And he was the powerful one! He'd just run over the damn cows, that would be easiest. He slammed in the gears. But here he found the road had magically cleared during his engagement with Pascal. The gray cows had chosen the path of least resistance and departed along the verge; the tethered cow had freed herself and was cropping grass, her tie line lying slack across the road. Bruno, with Pascal's taunts ringing in his ears, stamped on the gas pedal, rumbled down the road at a dangerous speed, and disappeared from sight.

Hugo's phone was ringing. "Hugo!" said Bruno's voice, full of wrath. "I've been trying to get you for ages! I can't find the *putain de* place. I don't want to wreck the wrong house. You better dump your cargo and come back here, quick. I'm waiting!"

"Okay," said Hugo, "where are you?"

Bruno looked about him. No street signs anywhere, just a lot of trees. "Middle of *putain de* nowhere," he answered.

"That's it," said Hugo.

Bruno was not in a mood to be amused. "Wise guy," he muttered, "just get rid of the old man and get back here!"

"Coming," Hugo replied meekly, and steering with one hand, he pulled the SUV off the road and brought it to a stop. In the back, Raymond opened his eyes and then closed them again, pretending to be still asleep. Hugo jerked open the door, and reaching in, grabbed his father by the shoulders and began to heave him up. Not wanting to fall, Raymond helped a little, leaning on Hugo and feigning a semi-comatose compliance. Hugo shifted him out of the car, took half-a-dozen steps with him, and deposited him on the ground. Raymond lay still in the grass and last year's leaves. The scent of the earth was comforting. Hugo hesitated. He had to get away from here before any cars came past. This was a little-used *départmentale*, but still, one might come along. What if his father died here? Just never woke up, or walked out in front of a car? Could he be blamed? No, no, he could always just say that he and his father had quarreled, his father had insisted on getting out there and then. What happened to him later couldn't possibly be his fault. He turned briskly, regained the car, and drove away.

Raymond opened his eyes and sat up. Well, it might have been worse: he'd had time to imagine a number of unpleasant possibilities as he lay in the car. What was abandonment on a country road? It happened to dogs and cats all the time. Better than euthanasia perhaps. Well, and what, now, was he to do about it? And why had Hugo left him here? Oh, just another of his pressure tactics, he supposed, or punishment for being drunk. What did it matter? And what could he do about it? Go to the police?

He sat in the grass below a plane tree sprouting thin wands of greenery. Its fellows stretched away along the asphalt in twin lines to the distant curves. Where was he? Far from the foothills, as this was lowland country. Between Rieux and Muret, he supposed. He imagined going to a police station. There would be polished desks, stacks of papers, computers, police officers in smart uniforms and high crowned hats. He, an old man, unshaven, tremulous, dirty, smelling of alcohol, would open the door. They would take him in with polite frozen faces and disinterested eyes. They would not listen to him.

"Monsieur," the officer would say to him, with weary disbelief, when he had explained himself, "you are accusing your son of exactly what? That he left you along the roadside when you were drunk? It is regrettable, perhaps, but not against the law." Shrugs, rustlings of paper to show that the policeman had other things to do. Raymond imagined himself mumbling something, the policeman raising his head, answering civilly still, but with growing impatience, "You say that first he set a guard on you and then he dumped you? *Eh bé*, monsieur, there is a contradiction there, *n'est-ce pas?* One minute you say you were a prisoner, the next that he wanted to get rid of you. You say that he is harassing and persecuting you. *Eh bé,* monsieur, I have two sons also, teenagers, and I can assure you that to harass and persecute one's parents is the usual behavior of children. But it is not a police matter—and we are very busy, as you can see." (More paper rustling.) The other station employees would glance at each other with ironical smiles, and Raymond would find himself shortly back on the street...

Raymond stood up. There was nothing to do but go back. He checked his pockets. No money. Well, he'd have to hitchhike, then. He stood a moment, tottering slightly. He'd stop the first car he met and ask directions: "*Excusez-moi,* monsieur, but where am I?" He would be like Cyrano de Bergerac, pretending to have fallen from the moon: '*Comme une bombe/Je tombe de la lune...j'en tombe.*'

The thought of Cyrano, who lost all but his panache, was strengthening. He straightened himself: Head-up, shoulders back—even with a hangover and a headache. Forward, march! I, Raymond Trencavel the Indomitable, shall not give in. He started walking, and the words, 'not give in, not give in, not give in,' served him as a marching song.

*

Amadea, like an automaton, came up Raymond's driveway and stopped beneath the trees, some eeriness about the place penetrating even to her altered state of awareness. It was so still here. The door of the little house stood wide open, but there was no sound of habitation. At her side, Guilhie pricked his ears toward the house, listening, and then looked inquiringly into her face, tail waving gently. Nothing moved. She wished even Thierry would appear.

She moved forward to the house and knocked on the door. "Hello? Anyone?" But she knew, even as she called, that there would be no answer. Although, after all, she told herself firmly, what was eerie in that? She had this terrible problem with her imagination. Probably they had just gone to town and would soon be back. She could just tie Guilhie up somewhere—assuming she could find a rope—and leave. But then, she didn't like to leave him like that: suppose they didn't come back for some reason? There was nothing to do, she decided, but wait. There was a chopping block in front of a woodshed, and she sat down on that. Guilhie settled in the fragrant wood chips at her feet, and, lost in their various thoughts, they remained immobile, time passing for them unheeded.

It was the sound of a motor that woke Amadea from her trance. She heard the motor, and almost simultaneously Guilhabert rose with such a deep roar of alarm and threat that her first reaction was to cringe and hold her ears. Her second was to catch hold of the dog's collar as he lunged forward, dragging her to her feet. A large truck, carrying a piece of heavy equipment, was lurching into the clearing. What more natural than a tractor on a farm? She didn't give it a thought. Here was someone who could give her information, no doubt, about M. Trencavel.

But the driver had leapt out of his cab and was striding briskly around the trailer, loosing chains and clamps with an iron bar. He appeared to be cursing. Amadea came around the front of the house and stood there uncertainly, trying to hold onto Guilhie, who pulled and barked, the short hair bristling along his back. The man ignored them.

Bruno was in a very bad mood. He had got tired of waiting for Hugo—like Louis XIV he was unaccustomed to waiting—and when a car appeared he had flagged it down and asked directions. "It was just there, around the bend," said the driver, "first road to the right, first drive to the right again, very close." So close he had decided not to wait, and here he was, and this was obviously the right place, but what was this girl doing here? This whole day had been one fiasco after another. Behind the tractor, he telephoned Hugo.

"A girl with a dog? *That* girl again? *That* dog?" Hugo's voice expressed disbelief. Was there no getting rid of them? "They're nobody," he said, ungrammatically but succinctly. "Get rid of them. Tell them to clear off."

Bruno clicked off his telephone, slid it into his pocket, and emerged from behind the tractor. "What are you doing here?" he roared for openers at Amadea. "Don't you know this is private property? Clear off before I call the police!"

"I was just..." Amadea began, shouting to make herself heard over the dog's angry barking. Then she broke off and her eyes widened in fright, as Bruno gestured with the iron bar..."I'm going, I'm going..."

She struggled with Guilhabert, who had decided she needed protection and was fighting with her to do his duty. His angry howls at the man were interspersed with urgent whines at Amadea—whines that meant, "Let me stop him." He was too strong for her. He yanked her to her knees and then he was out of her grasp and leaping toward Bruno.

Bruno raised the bar shoulder high—

"No!" screamed Amadea.

—and brought it down on Guilhie's head.

The dog fell to the ground and lay still. Bruno, shaking with nerves and anger, turned away and jumped onto the bed of the truck. He started up the bulldozer and backed it down the ramp far faster than was safe. He had set out this morning in perfect coolness to perform a simple razing job, but then he had met first the drunk, and then the dog. Two attacks and he was ready for anything, didn't care about anything anymore. He really wanted something to demolish.

Amadea, in tears, was kneeling beside the body of the dog. His eyes were closed and blood streamed down the side of his face, but she thought there was a heartbeat.

"Guilhie, Guilhie, don't die," she whispered, trying to stem the blood with her handkerchief. Where to get help for him and how? It was only then that she realized the bulldozer was heading straight towards her. She and Guilhie were blocking the only practicable approach to the house. The bulldozer, large, shiny blade hovering above the ground, was thirty feet away. Bruno was shouting something, but she couldn't hear it above the sound of the motor. He made "move aside" gestures with his arm. Amadea stared wildly at him, then back at the house, and then she knew what he was intending to do. She knew too, that M. Trencavel couldn't know about it; he couldn't have planned this. All his possessions were still inside; she'd seen the books and pans through the open door. Was it Thierry who had ordered this?—In revenge, because M. Trencavel had told him something that wasn't true? And what would the old man do, when his house was smashed? These thoughts passed through her head very rapidly, as she rose from beside the inert dog, and stood staring, open-mouthed, at Bruno. She couldn't let this happen. And besides, the dog was here, he would get run over.

Bruno made the impatient "move aside" gesture again. She could see his mouth moving angrily, but she didn't know what he was saying. If fright and anger could move Bruno out of his usual cool and calculating mood, so fright and pain had changed Amadea's sense of reason. She remained standing.

Bruno turned off the ignition and shouted above the noise of the dying motor, enunciating each word separately so there should be no mistake: "Get. Out. Of. The. Way. Or. I. Will. Run. You. Over." And he quickly flicked the ignition on again.

Amadea remained standing.

"Stupid, stupid, stupid!" thought Bruno, "*quelle conne, bon sang de merde,*" as he rammed in the gears. The worst kind of person to have to deal with. He'd back up and take a run at her: that would get her out of the way. If she wouldn't move—too bad. Accidents happened to stupid people who got in the way.

Lucien and Thierry, turning into the drive, saw the deep tracks of the flatbed and heard the sound of the bulldozer at the same time.

"He's there!" shouted Thierry, "We're too late! Hurry!"

The jeep tore up the ground, bouncing wildly over the ruts, and sped into the clearing, just as Bruno lowered his blade and headed for Amadea.

"No!" screamed Lucien, tumbling out of the jeep before it had even stopped. He raced across the distance separating him from the oncoming bulldozer and tackled Amadea, trying to pull her out of its path.

She struggled and kicked his shins. "Let go of me!"

"*Aïe!*" he cried, but tightened his grip and heaved her out of the way, holding her against his chest.

The bulldozer had stopped with a cough of dumped clutch and stood silent a yard away. Thierry jumped on the tractor and grabbed Bruno by the shirt front, while Bruno, in a fury, searched with his free hand for the crowbar. Lucien dropped Amadea in an unceremonious heap.

He ran to the bulldozer. "Stop!" he yelled, trying to force the two men apart, a hand on each chest. "Stop, Thierry!" he commanded, as Thierry tried to cuff Bruno by reaching around Lucien, and Bruno still sought for a weapon.

Another car arrived now at top speed, and slammed to a stop behind the jeep. Hugo jumped out.

"What's happening?" he shouted. Thierry let go of Bruno; Bruno, realizing the game was up, put down the crowbar; Lucien, pulling Thierry after him, stepped down from the tractor.

"Where's Raymond?" Thierry yelled at Hugo.

"What's it to you?" Hugo snarled back.

"It's something to *me*," said Lucien sharply, "and it may be of interest to the police, unless you can assure us that he's uninjured."

Hugo considered a moment, then answered sulkily, "He's all right."

"That's good," said Lucien, "Because enough damage has been done. Your partner was trying to run over this woman," he gestured towards Amadea, who still sat on the ground.

"*What?*" said Hugo. He stared at Amadea, at Lucien, and at Thierry, who all nodded their heads, and at Bruno, who avoided his gaze.

"You did *what?*" Hugo turned on his partner, his voice shrill.

"*You* said to do it!" Bruno countered angrily. His behavior of a moment ago was already beginning to seem incredible to him. He couldn't really have meant to run her over, could he? And yet it had been so close. "*You* said to bulldoze the house. Me, I'm only the operator."

"You're only the operator!? It was your idea," Hugo shouted back. "You said you were going to bulldoze the house, not run over people. You might have killed someone, and then what would have happened to me!?" He advanced on Bruno with clenched fists.

Lucien closed his eyes and shook his head in disbelief, then stepped between the two men, asserting his authority with a few words that stopped them. Obviously there was going to have to be some arbitration here. Agreements would have to be made; people put on their good behavior...He was going to have a lot of work here. And there was Raymond to think about, and Thierry, and Amadea.

Amadea...he looked about. She was bending over the prostrate body of the dog. She lifted her head and her eyes met his.

"What are you doing here?" he asked curiously.

"The dog came to me. I brought him back. He thought he was defending me. The man hit him." It was easier to speak in short sentences. "He's still alive," she said. "He needs to go to a vet."

Lucien turned to Thierry, "Help me get him into the jeep. Then you can take him to a vet. There's one in Valzères. It's on the right, after the gas station on the main street. Tell them I'll be along to pay for him, later." He gave Thierry his card. "Amadea had better go with you, in case he wakes up." He glanced at Amadea. She nodded. "Then you'd better go pick up M. Trencavel and bring him back here. Monsieur can no doubt tell us where to find him?" He turned and looked inquiringly at Hugo, who answered sulkily, realizing that this man could make a lot of trouble for him if he wanted to, "I left him on the *départmentale* between Rieux and Muret; he's probably still passed out there. Or maybe he's walking."

"You left him unconscious along the road?" asked Lucien.

"You dumped him?" asked Thierry.

Hugo shrugged, and trying not to look shamefaced, turned away and stood kicking his tires.

Lucien, with some difficulty, laid Guilhie across the back seat of the car. The dog stirred slightly. "I think he's coming to," he said to Amadea. "Will you sit back here with him?"

"Yes," said Amadea. She started past him toward the jeep, and then stopped. Her eyes fixed on the level of his lapels and couldn't get higher. She had to apologize for kicking him. Why had she done that? Partly so as not to leave the dog, partly perhaps from some subconscious feeling of resentment, but mostly, probably, from an ineradicable propensity to do the wrong thing.

"I'm sorry I kicked you," she murmured.

"My pleasure, mademoiselle," he answered gravely.

"I always seem to do the wrong thing," she went on, stepping toward the jeep. And feel the wrong thing, she added bitterly to herself. He held the door open and she slid onto the seat. Thierry started the engine.

"Listen, Amadea," Lucien began, "I have to talk with you." Or did he only think the words? She reached out and pulled the door shut. Thierry turned the vehicle around quickly and Lucien watched its tailgate disappear. Then he turned back to Hugo's vehicle, and then stepped over to the flatbed.

Hugo and Bruno seemed to have settled their immediate differences and were arguing in urgent undertones beside the house. Lucien could guess their conversation. They were debating how much he knew, how much they should submit to his authority, whether they shouldn't just tell him to go to hell, mind his own business, etc...or...

"Too many people know already..." Lucien heard Hugo hiss at Bruno. And Bruno, obviously wishing to disengage himself from the whole affair now, shrugged his shoulders repeatedly, and said to Hugo, "He's your father. It was your idea." Then he turned to Lucien. "You keep sticking your nose where it's got no business being, and you're going to get it broke one of these days. But this affair is Hugo's, not mine. I'm getting out of here."

"My affair?" demanded Hugo on a rising note, "My affair? It was your..."

"Shut up!" Bruno snapped back at him, "Just let me get out of here."

"No," said Lucien, "I think you'd both better stay till M. Trencavel appears. Then we're all going to talk."

"I don't have to stay here," said Bruno.

"Nor I," said Hugo, less certainly.

"Yes," said Lucien, "You do. Firstly, because if you don't, I, or any one of the large number of other people who know what you've been up to will make your activities public, and secondly"...he paused. Untruthfulness was not a habit with him, but he'd had an irritating day—"Secondly, because I've dropped your keys down the well."

*

By the time Amadea left the veterinary clinic it was evening. Guilhabert was still groggy but was recovering in a cage, with several stitches in his head. The young veterinarian had been all solicitude: "*Le pauvre petit*. What happened to him?"

Thierry had grunted, "Don't know. Found him like that."

Amadea had said nothing and the veterinarian had shaken his head and put away his stethoscope and pulled out syringes and gauze pads, and said that the dog should survive, and that he was going to anaesthetize him before sewing him up.

Amadea stepped out blankly onto the street, leaving behind the stifling medicinal atmosphere of the clinic. What now? She wondered vaguely if Thierry had found M. Trencavel yet, and what Lucien was doing.

She felt faint and remembered she had had nothing to eat all day. Perhaps her earlier actions had been not so much heroism as the dementia of inanition. She walked up the street till she found a restaurant, ordered dinner, and dawdled over it till dark. She had no idea that she had missed Lucien, who had been several times to the Cow Shed to seek her, and no idea that she'd missed the last bus back to Maugrebis. She left the restaurant and came out onto the street. It was misting and the evening had turned chilly.

A small white car pulled up beside her; someone was rolling down the window, speaking to her. She stared incuriously at the faces for a moment before it dawned on her that it was Marie, the woman who cleaned at the *manoir*, and her husband, and that they were offering her a ride home.

"What were you doing in Valzères?" asked Marie, turning in her seat to look back at Amadea with friendly interest.

"Oh, an errand," said Amadea vaguely and guiltily, and then it occurred to her that Marie probably didn't even know about Yves and Céleste and the broken legs, and as this seemed like a public-enough piece of news, she passed it on. The exclamations over the couple's departure and their bad luck lasted quite a ways; almost but not quite far enough. They were passing Maugrebis, driving up the hill.

"I can walk from here," said Amadea.

"No, no, we'll see you home. It's late now. Wouldn't you be afraid to walk in the dark?"

"No," said Amadea truthfully, "No, not at all."—Today—she added mentally.

"So you're staying alone at the *manoir*?"

"No, I've gone back to the Cow Shed."

"Oh? But..."

"M. d'Alembert has come. He's there. He'll let you in tomorrow, I expect."

"Oh. But I thought he was in Paris...What did he come for, I wonder?"

"It's hard to say."

"Is he staying long?"

"I don't know."

"Will you go back to the *manoir* when he leaves?"

"No," said Amadea, pushed to the wall, "No, I'm leaving tomorrow."

"*Aaaah oouui?*" Marie's eyes and mouth made three round circles.

Here at last, thank heavens, was the Cow Shed. Amadea got out and went indoors and went to bed.

22

She woke early, too early, and packed her bag, her over-strung nerves making her clumsy. Then she sat for a last time at the little wooden table and looked across at the *manoir*. Oh, Lucien. Was he sleeping there, or awake? It hadn't occurred to her till then to wonder how he had come to be at M. Trencavel's yesterday, or why he was with Thierry. Oh well, what did it matter? These people would all arrange their lives very well without her, or maybe Lucien would arrange everything. He would take care of Guilhie, too, she was sure of it. There was no need for her at all.

The *manoir* glinted as the morning sun slid over its façade. So it had been more *rêve* than *réalité*. French stories rarely ended happily, she knew, so why should her own? Suddenly she couldn't bear to be there any longer. She snatched up her bag and practically ran down the road.

She didn't know when the buses stopped, or where they went to. She would get on the first one that came along, she decided. She asked a passing villager: One appeared around nine, he said, but he couldn't say for sure where it went.

She had an hour. She decided to have breakfast at the bistro while waiting. As she walked down the hill, she heard the sound of a motorcycle coming up behind her. She turned and raised a hand to Thierry, who pulled up beside her and shut off his engine.

"Where are you going?" he said, gesturing toward her bag.

"Away," she replied, in a stifled voice, "But never mind me. Tell me what happened yesterday. Did you find M. Trencavel? Was he all right?"

"Yes. I found him not long after I left you and the dog, not far away at all. He'd been hitchhiking."

"And had his son really just dumped him?"

"*Oui. Épouvantable, non?* Me, I wouldn't have done that to my father." (Well, he hadn't had a father, but never mind, Thierry was fast growing in respectability).

"Why did he do it, I wonder?"

"Oh, you don't know. It was because Hugo—Raymond's son, that is—he and his partner wanted Raymond to let them develop his land, and he didn't want them to."

"Oh," said Amadea. "That was very wrong of them." And where did you come into it? she wondered vaguely.

Thierry was continuing proudly, leaning over his handlebars. "Monsieur d'Alembert made them agree to stay away from Raymond. Otherwise, we'll all go to the police. And I'm going to stay on with Raymond, to make sure no one bothers him." (Raymond had said he had behaved like a hero, Thierry remembered, heart swelling).

"Really?"

"Yes, and I'm going to work in the bakery."

"Really?"

"Monsieur d'Alembert arranged it. Sylvie says her uncle agreed at once because he needs someone strong for the deliveries. Her aunt hit the roof at first, she says, but then M. d'Alembert talked to her and she calmed down fast. Said she was all smiles when he left." Thierry hesitated a moment, and then added, almost shyly, "I have some ideas for selling Raymond's goat cheese on the bakery rounds. We could increase the herd—oh, lots of different things. I have lots of ideas."

"I think that's wonderful," said Amadea sincerely, "I wish you the best of luck." She extended her hand; he shook it, and coasted off down the hill with a backward wave.

She went into the bistro. There was a telephone in the corner. She remembered that she had one more thing to do before she left. She dialed a number and had a painful conversation with Lucien's grandmother. Then she found a table in the darkest corner, ordered breakfast, and tried hard, by sipping too hot coffee, to keep down the lump in her throat.

*

Madame put down the telephone and followed Joseph to the car. They pulled out into traffic.

"That Lucien is a fool," she said with some bitterness, almost to herself.

"Madame?" Joseph looked in the rear-view mirror, startled, his head sinking between his shoulders. Had the unthinkable occurred? It was seldom enough that Madame was moved to animadvert on anyone— and Lucien! This was very strange indeed. They drove a ways in silence. Then, "Joseph," said the marquise, in a sepulchral voice, "I give up. I shall get a maid."

*

"Well," said Loïc's mother, as she served her son a late breakfast in the d'Alembert kitchen, "it didn't come off between M. d'Alembert and the young companion. And I've heard the marquise was so hoping it would. Pity...Such a good man. He could make some woman very happy." She sighed, and shaking her head, went on with her dish drying.

"Well," said Loïc, digging in with hearty appetite, "but if he's not married, he can make several women happy, one after the other."

His mother flicked the dishcloth at him.

*

Lucien, knocking on the door of the Cow Shed, was met by silence. He paused to listen. Nothing, not a sound. He hammered on the wooden panels till the frame shook—not because he expected Amadea to open the door, but to relieve his feelings. The little house remained quiet. He strode back to the jeep and drove into the village. No one at the bus stop. He coasted down the street and then drove back up again, glancing in the windows of the bistro as he passed. No one. The first bus left at nine. He parked the car where he could see the stop and waited, one arm stretched over the steering wheel, outwardly relaxed and inwardly fuming. Eight-thirty, a quarter to nine, ten till, five till, three till, where was she? Perhaps she was taking the nine-ten to Tarbes then?

Someone was knocking on the off-side window. It was the baker's wife, curses. He opened the car door, stepped to the pavement, shook hands, agreed that it was a fine morning, that tomorrow was supposed to be even warmer, that it was very good that Thierry had showed up on time for his first day of work, that no, he didn't think it was taking a bit of a chance, he was sure the fellow would make an effort and that she would help him in every way possible...

*

Inside the bistro, Amadea came to with a start. That was the bus passing! She dropped some money on the table, threw a *"merci, au revoir"* over her shoulder to the proprietor, and ran for the bus, her bag slamming against her legs. She stepped on board, the doors hissed closed, and the bus moved off.

*

Lucien had been watching the face of the baker's wife for some time, nodding 'yes' and 'no' at regular intervals, more or less appropriately. He had to survey the bus stop; he let his gaze swivel again from her hypnotic snake eyes. The back of the bus was disappearing beyond the church. *"Merde!"* he said vehemently, stopping the baker's wife in mid-sentence. She stared at him in open-mouthed astonishment. He excused himself hastily and jumped back in his jeep.

If Amadea was on that bus, he could easily catch up with it, or in any case, he had only to follow it quietly to Toulouse. But if she wasn't? Suppose she was intending to take the bus for Tarbes that left in ten minutes? But if he waited for it, and she was on the bus that just left, then he might never catch up with her. She would reach Toulouse and then go who knows where; or she might get off before, in some smaller town. Lucien made up his mind: he had to see if she was on the bus that left. The jeep shot through town and onto the *départmentale*. A stretch of highway and he came shortly to a roundabout: he slowed, circled.

Would the bus take the *départmentale* all the way, or would it go by the *nationale*, or even by the small communal roads? He circled again, made up his mind, and sped off the roundabout. A length of empty road followed. No, surely, he would have caught the bus by now if it were going this way. He made a U-turn, returned to the roundabout, and allowed it to fling him out in a different direction. More empty road, and there, ahead of him, was the back of the bus. He put his foot down and the distance closed up rapidly. He was right on the bus's tail. He took his foot off the gas, and breathed a sigh of relief. But here, in the rear, he couldn't tell if Amadea were on board. He put his foot down again and pulled around to pass the bus, ranging alongside it while he surveyed the inside. No Amadea! He passed the bus. The sign on the front said "Montpellier.' It was the wrong bus! Cursing, he pulled his vehicle into the ditch, and allowed the bus to go by. Back to the roundabout and he was off in the last possible direction. The bus would be far ahead now; he doubted he could catch up with it, even if it were travelling slowly. He passed through a small town, and out again—if the bus had stopped here he might yet overtake it. But suppose she was taking the nine-ten? More driving, and there, at last, was the back of another bus. Let it be the right one! The distance closed, closed—no time to spend in the rear—he put his foot down and pulled to the left.

Amadea, sitting by the window, watched the plane trees flash past and the cow pastures unroll one after another, while the gray pavement continually disappeared below her, taking her away, far away. The bus was half-empty; surely she could cry a little without being noticed. But no, she mustn't let herself go, or...but—that was Lucien's jeep! It was! Its hood was creeping up alongside the bus, not passing. There was Lucien, he was looking up. Was he looking for her? But he wasn't looking where he was going! There was a truck coming! It would hit him head on!

"Lucien!" she heard herself screaming, pointlessly—he couldn't hear. "Lucien! No!"

The bus veered sharply to one side, throwing her against the glass; there was a sound of screeching tires, of horns, of the bus driver's shouted imprecations. Amadea stood up, searching for the jeep. Heads turned to stare out the window, to stare at her; necks were swiveling all over the bus. It was all right. No one was hurt. The jeep was behind the bus, following quietly, the truck disappearing into the distance, its driver holding down his horn to express his outrage.

Amadea stepped into the aisle and made her way to the bus driver.

"I would like to get off," she said, "please."

"Madame," said the bus driver stiffly, "what happened—that was not my fault. It is not I who drive like a madman, *moi*."

"No," said Amadea, "I know. It's my fault. Please just let me get off."

"Madame," said the bus driver, "this is not an official stopping place, you know. I can not stop here."

"Monsieur," said Amadea, in a tone of calm desperation, "I appreciate your point of view, but if you don't let me off, I think—yes, I really think—that I am going to scream again."

The bus driver muttered something that might have been "*saperlipopette*," and might very likely have been something much worse. He pulled the bus over brusquely and jerked open the doors.

Amadea descended. The bus departed, and she stood alone by the side of the road. The jeep had pulled over also. Lucien got out and came towards her. He stopped six feet away. She didn't say anything. He spoke first.

"Amadea, will you marry me?"

"No."

"No? Why not?"

"Because you don't love me." She hung her head.

"Amadea," said Lucien, "Amadea, I didn't know I loved you. But since yesterday, I have trespassed and lied and sworn at a woman and nearly driven a bus off the road. What more proof do you want? Amadea, I am turning to a life of crime. Save me. Will you?"

Amadea was not hard to convince. She started to laugh. "Really?"

"Yes. Absolutely. So…?"

"Yes."

And what happened then, happened as she had dreamed it would, and it was beautiful, as life is sometimes.

*

But after a time, one comes to. "Oh," said Amadea, coming to, "I left my bag on the bus!"

"It doesn't matter," said Lucien calmly, "I'm at your service now."

THE END